To,
Pat and Tom,

wishes.

George.

1st September, 1989.

£10

PERSONAL EFFECTS

George Walsh

A Square One Publication

First Published in 1989 by Square One Publications
Saga House, 29/31 Lowesmoor, Worcester WR1 2RS

© G. Walsh 1989
ISBN No. 1 872017 04 5

This book is copyright. No part of it may be reproduced in any form without permission in writing from the publishers except by a reviewer who wishes to quote brief passages in connection with a review written for inclusion in a newspaper, magazine, radio or television broadcast.

Printed by Billings & Son, Worcester
Typeset by Wyvern Typesetting, Worcester

PERSONAL EFFECTS is based on the wartime experiences of a number of airmen, one of whom was George Walsh. The people are real—though not necessarily their names. Most of the events really happened—though not in this precise chronological order.

The illustrations on the jacket are by kind permission of RAF Museum, Hendon, and the Royal Air Forces Escaping Society, 206 Brompton Road, London.

OPERATIONS RECORD BOOK

K.A.F. Form 540

(Unit or Formation) No. 144 Squadron

Page No. 78

No. of pages used for day ___

Place	Date	Time	Summary of Events	References to Appendices
Hemswell	16.4.41		The following Hampden aircraft of the squadron took off to attack Hampden 2U dockyards at KIEL:-	
		AD741		A.591 (Report)
		X3010	"	A.591
		AD745	"	A.592
		AD901	"	A.593
		AD811	"	A.594
		X3055	"	A.595
		P1164	"	A.596
		P1245	"	A.597
		X3130	"	A.598
		↑	The following other Duty was carried out:-	
			Gardening, One Hampden aircraft of the squadron took off to lay mines off KIEL.	
		00.15 hrs		
		↑	Personnel:-	
			P/O F/Lt. E.A. SMITH. D.F.C. 2nd Pilot. Sergeant TILLEY H. N° 745805.	
			Observer Sgt. WADDINGTON G.N° 903308.	
			Gunner W/Op/A.G. QUICK V.G. N° 745014.	
			Gunner W/Op/A.G. Sgt. CASE ... 845021 was made Captain of Aircraft.	
			This N.C.O. has twice been selected by the R.A.F. Hampden Remainder ...	

(signed) Talbot Brown

Extract from Operations Record Book — 16.4.41
144 Squadron

To my wife, Laura

*Murders of black, black, crows; Sharpening their beaks,
Spreading their wings, delivering their blows.
Most will return to nest, and strike again;
Others will fester in foreign earth.*

Chapter 1

It was one big step, one huge wrench; my young life was about to take off, quite literally. There was a lump in the throat as I shouted up the stairs. "I'm going now Mam." Her mumbled reply was lost in the sound of a passing milk float, the milkman filling the small assortment of jugs left on neighbours' door-steps. "Tell Dad I'll write as soon as I settle in at camp," were my last words as I slammed the front door behind me.

Earlier, because I found it impossible to sleep, my thoughts churning around and around, I had followed the doleful progress down the length of the street of the knocker up. He rattled the bedroom windows of the houses with his long bamboo cane, drearily intoning the time of day, "Five o'clock, five o'clock." Two pence a week he was paid for his services. Cheaper and more reliable than any alarm clock. He got the factory lasses to work on time, their looms would be set sharp on at six. Soon there would be the clatter of their clogs. First small groups clatter and chatter. Later an odd running single, trying to beat the clock and possibly the sack.

Dad had already been at work for more than two hours, his split shift started at 3 am, and by now he would have sorted, bagged up and begun his first delivery of letters. What a time to start work, in the middle of the bloody night. I had lain awake hoping he would disturb me to say good luck and his final goodbyes, truth was, he was dead set against me leaving home, and giving up a good job to boot.

Me, well I had other ideas. I was glad to be leaving, glad to be on the edge of something entirely new, even though the drums of war were beating loud and clear on the horizon. It was still early, and a beautiful summer morning. The tramcars into the centre of town were not yet running, pity, number ten would have dumped me right outside the main railway station, and I needed to catch the first train to Manchester. It would have to be Shank's pony. Forward march.

The end of August 1939 was not exactly the best time to be leaving the meagre comforts of home to enlist in the Royal Air Force as an aircrew volunteer, but my decision had been made, my services accepted and I was on my way to carry them through. The inspiration to become a flyer had its roots in a film going the rounds of the local cinemas called 'It's in the Air' starring George Formby, my favourite Lancashire comedian. Not that my reasons for doing so were as gormless as his. There were other reasons. Acute feelings of claustrophobia both with the environments of living in a small town and my job, which seemed to me to have little to offer. Dad had other ideas. They were the spurs for me to cut loose, to sever the link with the Post Office and my work as an engineer under training. Dad had been working for the Post Office for the last twenty years, still doing the same routine job, day after day, six days a week. I wanted something different. Just seventeen and a half years young, the flowering of those roots were certainly beyond any of my wildest dreams.

Closing the front door behind me, little did I realise it would be almost four years before I saw it again. Four years, during which time both my parents would be dead. My own young life changed considerably. Catapulted into action with bomber operations against Germany. Wounded and decorated for bravery as good measure.

First impression of life in the RAF was the reception centre at West Drayton, not too far away from London. Reception itself was clinical, the reception committee different to my expectations. Day one in retrospect seemed like a life time long interviewing starting and finishing in the dark. All new recruits, twenty of us, were processed like a sausage machine in reverse gear. It began with a de-skinning process from the head down. First the camp barber,

Sweeny Todd himself, haircut by braille. You could have any style you liked, as long as it was regulation short back and sides. We went in and out like a fiddler's elbow, a line of finished products looking like boiled eggs with handles. Shining pates, emphasising jug-handle ears.

The new intake shuffled for the rest of the day. Sick quarters next. The medics working downwards from ears, eyes, nose and throat. By lunchtime my belly, now stripped naked, thought my throat had been cut. There had been a quick glimpse of food as we shuffled past the airmen's dining hall, long trestle tables laden with bread and pots of marmalade, each pot being dive-bombed by flurries of bloated wasps. But we were not invited. Lunch time gone, everyone had progressed as far as arms—bare arms, stripped for action. This was the part that demanded courage. Courage to absorb a host of needles, needles of varying shapes and sizes. Rumours were rife, black water fever, yellow fever, cholera, smallpox—we were getting the lot. Cocktails of venom I could have well done without, my stomach was crying out for food. Don't they ever feed you in this man's Air Force? I convinced myself we were being fed intravenously. There were failures, the weaker stomachs. And the sight of all those clinical white trays of needles induced a quick roll off the top and they were carted away. It was only delaying the agony. Agony it was, despite the gyrations of the arms, to get the stuff moving around the system quicker, the stiffness was still there a week later.

By early afternoon, the thin blue line of buffs had gone further south, down to the nether regions. A line of masculinity parading limply, standing easy, each one looking sorely dejected, to be lifted roughly on the end of a pencil, and carefully studied by a gentleman in a white coat.

One wag next to me said it all, "He must have been a bird fancier, this will be the first time I've seen mine on a perch."

Next—cough. This was something called an FFI inspection, free from infection; someone further down the line, your typical barrack-room lawyer type, said it meant filthy foreskin inspection. We were learning.

Late afternoon everyone felt ravenous, but food was secondary, something bigger was brewing, you could sense it, there was an air of panic about, somebody higher up knew a lot more than we did, this was a rush job.

At last sustenance. We were all given a mug of hot sweet tea, obviously treatment for shock. Someone called Adolph Hitler was rampaging across Europe, the thin blue line had to be strengthened as quickly as possible, and volunteers for flying duties were like gold dust.

At the end of the day every man in the intake collapsed onto his bed. The bugle call to come to the cookhouse door was completely and unanimously ignored. All anyone wanted was to be left alone, left alone to suffer in silence. Had I done the right thing? Doubts were beginning to surface, too late, we had been attested, accepted the King's shilling and there was now no turning back.

Lying on my cot, both arms sore, swollen and throbbing, I remembered those last words shouted up the stairs to Mam. But I was feeling too damned miserable to write a letter home, it would have to wait. And wait it did, because war was only hours away, and then letter writing for a while would be declared obsolete. Poor Dad, he had such good plans for me in the Post Office, but no way did I want the Army, the Royal Corp of Signals in particular, a certainty for trained Post Office engineers.

Not one of us though had second thoughts, and once we had signed on the dotted, well and truly attested, we were on the move again. There was a degree of panic in the air, so off we went clutching a railway warrant away from the South East and for me back to the North of England. A motley bunch of airmen, still in civvies, sprogs we were christened but well and truly King's men. Gathered all together in the NAAFI with the rest of the station at RAF Padgate Warrington, most people assumed this was to be our first church parade. Prayers amidst the char and wads. How wrong can you get? The sombre chimes of Big Ben on the tannoy systems, were followed by the Prime Minister's declaration that we were at war with Germany. The announcement brought forth a few repeated Jesus Christs. We were praying after all. I'd been in the Air

Force for five whole days! This was now a completely different ball game.

"I came into the Air Force to fly," was a propitious opening gambit to anyone prepared to listen, but the only things that seemed to fly on that Sunday morning were blue arsed practicing landings around the pots of marmalade laid out for lunch in the Airmen's Mess. Blue bottles and wasps, when would I ever get to see an aeroplane? One thing was certain, I would be giving up marmalade for the duration.

Name and last three. It was like some gramophone record permanently stuck in the same groove. "You—do this—do that" suddenly became a popular pastime with hoary old drill Corporals and Sgts, even though none of us had yet been kitted out in Airforce blue. We were imposters, civilians with numbers, maybe there was an acute shortage of uniforms. Of course rumours abounded, but being confined to camp quickly dispelled any thoughts of the outside world. Before long, my dreams of flying into the sun with suitable background music were quickly brought down to earth by an obvious candidate for a concert party hammering out the Rustle of Spring on the beer sodden Naafi piano.

We were here to be taught the rudiments of square bashing, but there was no time to obey the maxim, if it moves salute it, if it doesn't paint it. Funny though how orders come through in the middle of the night.

Tucked up in your little pit, surrounded by snores, fears, sweaty socks, the doors burst open, the lights go on. "Wakey, Wakey, hands off cocks, pull on socks." It was funny the first time Corporal, but when Hitler looms large with every new rumour, innocent and callow youths begin to take a battering. "Right" bawls the voice framed in the doorway. "All of you heroes what volunteered to fly, out of bed, pack your kit and standby for further orders. The rest of you wankers, stay where you are, we've got nastier things on hand for you lot. Understood?" That was one quick course, not even time to hold a rifle. Somebody was in one hell of a hurry to get us kitted out with flying clothing.

"Christ! This is it!" I thought. "It's over the top tomorrow, and

I still haven't had time to write a letter home." Little did I know that Mam and Dad had taken a taxi to the station to try and buy me out of the service, their one and only son. They could have saved themselves the fare, since neither of them got beyond the barbed wire fence. The war was barely twenty four hours old.

Life was beginning to be one long travelogue. Few of us had heard of Calne before in the county of Wiltshire. For me the extent of my earlier journeys had been no further than Blackpool. But, that's what the railway warrant said, Calne, single third class to. Mind you someone in the party had heard of Harris's pork pies and sausages, but RAF Yatesbury, my home for the next six months, looked nothing like as appetising. After a long day's travelling and first sight under a blackened sky, the camp stood out in schematic outline as a conglomeration of low foreboding wooden huts, surrounding equally dark single storey buildings.

Each one of us still felt like imposters on arrival, still no issue of uniforms, most of us wondering what the hell had hit us. For me, George Formby had a lot to answer for. Maybe I was gormless. Rookies to a man!

The issue of uniform from the clothing stores the following day was a hit and miss affair. There was obviously an acute shortage of certain items of equipment. It seemed to be a survival of the slickest. Anyone unlucky enough to be out of the average mould got little or nothing to wear. Some were kitted out with old-type tunics, buttoned tight to the neck with puttees to match. I was lucky. We were certainly a rag-and-bobtail lot. It was a long time before uniforms were standard. But no way were we going to be allowed to be seen in public for some months ahead, so it was heads down, and back to school.

Chapter 2

RAF Yatesbury perched on a hillside in Wiltshire was No. 2 Electrical and Wireless School, No. 1 being the more prestigious outfit based at Cranwell in Lincolnshire. The camp smacked of jerry building thrown up in a hurry, semi-permanent buildings, housing a semi-permanent intake.

As new recruits we were immediately put into a squadron as part of a larger wing, and given a course number. The training in basic electrics, radio and morse, went on solidly for eight hours a day, seven days a week, with occasional breaks for a 48-hour pass. The hardest part of the course for most trainees was the ability to send and receive the morse code at speeds up to and beyond 18 words per minute. This surely must have been the origin of the dollali tap and most of the failures could never get up to the required speed of morse reception.

I counted myself one of the lucky ones. My previous training as a student engineer in the Post Office meant that the radio/electrical side of the course was relatively easy, allowing me to concentrate on transmitting and receiving the morse code.

That first winter of the war was a shocker. Isolated as we were, sitting on top of a hill, we froze. The whole of January and February was like one long winter survival course. Everything including each single blade of grass froze up solidly. There was no fresh water, and little fresh food. Sick parades were becoming longer and longer, diseases nastier and nastier. Meningitus was rampant.

The mutiny began when the entire camp was formed up on the parade square to be addressed by the Station Commander, who politely informed us how to be British. Someone in the rear rank, who obviously had other ideas, threw an orange, the missile scoring a bullseye on the nose of one startled Group Captain.

A solid square quickly dissolved into a ragged outcrop. Some airmen walked away, later to be court-martialled for absence, others simply deserted, never to be seen again. Later in the day a decision was made to suspend training until the weather had improved. Personnel living in the South of England on a line below Birmingham were granted an immediate seven days leave. Those like me, Northerners, were kept behind to provide for guard duties. No trains were running north of Brum. We were told the railway lines were blocked with snow and ice. It would be our turn for a week's leave when the southerners returned. If they ever did.

Of course after one week had gone by, and the weather had improved, our leave was cut to a weekend pass. There wasn't much one could do with a short weekend pass, and so every one of us to a man, some 300 airmen, made up our minds to have a week's leave come what may.

Later, this accounted for what must have been the one and only mass charge in the annals of the RAF when some 300 airmen were gathered together in the Airmen's mess and collectively charged with absence without leave. We were all doled out with the same punishment, admonished and the stoppage of one day's pay. I spent my leave in the smoke, London town, and it was worth every penny of it, considering my one day's pay was the magnificent sum of sixpence after deductions had been made. And yet our needs were few. We were fed and watered, worked hard and every Wednesday afternoon, sport's day, played hard.

The whole object was eventually to become a member of the senior course, having ploughed through all the intermediate tests and examinations, oral and practical, and to be able to look forward to that wonderful day when your name appeared on the flying detail. Up to this time, I had yet to see an aeroplane at close quarters.

The airfield at Yatesbury was some corner of a farmer's field, that was forever England. A simple strip of green earth down one end of a once ploughed field. The aircraft were old Dominie Rapides, and the pilots appeared to be a perfect match. A training flight was short and not altogether sweet; flying for the first time for a number of trainees had disastrous results, sick bags well in evidence, in here slob. Flight trainees after being kitted out for flying and packed into the bowels of the aircraft resembled a bunch of underripe bananas, spines curved by the tight fitting green-coloured parachute harness, known affectionately as the goonskin. The goonskin, into which clipped an observer-type parachute, was designed to raise the voice by two octaves, a desirable feature for would-be Wireless Operators. After a morning's detail, the nut-cracker suite wasn't exactly my favourite piece of music.

Aircraft radio equipments at the beginning of the war, looked primitive, were primitive, and seldom seemed to function properly. To change a transmitter or receiver frequency required the finesse of a brain surgeon and the dexterity of a safe cracker. The poor unfortunate trainee pushed or pulled pairs of small inductance coils into the body of the transmitter and the receiver. These coils fitted like gloves, a variety of which were housed in boxes, covering different frequency bands. In the air, with the aircraft bobbing up and down, the effect of changing them usually left the poor unwary student sitting on his arse, clutching a pair of coils, with the vague look of "what do I do now Corporal?" The instructors, who were mostly jumped up junior NCOs, told you in no uncertain terms. Our aged pilots had seen it all before, though they weren't exactly happy with the continual shifting of the centre of gravity.

On a cold day, wearing two pair of gloves, flying airmen for the use of, one silk pair of inners and one leather gauntlet, it required maximum effort to delicately tune the equipment to some remote ground station. The radio exchange if you were lucky, was bits of information in a special air ground code known as the Z code. This was something else to tax the retentive power of the minds of callow youths. Of course it had to end—the needs of the war demanded it. There were more exciting things around the corner, and the Air Force and its aircrews needed to expand rapidly, and Wireless Operators and Air Gunners were a vital part of that expansion programme.

It was a proud day when the course finished and we were presented with the cloth badge of office, a clenched fist with sparks emanating out of the fingers. It gave every one of us who had survived the six month's training maximum pleasure to wear it on the sleeve of our tunics. We were now fully-fledged tradesmen. It brought little perks too, able to stay up a little later in the evenings, admired by the lesser mortals in the Naafi, and a rise in your daily pay of an extra ninepence, badge pay. Members of the senior course strutted around the camp like peacocks, so that all and sundry could pay homage. The next round was eagerly awaited—a posting to enable us to practise our newly acquired skills.

This was the time for more rumours, postings overseas, home, a cushy number, somewhere close to where you lived. You could make some representation, but it made little difference, it was generally better to take pot luck, volunteering was a lost cause. My aim was paramount. I wanted the next step, an Air Gunnery course, and off into the wide blue yonder.

It was something of a let down when my posting notice appeared, to RAF Aston Down in the next county of Gloucestershire. My disappointment was lessened when I learned I had passed out as an Aircraftsman 1st Class, which in itself also increased my rate of pay.

RAF Aston Down, close to Stroud, was a small pre-war airfield situated on the top of a plateau near the village of Chalford. It was a fighter training station and the aircraft were suitably Gloster Gladiators. The station was bursting at the seams with bodies, and it meant that a number of airmen, me included, had to live under canvas, three airmen to a tent. My job was a ground controller, passing all kinds of information by radio to aircraft engaged on a variety of training exercises. Amongst the pilots under training were a number of well-known people, pilots who were later to write their history, as aces during the Battle of Britain, yet to come. These were the days of the phoney war, the "it would be over by Christmas" brigade were well to the fore. Early 1940, when life in the Air Force was full of glamour and the Brylcream boy spirit prevailed. There was little to do during the off duty hours, except walk and admire the countryside. There were some lovely old pubs on our doorstep, one in particular was called the Ragged Cot. It was the nearest hostelry to the camp and also the most popular watering hole. A delightful old fifteenth century inn where one rubbed shoulders with those special pilots, like Whitney-Straight, Guinness, Bader and others. Eavesdropping on their aircrew chat made me all the more determined to become one of them as soon as possible, and I continually made a nuisance of myself by badgering anyone prepared to listen, for my Air Gunnery course.

In spring a young man's fancy lightly turns to thoughts of love...

My home for the foreseeable future was a small khaki tent. Two other airmen shared it with me and we each had our allotted six inches of bedspace complete with wall-to-wall grass surrounds. My two companions, one engine fitter and another wireless operator, were very different birds of a feather. Aircraftsman second class Harry Gornall (Gormless), was a fellow Lancastrian. He had just finished his training as an aero-engine fitter and was fairly new on the station. A different animal altogether was the third member of our canvas home. Like me, Doug Chinnery was awaiting aircrew training, having been selected for pilot training. He rather looked down at this stage on would-be Wireless Operator Air Gunners, perhaps he would change his mind later on. Chinnery was straight out of the top drawer, public school, and, but for the war, would have been going up to Oxford. Later he would be commissioned, becoming something of an ace with Bomber Command.

Air Force life was not all work, though hours were long. The fair on Minchinhampton Common, close to the camp, was a huge attraction for two lonely airmen a long way away from home on a Saturday evening, so Harry and myself decided to go.

It must have been the beginning of a number of fateful decisions. I met my future wife at Minchinhampton Fair. Every year for centuries past a fair was held on the common, but the one in the spring of 1940 was to be the last one for the duration of the war.

"Let's split those two girls up," said Harry. "I'll take the brunette, you go for the blonde." The two girls in question were riding the dodgem cars. Of course I cocked up a simple instruction, didn't I? Guess who finished up with the brunette? Fate stepped in for the first time in my life on that lovely spring evening, my brunette was later to become my wife.

The station tannoy system crackled into life. "AC1 Walker will report to Station Headquarters immediately." My first thoughts were, bloody hell what had I done wrong? It wasn't usual to be summoned by tannoy to the big house unless there was something amiss. This is where the Station Warrant Officer and his cronies lurked. No one of our ilk went near the place, unless he wanted a quick dose of jankers. Admin wallahs did not like people who worked with aeroplanes, and the SWO and his minions were people to steer well clear of.

Warrant Officer Paddy O'Shea was the dreaded Station Warrant Officer. It was rumoured that he had eyes on stalks, like a monitor lizard. It was also rumoured that no Senior NCO would ever order a drink in the Sgts' Mess before Paddy O'Shea appeared. Mind you they never went thirsty, come rain or shine he appeared like a well-oiled clock. Affectionately known as Osh to his nearest and dearest, the smallest fan club in the world, our dear warrant officer was as thick as pig shit.

There was a story that one day he caught one of his airmen pinching one of his pencils. "Ah, caught you stealing the tools of my trade," bellowed Osh to a frightened erk. "What were you in Civvy Street, you horrible little man?"

"A draughtsman sir," replied the poor unfortunate airman.

"Oh, and how would you like it if I pinched your draughts." Apocryphal perhaps, but typical of Osh, a man to be avoided at all times.

Oh yes, my calling to Headquarters was the bit of news I had been longing to hear.

"Right lad," said the Admin Sgt. "Get yourself over to sick quarters, right away, if not sooner, for an aircrew medical, and if I were you lad, I'd tie a knot in it. You'll need all the wind and piss you can muster."

Fit Aircrew, what a lovely sound. I could have kissed the medical officer, but I'm sure he wouldn't have appreciated it. I walked into Stroud with a very light step to see my girlfriend, to give her my good news. She would have other views, but perhaps we were ships that passed in the night. All that day had been a dream. After my medical, I had been told to go over to stores to draw all my flying kit. Harry had insisted on taking a photograph with all my clobber on. It was impossible to sleep that night, my thoughts were whirling around, settling down at around twenty thousand feet. Doug Chinnery offered his congratulations less gratuitously, he was plainly jealous. I had beaten him to the punch. The plain truth was that the Air Force was needing them not feeding them, and the machine for processing volunteer tail end Charlies could move into top gear when it wanted to.

And so I said goodbye to my little six inches of bedspace, my girlfriend, my two oppos who shared the tent, and, with my one tatty suitcase and a well packed kit bag, began the long tiring journey to an Air Gunnery School—aircrew here I come. I was just eighteen years old.

Chapter 3

My posting notice told me to report to RAF West Freugh. The railway warrant was made out to Stranraer, which was somewhere beyond the confines of England. Scotland to me, a naive laddy from Lancashire, who hadn't been any further than Blackpool before the war, was definitely abroad.

The station, like most airfields, was in the back of beyond. Perched on the edge of Loch Ryan, it was a bloody long way north, and the furthest west I'd ever been. Courtesy of the railway it had taken me nearly thirty six hours to get there. It was dark, dank and blowing half a gale when I arrived. The camp, one more satelite conglomeration was totally blacked out. The cold wind whistled in from the sea, and after the usual paraphernalia of arriving, I was shown to a small wooden hut, my home for the next five weeks.

My question "What's the grub like?" was answered by one word " 'orrible." It was obvious I was going to bed without any supper. The hut was warm, a blazing stove glowed brightly in the centre of the room. I could just make out about twenty beds with lockers, ten either side. I moved into a vacant space, as quietly as possible, since the other occupants appeared to be all fast asleep. After a solid day and a half's travelling, I wouldn't need much rocking.

"Reveille is 0600," whispered the departing service policeman as he quietly shut the door.

Everyone around me began to stir long before the camp bugler sounded Reveille. Trying to understand any of the conversations going on around me was impossible. I thought "Bloody hell, if these bodies are all Scottish, the next four to five weeks are going to be difficult." In actual fact, the majority of the other course members were Polish. These were all seasoned airmen, all of whom had already been totally involved in air battles against the Germans over their own country and down through France, before escaping to carry on the fight from English shores.

Most of these gallant gentlemen would later form the nucleus of Wellington bomber squadrons after a short period of training. They were good, naturally the language problem had to be overcome, but they were all superb air gunners. I could never get over the fact that before retiring for the evening they wore hairnets and liberal doses of perfume. But anyone, but anyone, who tried to take the mickey, soon found themselves on the wrong end of a knuckle sandwich, so most people quickly realised it was safer to say now't.

Airborne gunnery training was carried out in Fairey Battles. The aircraft resembled a 'stretched' Hurricane and generally carried a crew of three; Pilot, Observer and Wireless Operator/Air Gunner. Navigation presented no problems, since on all the exercises we simply flew out to sea and blasted away at anything in sight. Navigator observers were never carried. Occasionally we were allowed to fire at a drogue towed by another aircraft the Westland Lysander. These exercises were assessed by the number of hits on the target, however, most of the time was spent attempting to cure a variety of machine gun stoppages, head stuck out of an open cockpit. The edict No. 1 stoppage-cock-and-fire was burned into my brain before the end of the course. The rest of the time spent in the classroom was filled with stripping, cleaning and assembling a variety of weapons. Filling magazines, and knowing every single part of a machine gun, was necessary before you successfully passed the course. I will never forget to my dying day where the rear sear spring retainer keeper belonged in the innards of a Browning light machine gun, and, how having dismantled it completely to a pile of moving and non-moving parts, having to put it all back together in less than ten minutes—blindfolded.

There was little danger of failing the course, since rear end bomber crew were in desperately short supply and training courses were being made shorter and shorter. At this time, April 1940, the majority of rear end aircrew in bomber Command were mainly aircraftsmen. Many an AC2 had been shot down since the beginning of hostilities, and as such, were made to work extremely hard in prisoner of war camps in Germany.

Only pilots and observers were either commissioned or senior NCOs. We, the rear enders were generally reckoned to be nothing more than ballast. Nevertheless, it was with a sense of great pride and belonging to an elite band of airmen, that at the end of the course, I was awarded my Air Gunner's badge. The coveted emblem was a small winged brass bullet to be worn above the Wireless Operator' insignia. With it went more pay, an extra shilling a day. Flying pay, riches indeed. Things were even getting better, for on the first of May, the Air Council decided that no member of aircrew would be below the rank of Sgt. I was promoted from an erk to a Senior NCO without firing a shot in anger. This was living indeed.

At the same time, a single wing brevet had been designed to be worn on the breast of the tunic with the letters AG within a laurel wreath and standing for Air Gunner. This would replace the old winged brass bullet.

There were two reasons for these far-reaching changes, one was to give protection to future aircrew who were unfortunate enough to be shot down and taken POW, the other was for recruiting purposes. It was not surprising that most young men volunteering for aircrew duties wanted to be pilots, and so the elevation in rank coupled with a brevet which was easily recognisable, proved to be a good recruiting slogan.

Myself, I'd been in the Air Force all of nine months, and already I was a member of the Sgts' Mess. Of course it was a very hard pill for hairy old groundcrew to swallow. Overnight, the Sgts' Mess was filled with lots of young aircrew who didn't have the same ideas about discipline, and the old timers who had taken years to reach the same exalted rank, bitterly resented it.

Customs and etiquette of the service had to be quickly learned. One custom was having to bow to the senior mess member present whenever you entered the mess prior to dinner each evening. This was a different world to the Airmen's Mess or the Naafi. Here you were waited on for meals, allowed to drink spirits at the bar, and had someone serve you early morning tea. George Formby was beginning to pay off.

I still hadn't had a spot of leave, and I wasn't going to get any either for some considerable time.

One course ended and another one on the horizon. Amazing the power of three stripes and an aircrew brevet, it made you hold up your head high with a feeling of intense pride, not bad for pulling the opposite sex either.

It was kit bag packing time again, getting closer and closer to the sharp end. This time it was back down south across the border, back to the land of the living. My next station had at least Operational in the unit's title, an Operational Training Unit, commonly known as an O.T.U. Sleepy Oxfordshire, and in particular RAF Upper Heyford, was tucked away midway between Oxford with its dreaming spires and the small country market town of Bicester.

The station had much more bustle than the last one, it sported three different types of aircraft, the Avro Anson, affectionately known as the Annie, the Handley Page Hereford and the same firm's Hampden bomber. It was here on the O.T.U. that trainees came together for the first time as bomber crews. As students we progressed from the Anson to the Hampden, and eventually, providing you survived all the hurdles, we were destined for squadrons in Number 5 Group of Bomber Command.

From a pilot's point of view it was understood that the Hereford and the Hampden were not exactly the best of aircraft to fly, the Hereford was a right bastard. The Anson on the other hand was comfortable, nice and gentle. RAF Upper Heyford had already its fair share of crashes, the little churchyard was beginning to become over-crowded. Most of the fatal crashes happened at night, generally during solo take-offs and landings. Night flying was entirely new ground for all of us, but it added that extra dimension towards becoming real operational aircrew.

I was crewed with a young Pilot Officer. The first time airborne in the Hereford ended ignominiously wheels up on its belly at a satellite airfield. A crash landing from the word go. No matter how hard the pilot tried to get the wheels down, they wouldn't budge.

We tried everything, even to urinating into the hydraulic tank when it was realised we had lost all the hydraulic fluid; this ruse sometimes worked, but not this time.

Imagine how my young pilot felt. Here he was with a completely sprog crew, including himself, with a total of about one hundred flying hours between the three of us, and he had to crash land an aircraft. Thank God it was daylight. Strange, there was no panic. Of course we were so wet behind the ears we didn't know any different. None of us had got to the frightened fartless stage yet, this was to come later. Our man at the controls just flopped it down with a minimum of fuss, and the three of us calmly walked away. Not as much as a tiny scratch, but my God that was worth a pint or two later in the Mess. What a line shoot. It was shortly after this the Hereford was removed from active duty and assigned to the aircraft's graveyard. It was exactly the same aircraft as the Hampden except it had water-cooled inline engines, where the Hampden had much more reliable air-cooled radial ones. The engines on the Hereford were the problem, very inefficient cooling and consequently always catching fire. Not to mention piss-poor hydraulics!

Most of the flying training on the course was cross country navigation exercises both by day and by night, where each crew member exercised his talents if he had any, by completing in an allotted time as much as possible of a laid down plan. Each exercise was different, becoming harder and more complicated as the course progressed.

For me as the Wireless Operator it was mostly the survival of the slickest. It meant establishing contact as quickly as possible with a variety of ground stations and especially the ability to assist the navigator by plying him with a succession of bearings and fixes. These were provided through contact with a number of ground stations with direction finding capabilities. The job was hard, and if you'll forgive the pun, you were very much the key man. These were early days, navigational techniques were crude and simple mostly dead reckoning. Aids were very sparse, it was absolutely essential for a Wireless Operator to provide DF information if a crew were to survive operations, there was a lot of responsibility on young shoulders, it worried me.

No thoughts were ever given to the ability of a night fighter to home onto telegraphy transmission. We had to learn the hard way and to adopt radio silence techniques later.

By this time of course the phoney war (the one predicted to be ended by Christmas, nobody said which year) was over. The Hun had overrun France and the Lowlands, we had survived Dunkirk and were completely on our own. The Brylcream boys were not very popular immediately after the retreat from Dunkirk with the majority of returning soldiers. It was early in July when completely out of the blue, the sound of church bells rang out announcing the Germans had invaded. We were told parachutists had dropped in all over the place. After spending a whole day awaiting their arrival later to be told it was all a rumour, one which had spread like wildfire. After coming up from the air raid shelters, sighs of relief all round.

Bad news in a letter from home. A double header in fact. Uncle Billy, one of Dad's brothers, and my favourite uncle, had been declared missing believed killed in the retreat from France. He'd gone over with the East Lancashires as part of the British Expeditionary Force shortly after the outbreak of war. To soften the blow he'd been recommended for the award of the Distinguished Conduct medal, to be presented to his wife by the Colonel of the Regiment.

Word had it that Uncle Billy had fought his own rearguard action to enable his troops to safely escape the advancing Germans.

I felt so sorry for Auntie Edna, they had no children, and she was such a timid sort.

The other news made my blood boil. Dad's other younger brother, Uncle Frank had declared himself to be a conscientious objector, and had been arrested. He refused to fight because of his Marxist principles, believing in the friendship existing between Russia and Germany. Dad said he was awaiting banishment to the Isle of Man together with a number of local supporters of the blackshirts of Oswald Mosley. I hope he rots away like the tail of the manx cat in his exile.

Dad promised to send me the local rag. The reporters had had a field day, and both my uncles had made front page news, both for entirely different reasons. That night I intended to drown my sorrows in drink.

What little off-duty time we were given was usually spent visiting Oxford. The plot was standard, a good meal, followed by a pub crawl ogling the local talent, before making a mad rush for the last bus back to camp, unless you were otherwise engaged with female company. This usually meant missing the last bus and a long walk back some fifteen miles, it was never worth it.

One night in particular was one to remember. The navigator and myself staggered out of the nearest pub to the bus station in good time to board the last bus home. We were almost there, when a voice, low, female, husky and American came out at us from a darkened doorway.

"Wanna drink boys?" the hidden voice said. What an invitation to well-oiled aircrew, this was too good to miss, last bus or no last bus. The both of us quickly homed on to the sound and followed it up the stairs to what can only be described as a luxury penthouse above a shopping arcade.

In the light of the room, both of us quickly realised that this beautifully dressed female was no Oxford harpie. This was not one of the girls who nightly did the round of pubs, known to most off-duty servicemen as prick teasers. No, this form before us was blonde, tall and gorgeous. However she was not alone. Lying in a heap on a settee was a male companion, who she introduced as her husband. In answer to the question if he was feeling alright she replied "Oh him; he's pissed out of his skull." Oops!

After a few drinks, this invitation was open sesame to the navigator who considered himself to be something of a lady killer. The last bus had long gone, but who cared, free booze coming up thick and fast and superb company. I began to smell a rat when the conversation turned to probing questions about military matters—seemed incongrous from the mouth of such a delightful bird. She however became quickly displeased with our non-committal answers, after all we knew little or nothing anyway, all that interested us was polishing off the free grog.

It was at this stage that the heap on the settee became suddenly sober, alive and nasty to boot, and the pair of us were smartly shown the door, before being booted out onto the street to face that long walk home.

In the sober light of dawn, the penny dropped, this was a classic case of being picked up by two German agents. The station Intelligence Officer was all ears when both of us plucked up enough courage the next day to fill him in with the details. The two people were immediately picked up, both American owners of a flourishing business in the arcade, but both Nazi sympathisers. It taught us a salutary lesson to keep our bloody traps shut at all times with strangers.

However all good things must come to an end and, by the end of October 1940, I was pronounced fit for operational duty as a fully fledged W/OP AG. Still awaiting my first leave, but on my one and only weekend off, I walked most of the way to Stroud to see my girlfriend, and after a few hours, walked all the way back. Young love hath no bounds.

The Signals Leader gave me the news "Right Sgt Walker, you are posted to sunny Donny, to No 7 Group (OTU) at RAF Finningley. Good Luck."

The Operational Training Unit was something of a hybrid, not exactly fully operational, but staffed with instructors who were all experienced flyers, most of whom had completed operations. It was designated an Advanced Flying Unit, and anywhere that could advance my seventy-five hours flying had to be worthwhile.

My assessments at the end of the Upper Heyford course weren't exactly anything to shout home about. As an Air Gunner I was below average, with the rider I'd done little air gunnery during the course. Little indeed. In fact I'd done none at all. So I considered the assessment unfair. As a Wireless Operator I was average, but once again the remarks were that I should be used as a Second Operator at first. I felt they'd assessed the wrong person, but I wasn't prepared to argue. At least I hadn't failed, and was one step nearer to operations against the enemy.

On arrival, and after getting the griff from the older hands, I rightly suspected that this was just another link prior to going on to a real operational squadron. Come to think of it, the majority of these were mostly nearer to the East Coast. Nevertheless the station had the feel about it, aircraft and crews flew out over enemy territory, actually crossed the English coast, most of them to return to tell the tale. The sorties were generally short ones, a quick look see at undefended targets, drop a few leaflets, and make a hasty retreat back to base.

All-night operational trips were entered in red ink in your flying log book. Daylight operations were entered in green. My flying log book entries were still all virgin blue. Crews spent only one month at Finningley, but one of the plusses was you were cheek by jowl with the real life operational aircrew, men who had already completed a tour of operations against the enemy. Mind you they were few and far between, but to me they were ten feet tall. As for us, we were a motley crew, four young men just thrown together and told to get on with it. Most of the time was spent hanging around the crew room waiting to fly. Sunny Donny didn't exactly live up to its name, with October fogs cancelling most flying details.

It was something of an anti-climax when it came. The crew heard it second hand from the pilot who had been called forward for a solo briefing. Gathering us all together in the crew room he whispered very quietly "We are on Ops tonight."

"Frying tonight," I thought.

"Where?" was the next question from the navigator.

"How the hell do I know," was the quick retort. "See you all at briefing at 1700 hours sharp."

I was given my instructions, "Get over to the armoury and draw your pigeons." Funny place to keep pigeons went through my head, guns and pigeons don't exactly mix. As the Wireless Operator I was responsible for signing out a basket of pigeons—two feathered friends to be precise. They were our message carriers if the aircraft was unfortunate enough to crash land over enemy territory or forced to ditch in the North Sea. God forbid, in October. Briefing was short and sweet. The sortie was to carry out a leaflet raid over the town of Eindhoven in occupied Holland. Christ, it was like delivering newspapers, although it didn't count as an operational sortie. A full tour for bomber crews was about thirty operations. Here I was, thinking about those magical thirty trips or two hundred hours operational flying and I hadn't even started. These early leaflet raids, generally by single aircraft, were known as nickels, can't for the life of me think why.

As I dutifully stowed away my basket of pigeons, who, by the noises they were making, seemed highly delighted at the prospect of becoming airborne, the thought crossed my mind that these two feathered friends had probably got more hours in over hostile territory than most people on the station. No medals for you Percy.

"Hey you lot—you lucky sods. You've been specially selected to be film stars. Report to the aircraft at 1500 hours sharp fully kitted up, parachute, the lot," all this from the Flight Commander. And so we became instant heroes as part of a documentary film to be called "Next of Kin"—an every day story about brave airmen and their long suffering families. I only hoped I would live long enough to see the finished product.

Bloody hell, if this was operations, there was nothing to it. We didn't even see a shot fired in anger. Away went the leaflets, I sent a message by W/T back to Group, telling them in code we had bombed the primary target, and we turned away for home and an early breakfast. Bombed indeed, we probably provided enough toilet paper for a month, but it was good training, with that extra touch of the unknown thrown in for good measure.

"What was it like?" Questions from other hopefulls. "Rough?"

"No, a piece of cake, bloody cold though at 10,000 feet with the cupola back."

I looked down at my bin gunner, a complete stranger, sitting for hours with his knees tucked under his chin, holding on to his single Vickers gun for support. Poor sod, it was a most uncomfortable position, it could be my turn before too long.

The crew of a Hampden bomber was different to crews of the other bomber aircraft, the Wellington and Whitley. 5 Group Bomber Command squadrons did not carry an observer as a navigator. For some reason the brass wouldn't have them. A Hampden crew was two pilots and two W/OP AGs, with one of the pilots assuming the duties of a navigator. It would have to change later no doubt, with the introduction of bigger aircraft and a shortage of pilots.

At this time there were no sophisticated aids to navigation other than loop bearings, stars and radio bearings and fixes from a number of direction finding ground stations. We did carry an observer once during training. He couldn't navigate around a piss pot and before long had us entangled inside the Coventry balloon barrage, nasty. I later heard he had completed a tour of operations as a bin gunner. This was not to say all observers were equally poor, but 5 Group wanted no part of them.

The idea of quickly expanding the number of operational crews was simple enough. A crew flew together on operations for about ten trips, the navigator pilot and bin gunner then formed the nucleus of a new crew, picking up two inexperienced members straight from training. An operational tour consisted of either 30 trips or 200 hours operational flying, whichever came first. Aircrew were then usually taken off operational flying and posted to a training job for a rest period to pass on their experience to new crews.

Of course many squadrons at this time had lots of pre-war aircrews, and these were usually experienced fliers. It was generally considered lucky if you managed to be crewed up with a pilot with lots of hours under his belt. Fate stepped in again for me and I was fortunate enough to be crewed up with one such pilot—Flt. Lt. Doughy Baker, of whom more later.

Chapter 4

And so at last, after just over one year in the Air Force, I was off to join my first operational squadron. My crew at Finningley was split up and posted to various squadrons in 5 Group. My own posting was to RAF Hemswell. There were two Hampden squadrons sharing the aerodrome at Hemswell in Lincolnshire. One was number 61 squadron and the other 144. I had been posted to the latter, the date was the first of November, 1940.

There was a quiet sinister air about the station as I settled in and reported to Station Headquarters to book myself in and pick up the inevitable arrival chit. Still clutching my chit I was told to report to the squadron crew room right away.

"Squadron Commander wants to see you immediately lad," said the adjutant. He was old, silver grey hair, a Flying Officer, and sporting first world war medals below his pilot wings. I noted too his small brass VR badges on his tunic lapels identifying him as a pre-war volunteer reserve. A great character who looked after all his squadron boys with the air and grace of a father figure. The Adj described himself as the greatest coggage basher in the business.

Squadron Leader Douglas Haigh, the Commanding Officer, was a different kettle of fish. Here before me was your dashing good looking pre-war regular Air Force Officer, full of bounce with a reputation as an expert aviator. The ribbon of the Distinguished Flying Cross sat beautifully under his pilot's wings. Later I was to learn he'd won it for a mission bombing at low level the Dortmund Emms canal. A Victoria Cross, the country's highest decoration, had also been awarded to a pilot of a 5 Group squadron for the same raid.

"Right Sgt Walker, welcome to 144, that's the good news. You're on ops tonight and that's the even better news."

I spluttered, "I haven't officially arrived yet Sir."

"Yes I'm aware of that lad, but bits of bumph take a poor second to operational requirements in my book, and you've been specially selected," he continued.

"Can I ask why Sir?" I started to say nervously.

"No you can't, but I'll tell you anyway. I'm desperately short of sparks and you can start earning your corn straight away. You'll be flying as first Wireless Operator with Flt. Lt. Baker, and you will be joining his flight, 'A' flight right away." The C.O. continued, "I want you to report to 'A' flight immediately, so go and make your mark with the flight commander. Let's hope your association with 144 squadron will be a long and happy one."

I murmured quietly, "Thank you sir," and was quickly ushered out. Looking back, it was the finest way to start a tour of operations, no time to ponder, no time to soak up the horror stories; but simply thrown in at the deep end before I had time to draw my breath.

Flight Lieutenant Desmond Alison Baker, to give him his full monicker, was something entirely different. Of course with a name like Baker he had to be called Doughy. Small, wiry, with a large drooping moustache, his figure matched his moustache to a tee, like a crumpled bag. I noticed his hands which were tiny with very thin wrists. I thought Jesus how can this character have the strength to lift a fully loaded bomber into the air, and fly it for the next eight hours. How wrong can you get? I was to learn later that he was a natural born flyer who flew by the seat of his pants. I was hopefully in good hands for my first real operation against the enemy.

"Sit yourself down lad, I don't bite," he said. "Welcome aboard Walker, this is the best flight of all, and you can consider yourself doubly lucky that you're getting some air under your arse with me tonight. How old are you lad?"

"Eighteen, Sir."

"Bloody hell, they get younger by the hour. What's that you're clutching?"

"My arrival chit Sir."

"You mean you haven't officially arrived yet?"

"No Sir."

"Christmas, I don't like these omens. Give me your chit," which he promptly filled in. "Right lad, take that over to the coggage bashers, hand it in, and then go get yourself measured for a parachute and an Irving jacket. When you've done that, get your head down for a couple of hours, and don't be late for briefing."

Briefing for tonight was at 1600 hours. Where would the target be for tonight? My first real operation against the enemy. Could I cope?—that was the next question. After all, unless wireless contact was established before leaving the east coast, you had to abort, and boy I didn't want that on my conscience.

Sleep was out of the question, so I side-stepped the idea of getting my head down. A number of others had come to the same conclusion. I wasn't quite sure if I was in the Mess ante room or a gambling den. Through the smoke and haze there were poker schools, brag schools, games of crown and anchor, all going on in various corners of the room.

There was plenty of money to be won or lost. Nobody was interested in me. Was this the shape of things to come? If you had money in your pocket and you were "frying tonight" there was little point in hanging on to it. Scanning the crew list, I found out that my bin gunner for tonight's show was one Sgt Chambers.

"Oh, Bill Chambers, that's him over there rattling the ivories," I was told.

I introduced myself. As soon as he opened his mouth, I realised he was a Geordie. Bill was from Newcastle. Later I learned he was also aiming to become a concert pianist, and the way he made music, probably a good one too. He was almost a veteran having already done twenty operations, every one with Doughy Baker. He quickly assured me that our Captain was one of the very best, if not *the* best pilot in the squadron, a real ace at the base. I was beginning to look forward to Operation number one.

The station briefing room was buzzing with noise. Two squadrons' crews were on the flare path tonight, ours and the sister squadron, number sixty-one. There was instant hush as the Station Commander took his place.

"Right chaps, settle down," he said. "Your target for tonight is Brest."

Someone close by said "A piece of cake." A real live Group Captain, well decorated too, a rare bird in my book. I stifled a chuckle, remembering the last time my target was the same place, none too successful either. I was brought back to reality by the Station Navigation Officer giving us his specialist briefing on the route outbound to the target, and more importantly, the shorter and more direct route for returning to base.

It all sounded so easy, everything conveniently covered in a little over five minutes. My lot was next, signals. It followed the standard pattern emphasised to a boring degree during training. It was stressed how important it was to contact Group before coasting out, abort otherwise and probably jettison your bombs, kill a few fish, God I hope not. We were told the content of the signal to send having bombed our primary target, and similarly one for bombing the secondary, time permitting, both in bomber code. As the communicator, I picked up the colours of the day, together with the letters to reply to any challenges from friendly shipping, frequencies and call signs to use with ground stations. All this information was on flimsy rice paper, airmen for the eating of. Finally, we had a short sharp briefing from the intelligence wallah. Full of apologies for his lack of information. However, since most of this trip would be over the oggin, there wasn't too much he could say.

We were all waiting patiently to have the 'piece of cake' explained. It was left to the Station Navigation Officer to fill us in with the details. He stroked his long curly moustache. "Right chaps, tonight you're all going gardening."

Gardening, I thought to myself, what's the hell that got to do with blasting old Jerry? The answer, soon apparent, caused a sudden hush and a sucking of teeth from a number of experienced crew members.

"Gentlemen, the two pocket battleships the Scharnhorst and Gneisnau have quietly slipped into dry dock at Brest and we want to keep them bottled up there. So your task for tonight is one of laying mines outside the harbour in the positions marked on your target maps." He continued, "The secondary target, once you've dropped your mine will be Lanveoc airfield with your two 500 lb wing bombs. We have reason to believe the Luftwaffe have moved in with a squadron of JU 88 bombers." He paused, waiting for his pearls of wisdom to be digested. "Any questions? No? OK chaps, good luck. Wish I was coming with you." This produced a burst of good natured laughter all round.

The met man was the last link in the specialist briefing chain. He intoned in met symbols, which to me all sounded reasonable, not much to worry about, no nasties en route, pretty black but clear enough for the navigator to be able to pin-point leaving the British coast and a good view of the target area. A clear sky meant we could see the stars for astra navigation. "Per Ardua Ad Astra"—is that what it meant?

I wasn't listening too hard, thinking more about my work ahead, praying all my equipment worked. I caught ". . . and finally the weather for your return should be reasonable. If you have to divert, all the airfields in Cornwall will be fit. Have a good flight."

The Wing Co. was on his feet. "OK chaps transport at Messes at 2200 hours, first aircraft off at 2359, and from now on, nobody, but nobody goes anywhere near a telephone. Nothing goes further than this briefing room, understood? See you all tomorrow morning for eggs and bacon."

There were things to do before I joined the others in the Mess for fried egg, a pre-flight meal. I checked the crew's helmets in the parachute section, walked over to the armoury for a discussion on ammo and magazines, collected my signals satchel with all my bits and pieces, did a quick check at the aircraft to see if my boxes of coils were all stowed, looked at the aerials, and finally satisfied, repaired to the Mess.

I would look forward to this meal later on when food rationing began to bite and operational aircrew were the only recipients of fried eggs.

Over the meal, Bill Chambers filled me in with personal details of the two barons who made up the rest of the crew. Here I was crewed up with three people, each one of which oozed charisma. Flt. Lt. Doughy Baker, probably the most experienced bomber pilot on the station, a married man, whose wife was at this very moment starring in a revue at the Windmill Theatre in London. She was billed as the pocket Venus, a household name in theatreland, and a gorgeous platinum blonde to boot. Doughy was very much in love, both with the Air Force and his lovely wife, but not necessarily in that order.

Pilot Officer Tony Black, our second pilot-cum-navigator, was the son of a very famous father, a well-known impressario of the London theatre scene. Tony was engaged to one of the forces' favourites. She too was presently starring in a musical comedy in the West End, another gorgeous blonde. Tony's girlfriend had special dispensation to visit the station at any time, to wave us off. I couldn't wait to meet both of them—pilots obviously preferred blondes.

"Transport" the cry rang around the Mess. Someone said "Let's get this show on the road." I'd just finished writing the odd letter home, and one to my girlfriend, nothing maudlin, or philosophical, just general chat mostly about my coming forays into Lincoln and the surrounding countryside.

There was a good piss up going on in the ante room, tomorrow was pay day. Tonight they didn't have to brave the elements, reserved for the rest of us. As we piled out of the Mess and into the back of a three ton truck, the strains of the service ballad, *"If your engine cuts out you've got no balls at all"* floated out into the still black night. The makeshift benches in the back of the crew transport were most uncomfortable, designed to chill the bones, and I began to shiver. I was not alone, nerves maybe. Nobody spoke, no instant repartee, as we trundled along to the parachute section to be kitted out. There was a cloying smell of carbolic, which for two of the airmen tonight would be the last bath they would ever take on this mortal soil.

Flt. Lt. Doughy Baker always planned to be first away. We taxied out immediately the green Verey signal had crackled into the night sky. How the hell did he know where to go, the night was a black as a whore's drawers.

I listened to other aircraft of 5 Group on the radio, transmitting on the special frequency, already airborne and on their way, some to other targets in Deutschland. They would be bombing railway yards in the Ruhr valley. The duty pilot flashed us a green on the aldis lamp at the take-off point. "OK Wireless and Gunner, you both strapped in OK?—acknowledge, skipper here."

"OK skipper from both of us."

"We'll be off in two minutes. As soon as we get airborne WOP get W/T go."

"OK skipper," I answered.

The Hampden bomber was built like the shape of a champagne glass. The very slender back end of the fuselage with its twin boom, lifted into the air and vibrated as soon as full power was applied on the engines. My cupola was pulled back open so that I could operate my guns if necessary. These were twin Vickers on a scarf ring mounting.

The Luftwaffe at this time were occasionally sneaky, putting a Junkers 88 in with departing bombers and shooting the odd one or two down. These were intruders. We had to be always prepared to engage. I gave a thumbs up to Bill sitting underneath me like a screwed up ball, and away we went. The take-off was smooth, though the run seemed endless, but with a full bomb load on it was only to be expected.

"W/T go OK skipper, listen out to Darkie."

"Christ that was quick WOP—OK I'll tune to sixty six four. What's the first course Nav?"

And so we were on our way, and my blooding was about to begin. Incidentally, Darkie was an emergency channel which could very quickly provide navigational assistance to aircraft who got themselves lost, and plenty did in those early days without sophisticated navigational aids.

Remembering the words at briefing, 'a piece of cake', I got to thinking about what the hell were pocket battleships. The name belied the immense fire power we were to feel directed towards us during a later sortie.

We crossed the coast at Culdrose in Cornwall. By this time, the aircraft had staggered up to 10,000 feet, and it was bloody cold inside and outside. Ice was beginning to form on the leading edges, upsetting the airflow, which did not make for smooth flying. I cursed myself for drinking far too many cups of tea before departure, the intense cold was affecting my overful bladder. Tapping my under gunner on the shoulder I shouted to him, "Keep your eyes closed Bill, I must have a piss."

"A nervous one," he answered.

Practising the call of nature was a hit and miss affair and usually the poor old bin gunner, unless he was warned beforehand, got an eyeful.

The navigator required some assistance so I got him some bearings from a number of radio beacons. Having passed them on, he thanked me and plotted them. Visibility was good enough for him not to worry too much about navigation.

"OK gunners, go ahead and test your guns," ordered the skipper. Both of us cocked the twin Vickers and fired a short burst, watching the tracers disappear into the night as streaks of coloured lights. The smell of cordite filtered back and stayed around for a few minutes, the gun barrels were nice and warm. We both reported in, guns serviceable, settling down until the next bit of excitement. It was bloody cold, like sitting in an open cockpit. My hands were beginning to feel numb so I tried to get the circulation going, it was probably nerves.

The intercom crackled again, "Right young Walker, look out to port at nine o'clock. Can you see the searchlights in the distance."

"Yes sir," I answered the pilot, only to be quickly rebuked.

"Don't call me sir lad in the air. I'm skipper. Got it? Let's have some good R/t discipline."

"Sorry skipper," I replied.

"OK you'll see someone's getting a pounding and there's plenty of flak around, so keep your eyes peeled, we don't want to get bounced."

The rest of my first real operation was uneventful. We descended smoothly into the target area, laid the mine, dropped our two wing bombs on the airfield on the coast, and quietly climbed away. My task of providing assistance to the navigator was fulfilled to the letter, and some four hours later we landed back safely at Hemswell.

Easy, easy, a veritable piece of cake. Filling in my flying log book in red ink, with 'Operations—mine laying Brest' in the remarks column was even more exciting. I was on my way. I was now productive aircrew, earning my corn. Bomber aircrew had an inbuilt fear of three phases during any tour of operations; it was getting over number one, number thirteen and most important of all, the final one, before a well-earned rest. The stories were legion of those who didn't make it. "Well done lad" from the skipper, sent me off to bed very happy. I'd been accepted.

There were of course a thin line of characters who never wanted a rest, characters who were always wound up like a clockwork spring, couldn't relax. Operations were like a drug, it had to be taken all the time. Arthur Paxton was one. To give him his full title, Flight Sergeant Arthur Paxton DFM, was the deputy squadron signals leader. Pax to his friends, his nickname was a complete transgression of its Latin equivalent. This man was no peaceful being, he was sated with a bitter hatred of the German race, and simply wanted to carry on proving it.

His sense of duty had to be admired, but underneath most people felt he would eventually get the chop, the reaper would not be denied ad infinitum. Pax had already completed one tour of operations, recognised by the award of the DFM. That little purple striped ribbon worn with pride did not come up with the rations for Wireless Operator Air Gunners. Paxton was a gem, one of the most helpful characters I was ever to meet and we were to remain close friends for a long time to come. Considering this was still early days, early November 1940, Pax was already a legend. He would volunteer to take the place of any Wireless Operator who fell by the wayside, either ill, sick, dying or dead.

It was on one such operation that Pax was to be awarded an immediate bar to his DFM, and this is how it happened.

Chapter 5

Tubby Wilson was different. To give him his full rank, Flight Sergeant Anthony James Wilson, was probably about to make service history. The differences were readily noticeable. Apart from the fact he was a roly poly figure, he was also much older than the majority of aircrew on either of the two squadrons on the station. Tubby was married, a family man with two small children, and unofficially he lived off the station, a practice generally taboo for operational aircrews.

Tubby and his crew had had a rough old tour to date, and together they had completed twenty missions. On one occasion, a daylight raid against the naval base at Sylt, his aircraft and crew were the only survivors from a formation of twelve aircraft sent to bomb the docks. The formation was bounced by ME 109 fighters, whose pilots quickly realised the bombers' inadequacy in fire power. Neither bottom or top guns could fire beyond the trailing edges of the wings, as the fighters carried out cross over beam attacks. Tubby's rear under gunner took his red hot gun from its mounting, pushed it through the fuselage amidships, put on a magazine and blazed blindly away. They were left alone. During later daylight raids, two panels were cut amidships, beam guns fitted and an extra gunner carried. However, shortly after this, primarily due to unacceptable heavy losses of aircraft and crews, daylight raids were suspended.

Tubby Wilson and his crew however would never complete those magical thirty operations and a well earned rest. I was friendly with his WOP/AG and sensed there was something wrong, but I didn't have to ask him what was bothering him, because he confessed to me one evening after a few beers. He was thinking of requesting a change of crew. This was unheard of. Whatever was bothering him was very serious indeed.

"What's the problem?" I asked. When he eventually filled me in with the details, I was shattered. It transpired that they had flown their last three sorties completely over the North Sea, where they dropped the bomb load, flown the required number of hours before returning to base, and concocted a plausible story for the benefit of the Intelligence staff during interrogation. It was unbelievable, and obviously Flt. Sgt. Wilson was on the edge of a nervous breakdown.

Tubby Wilson's Wireless Operator went sick before the next operation and Arthur Paxton was called in to deputise. Pax knew by now what was happening, and had been specially briefed by the Station Commander to carry out certain instructions.

Bomber aircraft, for their own protection against being fired upon by friendly forces, were fitted with a piece of radar equipment known as the IFF. The abbreviation stood for Interrogation Friend or Foe. The little black box was secondary surveillance radar equipment which allowed our own radar stations and certain ships to interrogate an aircraft, either as friendly or an enemy one. We were briefed to switch it off after coasting out and to switch it on again before coasting in when returning from operations.

Paxton's brief was simple. He would leave the IFF equipment on the whole time, allowing Group to track the aircraft at all times and eventually produce a radar plot as evidence in a probable subsequent court martial.

The target was the docks and shipping at Heligoland Bight, with enough fuel carried to allow both the simulated operation and the real live one, if Tubby still intended to drop his bombs over the North Sea before returning to base. Wilson's nerve had obviously gone and once again he intended to offload his bombs in the North Sea. Arthur Paxton had other ideas.

By a pre-arranged code word known only to Group and Arthur Paxton, a message was relayed by W/T to the aircraft that Headquarters were satisfied with the evidence and the aircraft should return to base. This is where Flt. Sgt. Arthur Paxton took charge of one bomber crew avoiding the authority of both the Captain and

Group Headquarters. Removing the Verey pistol from its stowage, he loaded it with a cartridge.

Making his way to the cockpit, he asked the pilot, "What the bloody hell is going on?"

Wilson, quickly realising the game was up and his bluff had been called, ordered the co-pilot to drop the bombs and give him a course for home. That order was just as quickly countermanded by Pax, who, pointing the Verey pistol to Wilson's head, told him in no uncertain terms; "Tonight you are going to the target unless you want your bloody head blowing off." From there on, into the target and return, the Wireless Operator was in sole command of a bomber aircraft.

On return to base, Wilson was charged with cowardice in the face of the enemy and was the first aircrew member to be labelled with the insidious term 'lack of moral fibre', LMF for short. One of the first shell shock victims of the air, he was later court martialled, sentenced to two years hard labour and discharged from the Royal Air Force with ignominy. His crew were all punished by severe reprimand and each one sent away for a period of punishment training to an Aircrew Discipline Centre. Flt. Sgt. Paxton was awarded an immediate bar to his DFM.

Chapter 6

Our masters had not yet got around to making full use of the phrase 'maximum effort' and, in retrospect, operating during the early stages of the war was relatively easy. By easy I mean we were not expected to fly night after night, but were generally rested after each operation, which could last for two or three days, before you were detailed again.

Naturally we all made the most of stand-down periods. This usually meant nightly prangs to Air Force City, the ancient city of Lincoln, and a pub crawl around the favourite hostelries. Each night would generally end up in the local dance hall sizing up the talent on offer. There was already tremendous rivalry between different stations and squadron aircrews, and the stories and characters became legend as the war progressed.

Lincoln was also a favourite place for informers who sympathised with the German cause and unfortunately many a loose tongue cost dearly the lives of brave young bomber crews. The war was still being played as a game, not to be taken too seriously by its main protagonists.

The memory of seeing my first Luftwaffe aircraft being shot down was quite unreal. The aircraft, a Junkers 88, seemed to dawdle over the city out of a clear blue sky, shooting down a Hurricane on its tail before being hacked down itself by a Spitfire, the pilot executing a perfect victory roll to celebrate his kill. There was a spontaneous cheering from onlookers watching the German aircrew escaping from a blazing aircraft by parachute, floating gently down to mother earth. I counted the chutes—one, two, three—there was one missing. The aircraft was descending slowly in a flat spin. Come on, come on, I almost shouted, get out, get out. A small black bundle left almost in answer to my plea, but his chute didn't open. I couldn't watch it hit the ground.

Later on I saw the enemy airmen who were locked away for the night in the main guardroom. They were typical, tall, arrogant, blonde Ayrians, and yes we had an affinity with them as fellow flyers, after all, the blitz had still to come and the battle of Berlin a long time ahead.

We flew together as a crew for the next ten operations, eight of which were against the pocket battleships the Scharnhost and Gneisnau still bottled up in dry dock at Brest. Not one of these eight sorties was as easy as the first one, neither were they all concerned with the laying of mines outside the harbour. The next operation, and my second, was a bombing raid carrying armour piercing bombs against the ships themselves. And naturally the area around them, and the docks themselves were very heavily defended.

Over the target area I was quickly to become a devout Christian and a coward at one and the same time. The plan was to go in low just above one hundred feet over the top of the battleships themselves. This was Coastal Command stuff, tactics alien to high level bomber crews, and we were all very apprehensive. The gaily coloured anti aircraft shells, in addition to what the ships threw at us, rattled against the side of the aircraft. My instinct as the fireworks crossed over seemingly just above my head, was to duck and kneel and say a quick prayer. They appeared so close, and lit up the whole of the aircraft. There was an acute silence all round, none of us were enjoying this one. Another aircraft to starboard suddenly exploded in a ball of fire. I could almost touch it. It was too low for the crew to bale out, and I watched it all the way down, a flaming torch as it smashed into the ground exploding with a tremendous impact. With the cupola back, not only could I hear the whoosh and crackle of exploding ammuniton, I could also smell it. This was getting far too serious, somebody didn't like us. Thank God the Hampden wasn't too big a target.

"Hold on crew," the intercom crackled. "I'm going to do a split arse turn out of this, otherwise we stand a good chance of buying it." The bomb load had gone somewhere close to the target area and the aircraft was light enough for such a manoeuvre. At the same time there was no problem with high ground, no chance of meeting a cloud with a solid centre.

It's an entirely different ball game in the back of an aircraft looking rearwards, rather than looking dead ahead with your hands on the pole. Bill Chambers almost finished up in my lap and was instantly airsick all over me. The ploy had however worked and we were soon heading out to sea setting course for East Anglia and home. I could almost taste those eggs and bacon.

When we settled down, Doughy apologised. "Sorry crew, but that was necessary. Everything OK at the back end? You feeling OK now bin gunner?"

"Ok skipper."

The skipper continued, "I only hope the fuselage has stood up to it. We'll soon know." He slowly climbed the aircraft up to 8000 feet and settled it down for the flight home. Group was quickly told we had bombed the primary target and I busied myself gettings aids for the navigator.

My Piscean intuition told me instantly something was wrong. The beast was beginning to behave like a ruptured crab. There was a problem up the sharp end.

"WOP."

"Yes Skipper," I answered.

"Have you good contact with Group still?"

"Yes Skipper."

"Right. I'm never going to nurse this ship back to Hemswell. I want a diversion into St Eval, the nearest airfield. Get to it OK?"

A quick call nervously tapped out to Group, produced an equally quick response.

"Sorry Skipper, St Eval is out, low cloud and poor visibility. We've been diverted to Tangmere."

"Damn it, I hope we can make it. It's possible we may have to ditch, I'm having one hell of a job to maintain height."

Christ, ditch in the middle of the oggin in mid November, what a prospect to look forward to. I switched to the master D/F station and sent out an emergency message. They acknowledged, instructing me to stay with them. The emergency organisation went into top gear and plenty of good Class A fixes were passed on. At least if we had to become members of the goldfish club, they would know where to search. The split arse turn away from the target had affected the navigator sitting in the nose. He had been flung against the fuselage and he reckoned he could have suffered a broken ankle.

"OK," from the boss, "whilst we've got time on our hands, let's go through dinghy drills. I want no cock ups, let's get it right." We were certainly blooded tonight alright. "I take it everyone can swim?"

"Sorry skipper," from Bill Chambers. "If I'd wanted to swim, I'd have joined the fishheads."

Bloody hell, a navigator with a suspected broken ankle and a Gunner who couldn't swim. Thank God for Mae West.

"OK WOP, break out our feathered friends and let's get them ready with the right information." I'd forgotten all about our basket of pigeons. They were still safely stowed, clucking madly away, unconcerned. I couldn't believe my eyes, pigeons also having feelings—one had laid an egg. We now had an added responsibility with a family on our hands.

Drifting across the English coast at below two thousand feet, the skipper was having one hell of a job trying to keep the aircraft straight and level. Landing this beast was going to need every ounce of skill and airmanship. A very shallow turn to port and the navigator saw Tangmere dead ahead. There was no response to my call for landing instructions from the aerodrome tower. However the chance light was on, illuminating the landing run.

"I'm going in," said the skipper. "Everybody prepare for a possible crash landing. Brace, Brace."

It was a beaut. Sighs of relief all round, we taxied in without assistance and finding a dispersal, shut down the engines. Congratulations were in order for the boss on his performance. It was eerie, there was not a soul around, no ground crew to check the aircraft, no transport to take us for de-briefing, it was ghost-like. There was a light ground mist, which added to the effect, and shapes of other aircraft around us could be made out, but not one sign of personnel.

A decision was taken to make our way to respective Messes, leaving behind our injured Navigator comfortable in the aircraft, to be picked up by ambulance from sick quarters. The Sgts' and Officers Messes were either empty or nobody was bothering to answer the telephone. This was not on, operational aircrew were entitled to a fried egg after successfully completing an operation. Later on when food was scarce, 'frying tonight' became an aircrew catchphrase.

It took some time before we eventually ran someone to ground, albeit one oversized, overweight Cpl. who described himself as skeleton staff—some skeleton! "What's going on?" we all enquired. He told us the Luftwaffe generally bombed the airfield every night without fail, and each night the place was evacuated, except for one or two duty personnel. Tonight he was C.O., head cook and bottle washer. All the remaining aircrews who had arrived earlier had been hurriedly moved into transit accommodation well away from the aerodrome. Bill and myself settled into the Sgts' Mess and cooked ourselves one enormous breakfast, before getting heads down in large comfortable leather chairs for a few hours well earned kip.

The co-pilot suffered a badly sprained ankle and was declared fit to return to base the following morning, soon after the station came back to life. However, inspection of the aircraft was not good. The airframe was in a much worse state than we expected, pock marked with holes. We had been peppered from stem to stern with light anti-aircraft fire. One of the flaps was suffering from brewer's droop, no wonder it made the skipper sweat his balls off trying to keep it straight and level. This had been a magnificent piece of flying in anybody's book. Looking at the full extent of damage, a quiet Ave was offered up by one and all.

The following morning we fed and watered our family of pigeons and made preparations to return to base, courtesy of the railway. Doughy Baker had other ideas. He pulled a few strings and before too long, the station Anson was on its way to pick us up. Home in style. Actually, Doughy wanted to hot foot it down to the Windmill Theatre to watch his wife performing in a new revue. Her performance must have matched his own, because on his return to camp he sported a pair of her finest silk cami-knickers. We flew them from the aerial mast as our very own standard.

Operations number two having been duly recorded in red ink in my log book, it was suitably embellished in the remarks column with an aside about being hit by anti-aircraft fire. We reckoned this deserved a small celebration, a line shoot too good to miss. So it was hot foot down to Lincoln for one big piss up, to Bomber City. Operational crew were never allowed to stray too far away from base, so Lincoln being the nearest big town was always full of bomber crews.

The Barons used the Saracen's Head, the snake pit, and we peasants had adopted the Crown next door to the local dance hall. Occasionally the twain would meet, mostly at the local hop when the pubs had closed, and the name of the game was to latch onto a piece of crumpet. More often than not, game set and match was awarded to the peasants; local girls were choosy!

Back at Hemswell, things were beginning to get too serious. No longer were crews allowed after morning checks to disappear back to Messes for games of chance etc. Lectures were organised on a variety of subjects, subjects which at the time seemed awfully boring, but which later on when it was no longer a game and heavy losses were being sustained, made an awful lot of sense.

Aircraft recognition techniques, showing us silhouettes of enemy aircraft gave us ranges at which to open fire if attacked. Intelligence briefs, ship recognition, what to do in the event of being taken prisoner of war—these were all discussed. How to use a parachute and to land safely, how to try and evade capture by the Germans. Some of this information was to become invaluable to me later on when I had to bale out in anger and become a member of the exclusive caterpillar club. I never dreamt though that I would hit the silk for a second time, qualifying me for a bar.

Chapter 7

The rest of my crew were now on the home stretch with only eight more trips to go before finishing their tour of operations. It was unbelievable that the next six operations for all of us were all to be mounted against those two bloody battleships now nicknamed the Salmon and Gluckstein, still in dry dock at Brest.

Our masters were determined either to destroy them, some hope, or failing that, keep them immobile and so allowing freer passage on the high seas for our own convoys, which, with hunter killer submarine packs prowling, were taking a beating. Briefing was beginning to sound like a well worn gramophone record with the needle stuck in the same groove. Brest again, a piece of cake, the slices were already stale. The targets alternated between mine laying and straightforward bombing with a maximum bomb load of four 500 lb bombs.

Gardening was relatively easy, but remembering my second sortie, I was always uneasy when Lanveoc airfield had been designated as the secondary target. A for Apple, our own aircraft was always beautifully behaved. We were fortunate to have an excellent ground crew, all pre-war fitters and riggers, hand-picked by Doughy, and why not—it was his prerogative as Flight Commander. It was always a good sign when your ground crew volunteered to fly on pre-flight checks before actual operations. It inspired confidence all round, especially to aircrew.

By some strange quirk I was not looking forward to operation number eight. This was to be the last one for all of us as a crew. It meant that I would be floating, waiting to be crewed up again, probably next time with a sprog crew. Fate held the pack of cards and I wondered which one would be dealt to me.

It was a daylight departure and standing on the touchline, hair blowing in the wind, waving us regally goodbye was Tony Black's girlfriend. This was the first time I had seen her in the flesh, although I had followed her success in most of the newspapers. What a figure, she was gorgeous. She gave us all a lift standing there, and, as the power went on and the tail lifted into the air, brakes off and we rolled away, it was almost a pleasure to go to war.

Our own 'royal standard', the pocket Venus's cami-knickers, fluttered proudly in reply. Nothing was said about this being the last trip, but there was an air about it, which I didn't like. My Piscean intuition was twitching away like mad. The trip itself was an absolute doddle. Everything went right, we dropped the mine and the bombs, and Doughy headed the nose for home.

Even in the circuit back at base there were no congratulations. Aircrews are susperstitious creatures, let's get this kite on the ground, back in dispersal, before anyone dare open his mouth.

The tense message booming out in a quiet frequency from the tower shook me to the core. "A for Apple, A for Apple dowse your navigation lights, there's an intruder overhead." In the Hampden, control of both R/T transmitter and receiver was handled by the pilot. The remote switch for both equipments including the volume control was in the cockpit, just to the skipper's left hand. For some strange reason, call it fate, call it poor airmanship, call it what you will, Flt. Lt. Doughy Baker committed his first and last act of not being on the ball, he failed to react.

I intersposed swiftly, "Skipper, tower is calling you, switch off your navigation lights." That vital message from the ground was acted upon too late.

All the cards were stacked against us, we had to be the first aircraft back in the circuit. None of us saw the JU 88 that shot us down. It attacked us from a head on position and with all our lights on, we were a sitting target. We were the first of five aircraft the intruder was to successfully destroy that awful winter's night. The enemy crew eventually got too cocky and after a low level straffing of Scampton airfield, was shot down itself by a ground gunner manning a Bofors gun.

Ourselves, we were raked completely from front to rear with

cannon and machine gun fire. There was no reply on intercom from the front end, so I immediately assumed both pilots had either been killed or seriously wounded. Poor old 'A for Apple' was very much on fire. It was becoming too close for comfort. The aircraft fortunately was descending slowly in a shallow dive away from the airfield boundary. Bill Chambers looked up at me with complete bewilderment in his eyes, the look said it all, absolute shock.

I signalled him to put on his chest parachute, to jettison the door and to bale out. He had to leave before me otherwise I was trapped. Bill was obviously badly wounded, unable to respond. I signalled again, time was running out for both of us. "Get out, get out," I shouted, but he didn't move. "Christ this is it," I muttered. But no, something, someone spurred me on, I must not give up and finish up in a burning heap. Picking up Bill's parachute from its stowage, I quickly clipped it on his chest, jettisoning the side door at the same time. He sat up with a sudden rush of air, and I gently but firmly rolled him out of the aircraft, pulling his rip cord at the same time. My hand was covered in blood, I'd been wounded. But I soon realised that Bill my under gunner had been hit in the back. It's amazing how fast you can move when the chips are down, and by God they were certainly down for the crew of 'A for Apple' that night.

I rolled out of the aircraft, pulled the rip cord of my chute immediately and before I had time to draw breath, had slammed into mother earth with one hell of a crump. The aircraft crashed shortly afterwards in the next field, with a large violent and colourful explosion. It wasn't November the fifth but this was our very own fireworks display, as well as a funeral pyre for Doughy Baker, our gallant skipper.

Trying to walk was impossible. I assumed I had broken a leg or an ankle. Blood was running from a head wound, my left knee was oozing blood also through my flying suit, and I didn't like the look of my left hand which had been badly mauled, two fingers had either been shot away or had been broken by bullet wounds. I was alive though, but not entirely kicking.

The next thing that happened as I lay in this potato patch feeling very sorry for myself was the arrival of two members of the Local Defence Volunteers (LDV). Both were armed with rifles which they cautiously and threateningly poked towards me with their outstretched arms. Both were convinced I was German, a Luftwaffe member, and it took a few choice Anglo-Saxon swear words to make them change their minds.

"Get the blood tub over from Hemswell," I urged. "Have you got a phone in your cottage?" I asked them. They reluctantly carried me back and then began a lengthy argument once indoors whether it would be right to use bandages since they were ARP property.

By this time I couldn't have cared less what they used. All I wanted was to get into an ambulance and be on my way back to the comfort and medical expertise of sick-quarters. Eventually an ambulance and the doctor arrived, and we began a very bumpy journey to the nearest military hospital. The services had taken over a stately home at a place called Rauceby, which had been quickly converted into a hospital. After filling in the usual forms stating next of kin, religion etc., I was bundled off to the operating theatre for surgery to my wounded limbs.

When I came to the following day, I heard the whole grisly saga of what had happened the previous night. "What was the fate of my other crew members?" was the first question on my lips. Bill Chambers and Tony Black had both survived, but both had been very badly wounded, much worse than me.

Bill had lost one hand and he would never walk again, and finished up in a wheelchair for the rest of his life. A bullet in his back had severed his spinal cord. No more fine music for Bill to play on the piano, life was cruel. Tony Black sustained severe injuries to his vital reproductive organs by a direct hit from a cannon shell. Shortly after this he was cruelly to receive a 'Dear John' letter from his fiancée. I don't know which hurt the most. Later, after a long period of convalescence, he was invalided from the service and entered a monastery to serve another cause.

Poor old Doughy Baker did not survive his last trip. Our gallant skipper was not wounded at all, but stayed with a crippled aircraft to give us all a chance. When he knew we had all gone, he baled out, but at such a low altitude, his parachute failed to open and coming in head first, he broke his neck. A sad ending for a very brave pilot.

Flt. Lt. Baker was awarded an immediate and posthumous George Cross. Bill Chambers collected a Distinguished Flying Medal, and Tony Black and myself a mention in despatches.

My parents were immediately sent a telegram informing them I had been wounded in action, and to visit me as soon as possible. Naturally they assumed the worst had happened. Train journeys during the war, particularly ones which involved a journey across the country from Lancashire to East Anglia, could take a very long time. My parents arrived at Grantham railway station shortly before midnight, to be told that the next train to Lincoln was the milk train the following day. Mum and Dad settled down for a long cold wait on a station bench to await its arrival. The Air Raid Warden on his final rounds was a friendly chap and after sympathetically listening to their story, told them he couldn't possibly allow them to stay on a cold draughty railway station for the rest of the night. Mum and Dad must come home with him and have a bed for the night. My parents slept that night over a little greengrocer's shop in the centre of Grantham, and were served breakfast the following morning by a charming young lady before she went off to the local girls' grammar school. Mr and Mrs Roberts and their charming daughter Margaret were remembered for their great kindness to perfect strangers. Margaret later married Denis Thatcher.

My parents arrived at the hospital to be told I was in theatre. Yes, I was in the theatre, not being operated upon, but was in fact enjoying an afternoon's entertainment by a visiting concert party. Elsie and Doris Waters, alias Gert and Daisy, were the stars. When they were told I had saved my life by baling out, Gert said, "Bert would have made a good parachutist, he was always hanging around waiting for them to open."

It had been some time since I had last written to my girlfriend. She in turn had asked a friend working in the RAF records office to look me up. My girlfriend was later told I was reported 'Missing believed killed in action'. She could of course have accepted the explanation but no, kismet was once again on my side. Laura immediately wrote to my last address and before too long the letter arrived with me at Rauceby.

Hospitalisation in a stately home, with all its many amenities and marvellous surroundings, had a wonderful rehabilitation effect on most of its inmates. However, not all enjoyed the caring that was lavished upon them. My nearest bedmate, a fellow aircrew member, had sustained nothing more than a simple fractured leg in an aircraft crash. We were the only two Air Force aircrew in the hospital and the staff were most attentive, especially to me, I was their hero. My bedmate was determined however he was never going to fly again. He was a classic case of malingering. The staff constantly upheld me to him as a fighter who was determined to fight again, without avail. The man was a loser, he had a death wish. Before I left hospital after less than a month, his leg had been amputated, after which he simply went downhill and I was to learn later he eventually died. What a sad waste of a human life.

The bullet in my left knee was my most serious injury. It smashed a cartilage which had to be removed, but I was young and strong and within three weeks was declared fit enough to be discharged back to full flying duties. My fingers had been slightly affected, but constant exercise would soon have them supple enough to wear leather gauntlets. I would always have a small wound on the right side of my head caused by ricochet. I was lucky.

Given one weeks sick leave, my decision was to spend it with my girlfriend and family rather than go home to Blackburn. My decision in one respect was a bad one, I was never to see my parents again. The house was destroyed with most of the road by a single land mine, with Mum and Dad buried underneath the rubble.

This was a spur for me to get back to full flying duties as soon as possible. I had a tour of operations to finish, and the sooner it began again, to avenge the death of my parents, the better.

During my leave, a telegram arrived telling me to report to another station when my leave had finished. The squadron had in the meantime moved out of Hemswell and into a new base in Rutland. Our old station had been handed over lock stock and barrel to the first squadron of Vickers Wellington Bombers to be fully manned by Polish aircrews.

Even in such a short time of absence, the squadron had changed, expanding rapidly. There were now three flights, A, B and C. I was to stay with A flight and had been appointed to the position of Deputy Signals Leader even though I had only completed less than ten operations. I was considered an experienced squadron Wireless Operator.

It is said that one volunteer is worth ten pressed men, so I immediately volunteered to become crewed up with one of the new crews. This made me the only crew member with any operational know how, a point to stand us in good stead for the next round to come. My pilot for the second round was barely nineteen years of age, still older than me and a Sgt. Pilot to boot. The other two crew members were marginally older, we were a very young crew indeed.

Sgt. Allan Kirkby was not long out of Harrow, the tide mark was still showing. He was born to lead, at least that was his opinion, but he was to be led by the nose by no less than a secondary school boy on a number of occasions before his next birthday.

Sgt. Jack Hunter, the Navigator Co-pilot, was a bit of a rough diamond. A fellow Lancastrian, his family background was steeped in the fishing grounds of the Irish seas, rather than the air above it. He told us he was distantly related to one of the top American families, his family having been in the trawling business based in Fleetwood for many generations. Jack himself had been sitting on the sidelines enjoying its patronage as the spoiled boss's son and heir. Jack Hunter was not the bomber type, a point he constantly drove home. He saw himself as one of the wide blue yonder boys, chasing Huns, shouting Tally Ho, not entirely happy with the possibility of having a crew around him. His forte was the solo type of flying with no one else to worry about but himself. He was a typical fighter pilot who, by some unfortunate cock up in administration, found himself saddled with bomber operations. I worried about him. Could he cope as a Navigator—his job was important, very important indeed. Jack fortunately never made it as bomber captain, but was to go on to flying Spitfires over the jungles of Burma. During the short time he was with us, we nicknamed him Happy Jacko.

The fourth crew member was an enigma to say the least. Sgt. Taffy Richards was ex miner, ex Borstal, and Cardiff Tiger Bay. Taffy was the senior crewman, if you call twenty years of age senior. Short, dark and wizened, Taffy had already seen a lot of life, most of it seedy. The majority of W/OP Air Gunners were not generally blessed with too much grey matter, Richards was no exception. There was little doubt though he was a character in his own right. I felt sure he was either a redundant gypsy or running away from something or someone even more mysterious or nasty. A chain smoker, his remaining teeth matched perfectly his badly nicotined stained fingers. Gratuitously known in the crew room as the man who had worn out two bodies with the same face, he was utterly without fear. Time meant nothing to Taffy Richards, he spent most of his off duty hours either drunk or playing poker. If there was a card game, you could bet your bottom dollar through the haze and the fug would be the deadpan face of our bin gunner, a cigarette dangling from his lips. He very rarely spoke, except to up the ante. Taffy never ever discussed operations or the possibility of being despatched to the land of his fathers. He simply appeared when required to do so, with the minimum of fuss. I adopted him from square one, generally to keep him out of trouble. I saw to it he was around when we were detailed for flying or any other duty. Allan Kirkby, the skipper, could never get through to him, not for want of trying mind you. They were on different planes and finally Kirkby gave in and accepted the fact he was lumbered with him as his bin gunner. Taffy was an enigma, there was little doubt about that. On rare occasions when he opened up to me, mostly when he was three parts pissed, his knowledge of classical music astounded me, and like most members of the Welsh race, Taffy had a beautiful voice.

Breaking the duck with my second crew when it came was the big one, a shock to the system. There was more than a certain amount of fear and trepidation when we knew the target was Berlin. For nearly six weeks I had been off operations, and to be re-christened with a trip to the capital of Deutschland, with a completely new crew as well, raised the adrenalin more than some. Most of the other bomber groups were involved, so there would be Wellingtons, Whitleys and Hampdens on stream tonight.

The raid was to be a reprisal for a Luftwaffe attack on London. Tit for tat, to prove to the fat Herman that the RAF could hit Berlin just as easy and just as hard. The Hampden unfortunately was not the best of aircraft to be targetted all the way to Berlin and back. Navigation, mostly suspect, had to be absolutely spot on and because the fuel intake needed to be maximum, the bomb load was the minimum of just one tiny bomb plus incendiaries. This was a prestige operation really, more to raise the spirits of people at home, a still shell-shocked nation, rather than inflict any real damage to the enemy's capital city. Berlin had in fact been bombed at least three times before, but had suffered only minor damage.

The target was the main railway station at Templehoff, the stradling of which could hit other important buildings around it. Intelligence hinted that both Adolph and his Reich Marshal, together with important members of the party, would be at a function in the city. The hope was to embarrass Goering who repeatedly said the RAF would never be able to attack Berlin.

The weather had to be good, this was very important. Bad weather could mean poor navigation and a bigger loss rate. We all needed good pin points for a successful sortie. Take off was early, scheduled for 1500 hours, in order to give us at least a good two hours of daylight and allow us to cross the Dutch coast at dusk, a good sighting in. I was a little worried about the professional skill of the navigator, Jack Hunter, who did not impress any of us on a recent night cross country planned as a work up together. We were at one stage completely lost in the middle of a balloon barrage. None of us was impressed by the performance. We thanked our lucky stars it was a brilliant moonlight night and we visually threaded our way past the swaying balloon cables. Darkie was well used on that occasion.

We were a select band of aircraft and crews targetted against the Reichstag that night, with a spoof raid mounted against a secondary target as a precautionary and diversionary measure.

Taffy our tame gunner had been given another job to do tonight which put a stop to him having a crafty fag during flight. The extra task was the carrying of small packages of what looked like cream crackers, which had to be kept moist at all times. Taffy had to keep dipping them into a bucket of water, which shared his tiny position. These small incendiary devices, which apparently if they became dry would burst spontaneously into flames, were to be tossed out by Taffy over areas of forest with the idea of setting wooded areas alight. Poor old Taffy, his fingers were numb with the cold long before we reached the release point. He could have suffered a bad case of frostbite. No one ever told us if they were successful or not, but since they were withdrawn shortly after this, it was safe to assume they weren't and the boffins would have to go back to the drawing board.

On a later raid which routed over the top of Rotterdam, Taffy and myself tossed out of the aircraft small packets of tea to celebrate Queen Wilhelmina's birthday, in addition to raising the spirits of our Dutch compatriots.

The majority of aircraft lost on previous raids to Berlin had been due to a number of reasons, most of which had little or nothing to do with direct enemy action. Vile weather was the paramount cause on one raid, when a number of crews simply got themselves lost, ran out of fuel and either crash landed in occupied Europe or ditched the aircraft in the North Sea never to be recovered.

There was one embarrassing occasion when an ace crew had set fire to their aircraft and destroyed all their codes assuming they were in enemy territory. They evaded for three days before they realised they were in England. Finger trouble all round. It could have been different if we had sophisticated navigational aids to help us, but we hadn't, and those at our disposal were being constantly jammed by the German signals organisation.

Time drags when after the initial briefing, there is a long wait before transport arrives to take you out to the aircraft. Sometimes there were hours to kill. Interesting how aircrews fill them in, we lived from one day to the next, no one could make any long term plans.

The skipper was a loner, overawed by all that responsibility placed on his young shoulders. He would lose himself by walking around the airfield all alone with his thoughts, he was not the type to get close to any one of us. Basically he was very shy, somewhat immature for the job in hand.

Taffy Richards as we all knew had to get into a card game. Poker he loved, it was an obsession with him. I'd given up worrying or wondering if he ever slept. If there was a thick cloud of smoke, he would be in the middle of it, crouched over the table together with a school of about five other aircrew. In the centre of the table there was invariably a large pot of pound notes. The stakes were high, maybe they had the right idea, after all it was a day to day existence.

The Co-pilot was different again. Happy Jacko spent most of his waiting time horizontal on his sack in the Mess, either staring at the ceiling or reading 'Health through Strength' magazines. It takes all sorts. I filled in my waiting moments writing letters, reading a book or playing a game of snooker. My outside interests were either cricket or football, representing the station or the Group.

"Transport" the tannoy spluttered into life. Packed into the back of the three-tonner, we drew away from the Mess forecourt and the adrenalin began to flow. The strains of a ribald song hammered out on the Mess piano wafted across, somebody not on the battle order was enjoying themselves.

Taffy had made a pile of money at poker. He was a natural card player. He assured me he would be having himself one ginormous piss up on the proceeds tomorrow night in Lincoln. "There's confidence for you boyo," I said in a lilting Welsh accent. The skipper looked scrubbed and shone like a new pin. This was to be his baptism of fire, I prayed he would be up to it. Nobody spoke, we all had our own private thoughts. Next stop, parachute section, I collected the pigeons who were clucking madly away. Taffy fed them both a piece of chocolate from his ration. They loved it. He chain smoked his last packet of five Woodbines. It was going to be a long ride before the pigeons came home to roost, praise the Lord.

The day was cold and crisp, a lovely clear sky, The Met man promised us a bomber's moon. There was nothing more to add to earlier briefing except to wish us luck and to tell us we would be making the news both in press and radio on our return.

Sitting in the aircraft having completed all pre-flight checks, we awaited the firing of the start gun from Aerodrome control tower. A red light meant a scrub, a white one standby, and a green Verey light start engines and taxi out for take-off.

A short discussion on intercom between the two at the sharp end, on the initial course to steer after take-off, height to fly etc. The two of us in the back were told to be extra vigilant for the first three hours, most of which would be during daylight and dusk.

"There's the green light, skipper," from the Navigator.

"OK crew, starting engines."

A quick thumbs up from the ground crew and the port engine spluttered and crackled into life, a shower of sparks flying off into the slipstream. After both engines were started, running up checks were carried out. I read off the checks to be completed from a check list, so that the pilot did not forget anything before taxiing out to the take-off point. The Duty Pilot, standing to one side of the take-off run, flashed us a green on his Aldis lamp and waved his hand in salute. Throttles open, brakes full on, the tail boom lifted and vibrated madly, release of brakes, and we were on our way snaking down the airfield.

The aircraft lifted off quite comfortably. Sitting strapped in the back, watching the ground streak away in a shower of sparks, was a sensation designed to set the pulse racing. Some take-offs were long and heavy, this one was much better. We climbed slowly away, course set for overhead the port of Boston, and coasting out, climbing steadily to a cruising altitude of 10,000 feet. I gave Group a quick radio check and felt good when the ground operator replied to me with an equally quick acknowledgement. We were on our way.

"W/T go skipper."

"Well done W/OP. Listen out," he replied.

Out over the North Sea, once we were clear of the shipping lanes, both of us tested our guns, each firing a short burst to warm them up. Soon we would be coasting in across the Zuider Zee and enemy coast ahead. Sitting for hours on end in an open cockpit, perched on no more than a padded stool isn't exactly exciting, especially when there is nothing going on around you. I busied myself by taking loop bearings but the Navigator wasn't ecstatic about them, grunting in approval after I passed them on. It was true to say that during the early days of the war, the most exciting periods of operations were during take-off, the short time over the target, and the landing back home. During take-off and landing phases, it was becoming more and more prevalent that you could be joined by the Luftwaffe engaged on intruder operations. They looked for sitting ducks and they were successful on many occasions. However, like us, the Germans had yet to improve on night fighter tactics and the ability to shoot down aircraft over their own territory, but both sides were learning fast.

Even so, a far ranging target such as Berlin presented a number of problems. Crews ran the gauntlet of miles of searchlights. Searchlight Alley it was nicknamed, interspersed with spouts of light and heavy flak. This was jousting brought swiftly up to date and we were the modern day knights cloaked in camouflaged armour.

Bomber crews airborne are a silent race, trained to say as little as possible. Good R/T discipline, always alert and to pass information as quickly and as succinctly as possible. This is why time would drag, ninety per cent boredom, ten per cent sheer panic. This would be changed considerably as the conflict became much more a battle and less like a game.

Adrenalin would flow in short sharp bursts, punctuated by a euphoria of different smells. At least in my position, cupola back, I could filter the stronger ones out. Back to reality it was bloody cold and we have another six and a half hours ahead of us.

The good weather we were promised at Met briefing all the way to the target was adrift. Beyond the Dutch coast it quite suddenly changed to a cloud-covered sky, maybe the Hun was manufacturing it. The low cumulus cloud was well illuminated with ranks of searchlight beams, probing away to discourage low level aircraft. Light flak came spewing through the tops sporadically, obviously defending important installations down below our flight path. Taffy was asleep below me, he never moved an inch. There was slight nervous twitch in both the skipper's and the Navigator's voices, it was only to be expected. The flak and yellow tracers were well off target so there was little to worry about, as long as those two radial engines kept purring away.

This was a reasonably big raid tonight on Berlin, with over two hundred aircraft heading its way. With luck it should be a wizard prang, but this continuous cloud cover was a disaster for accurate pin points. Assistance from loop bearings was out since the Hun had been jamming frequencies, so they were discounted. The big city would have to be bombed by dead reckoning, unless mercifully cloud cover lifted long enough to see the ground.

No such luck, the weather was not on our side tonight and so the bombs and incendiaries went down on estimated time and the glow below. This was a bloody long way without the satisfaction of seeing Berlin below. All of us were disappointed.

Later reports from neutral observers based in the German capital were not encouraging, the majority of bombs having landed well away from the city. Altogether a most disappointing raid. This was unfortunately par for the course until the boffins came up with better guidance systems.

My first task over the target was to transmit a coded message back to Group Headquarters telling them we had bombed the primary target, and sadly having to log a distress message from one of our own aircraft which had been hit and was on fire. The final transmission was simply baling out. Poor bastards, the reception committee down below would be none too glad to see them.

The squadron lost two aircraft, one over Berlin and another crew ditched their aircraft in the North Sea. Both crews were reported 'Missing, believed killed in action'. Eight more brave aircrew. We were to learn later that the crew lost over the target area had all been taken prisoners, to spend the rest of the war no doubt in Stalag III.

On the way back to base, the weather took a bloody miserable turn for the worst. Heavy rain and sleet, with severe airframe icing, forced the skipper to gradually fly lower and lower. Down, down we drifted, stabilising at around two thousand feet. Buffetting by gale force winds, thank Christ they weren't directly on the nose, fuel reserves were finely tuned.

This was one time I needed to earn my corn, plenty of bearings and fixes were a definite must. The good Lord was in my corner and I provided the Navigator with some excellent Class A bearings. He was relieved because his plot had fallen apart, it was the difference between hitting the English coast and floundering around the North Sea.

We were the last aircraft to land at base, some of the more experienced crews had already written us off. It was a good start for a sprog crew and one from which we would learn some valuable lessons.

The Navigator, after briefing, just said "Thanks George, you saved our bacon." The skipper had done a good job under pretty adverse weather conditions. He was like a dog with two pricks. Taffy went off to bed and got himself pissed out of his mind in Lincoln the same evening. Poker had its good points. I retired to my bed, very tired, happy that my skills had paid off. I was chuffed entering operations—Berlin in red ink in my flying book.

The next three trips were something of a busman's holiday.

Adolph and certainly his Reich Marshal Göering did not like the RAF bombing his capital city. This was a severe affront to the German people. He swore in his passionate way the Luftwaffe would by reprisal flatten every British city to the ground. Some German bomber squadrons were moved to bases in France and Holland from where they began to mount night bombing attacks on major cities, Bristol, Birmingham, Liverpool, Manchester, Coventry, Sheffield and London. Our own night fighter squadrons were very thin on the ground. In truth, it was never envisaged they would be needed. There were few pilots who even had experience of flying a fighter by night, let alone operating it in anger against a force of bombers. The Luftwaffe had it good. They were able to mount air raids with very few losses. This is where we instantly changed role. Hampden aircraft and crews of 5 Group Bomber Command were drafted into the battle over Britain. The mind boggled, but it happened. Medium bombers were utilised as night fighters.

Carrying a crew of five, one extra mid-gunner amidships, we were routed in the air by a specially coded message to the city under attack. We then patrolled over the top, hoping to be in position to shoot down an enemy aircraft preferably before he dropped his bombs. Both anti-aircraft guns and searchlights would not be in action for a specific period of time, after all we didn't want to shoot down our own aircraft.

The first sortie was Liverpool. The night was as black as pitch and we soon realised that the sky is an awfully big place. We flew specific flight patterns, but nothing was seen before being recalled to base.

From our grandstand view we watched the port and dock area of Liverpool being steadily plastered with incendiary and high explosive bombs. Not a pretty sight, but we couldn't do a thing about it.

The next two nights there was a similar performance only the target in each case was different, firstly Coventry and finally Sheffield. It was fraudulent having to enter these three sorties as night operations, so much so that I quietly forgot them. The second Christmas of the war was at close hand and I was beginning to feel lucky enough to enjoy it.

The local hostelry, a very nice pub, was close to the airfield and mine host could still provide an excellent bill of fare. Naturally everyone looked forward to spending Christmas at home, but unfortunately our masters had other ideas.

We stood by to mount a raid on Christmas Eve, but whether it was the Christmas spirit or the foul weather over the continent which changed the minds of the top brass we will never know, suffice to say that there was a big scrub all round. We could all rest easy.

Christmas festivities on Air Force camps are usually splendid affairs. Christmas of 1940, the second one of the war, was no exception. It doesn't make up for not spending the festive season at home with loved ones, but this one in particular we all needed to laugh, to forget for those short moments the seriousness of the world beyond the camp gates. It was a round of parties from start to finish, good natured with plenty of grub provided by overworked and underpaid kitchen staff.

This war was different; directed against a civil population by Reich Marshal Göering. For us, still bombing military targets, still playing the game, before too long the Queensbury rules would have to be shelved for the duration.

The county of Rutland, the smallest county in the land, was flattish and damp, similar to Lincolnshire. It drew around it a cloak of fog during the first weeks of the new year. Fog meant we kept our arses on the deck. RAF crews were not trained to fly off under pea soup conditions to attack the enemy. It had been tried, but the end result was the loss of an aircraft and its crew.

One of the squadron's experienced crews pressed on regardless, took off for a mission in thick fog hoping to be able to land away on their return to base, when Met forecast the weather would improve, certainly on the South coast. It had to happen, fate or simply bad luck. Shortly after take-off, the aircraft immediately lost an engine and, since the majority of Hampden pilots were not particularly well trained in the art of flying on one engine, especially one with a full bomb load aboard, the aircraft stalled and crashed beyond the airfield, leaving the squadron short of one crew, one aircraft, and a Station Commander with egg on his face. That ploy was not tried again for a considerable time. The grounding allowed overworked groundcrews to begin to sort out a large number of minor maintenance snags which had been carried as acceptable risks. The bad weather in some respects was therefore a blessing in disguise.

New aircraft equipment, radio and radar were beginning to appear and lectures filled in the working hours. The rest period was good, games and parties were organised between rival squadrons. It all raised morale, which was sorely needed. We even had the first of a series of concerts by visiting cabaret artistes. The town of Stamford was drunk dry. Happy days.

On the other hand, our Co-pilot Jack Hunter was distinctly unhappy about his role of having to fly as Navigator, he felt emasculated. I could sympathise, but until the system was changed, there was nothing he could do except witter about it—this he did at every opportunity. It would be sometime ahead before an aircrew member and wearing a single wing brevet as Navigator would be introduced. It didn't make too much sense to carry two pilots, especially when these were in short supply and in great demand. Truth was that Jack was a reasonably good navigator. The niggle for him if truth be known was that one day he would take a full crew of his own, and that responsibility was depressing him.

Sgt. Taffy Richards on the other hand had no great pretentions in accepting any new responsibilities by becoming a first Wireless Operator. Taffy was happy enough tucked up in his posiion as my under-gunner, which providing he kept awake during flight, did not tax his grey matter too much.

At some stage however I would have to see what he was made of and if he could cope. The skipper was beginning to find his feet, impetuous at times, and beginning to volunteer his crew for all kinds of extraneous duties without discussing it with the rest of us. A little more co-operation was needed. We had diplomatically to put him in his place.

The weather improved during the last week of January. New crews were beginning to swell the squadron's ranks and some of the older hands had started to look forward to the end of a tour of operations and a well earned rest.

My good buddy Arthur Paxton had become commissioned as a Pilot Officer and had taken over the reins of Squadron Signals Leader, with me as his deputy. Spare time was spent giving lectures to the new boys on newly introduced radio equipment. Two aircraft had been modified with a modern transmitter and receiver, designed by the firm of Marconi. The controls were in three different colours, red, blue and yellow, for ease of operation and reference. We nicknamed them idiot switches.

As they say, I was 'specially chosen' to be the first Wireless Operator to try out the new equipment on operations. It worked like a dream. A local firm had also designed an electrical gun mounting, so that by simply pressing a button, we could now freely move the twin Vicker machine guns. Things were looking up, roll on better navigational aids, they were a paramount requirement.

Earlier I mentioned the local pub where the landlord was always extremely friendly to the squadron aircrews. It was an enormous shock to everyone when he was taken into custody and charged with being a German agent. Immediately prior to arrest he was seen taking pot shots with a rifle at army despatch riders.

'Be like Dad, keep Mum' was a slogan which now had some real meaning to everyone serving on the station. A little box arrived for me through the official mail. I assumed it would be the emblem of an oak leaf—my mention in despatches. The contents turned out to be a small gold caterpillar brooch, complete with two ruby eyes. The back was suitably engraved with my number, rank and name. I was proud to wear it in my tie, a recognition to the cognescenti I had saved my life by hitting the silk and baling out. Club members were at this time part of an exclusive club, but one which, if you will forgive the pun, was to increase considerably by leaps and bounds as the war progressed.

It was unusual to see an RAF aircrew Sgt. wearing the Military Medal. The MM decoration was generally a preserve of the army. Squadron aircrews were however treated to a most interesting talk by the recipient on a variety of aspects to do with escape and evasion from behind enemy lines.

Our evader had the unique distinction of being the first member of aircrew to have walked out of occupied Europe. The good advice he proffered made a lot of sense. I memorised it well, little realising at the time I would have to put his advice into practice myself.

The nearest rival squadrons just down the road were based at RAF Scampton. The squadrons were number 49 and 83. 83 Squadron now sported two Victoria Crosses, one of which had been awarded to a Sgt. Wireless Operator Air Gunner. He had bravely beat out a fire in the back of an aircraft with his bare hands, enabling the pilot to safely fly the aircraft back to base. The remaining two crew members had baled out over enemy territory. His pilot on return was awarded an immediate DFC, later to be killed on operations before he could collect it. The Wireless Operator who was badly burned was hospitalised, and the award of the country's highest decoration, the VC, to a 'jeep' was a tremendous boost to badly needed aircrew, particularly Air Gunners and Wireless Operator Gunners. A jeep was an affectionate term for WOP/AG.

Bomber Command sorely needed new aircraft, aircraft able to carry larger bomb loads. We needed aircraft able to strike deeper into enemy territory. The pre-war trio of medium bombers, Whitley, Wellington and Hampden, were all becoming obsolete, too old, and becoming harder to maintain. There were rumours of new aircraft on the stocks and around the corner. Mention had been made of some with four engines—what a boost to morale that would be. It was curtains if you lost an engine in the Hampden, the Mess song said it all, "If your engine cuts out, you've got no balls at all." The Americans had the Flying Fortress and we wanted one ourselves. Apparently the firm of Shorts had something on the design board, let's hope it came to 5 Group along with some good aids to navigation.

Bomber Command was also growing with each passing day. Aerodromes were springing up all over the counties of East Anglia. We talked about satellite airfields where aircraft were occasionally despatched to all day for training exercises.

During the shortest month of February, when it wasn't snowing and the grass airfield had been cleared, we flew a further four sorties. For the first time we began to bomb the Ruhr valley, although the battle of the Ruhr was still to come. The area contained the industrial might of Germany, with masses of searchlights and barrages of heavy and light anti-aircraft fire. We entered Geilenkirchen, Essen, Dusseldorf and Duisburg in our respective log books. I was halfway through a tour of operations, fifteen trips against the enemy, fifteen more to go.

During the last raid on Duisburg the whole situation was eerie. There was no flak at all during the time we were close to the target, during the bombing run and long after leaving the target area. And yet all around us each one of us saw aircraft being shot down in flames. We were all puzzled. What new and horrendous weapons had the enemy found? Intelligence sat up and took notice during debriefing. They had their views, but were giving little away. Later on we were told why aircraft were being so mysteriously blasted to kingdom come. Night Fighters were out in force, and they were being homed on to our radio transmissions by ground controllers. This was shattering news for all and sundry. The planners had to come up with new procedures, and fast. The result was no more open radio transmissions over the target. Radio silence techniques were introduced until we crossed the Dutch coast on the way home. The question had also to be raised why, prior to operations, all Wireless Operators religiously carried out air ground tests on vital radio equipment. These checks were an absolute give away to enemy signals intelligence when forecasting operations against themselves. The consequence of this was the design by the boffins of a dummy aerial, ensuring equipment could be checked out but would not radiate too far. Spoof transmissions were introduced to fool the enemy and to our own advantage.

Two newcomers joined the squadron at the beginning of March. Both were American, seconded from the American Army Air Corps. They were both airgunners from Flying Fortress squadrons.

Taffy welcomed both of them with open arms, they were both avid poker players. Taffy's game improved no end and under their aegis he began cleaning up. He began to chatter in an endless stream of poker hands. Occasionally during a lull in flying I would sit down and watch the school operate. Each player was deadly serious, with mountains of money passing backwards and forwards. "You can't take it with you," Taffy would say with a shrug of his shoulders when he was on a losing streak, which was not very often. Allan, our straight-laced pilot, didn't like it one little bit. The knowledge that he had an impetuous gambler in his crew annoyed him no end. We were all on one big gamble, so what the hell. His off duty pursuits were poles apart, the front and back end of the aircraft were one hundred and eighty degrees adrift when it came to off duty interest.

Hank Johnson, the American Master Sgt. was blooded on the next operation. The two pocket battleships were both still holed up in dry dock at Brest. Intelligence information indicated the possibility of the pair of them being rapidly prepared for a possible move, either back to Germany or a Baltic base in Norway. The hierachy had obviously decided that our efforts to sink the bastards to date could not be allowed to go to waste. They must be reminded we hadn't forgotten them.

Nothing as easy or as simple as gardening, the laying of more mines, was on the cards. This time something was different, something new. A small bomber force would be saturating the area with anti-personnel incendiary bombs. Take-off was scheduled for 1900 hours, the date the twelfth of March, under conditions of full radio silence. The night was brilliant, a full moon in a crystal clear sky. As the stream flying below one thousand feet headed across the Bay of Biscay, the low height provided that extra bit of protection from prying radars. A bomber's moon was dreaded later on, when night fighters were out in force against bomber streams.

Taffy much to his annoyance was asked to stand down. He was livid and blamed the skipper who he said had it in for him. I was a bit annoyed too, Taffy was good luck.

All this was completely new to Hank, my under gunner, who for the first time in his flying career was actually airborne at night, and also for the very first time against an enemy to boot. Most Master Sgts. seem to be big men and Hank was no exception. Tucked away below me in the bin gunner's position, he filled every inch of space, and then some. Remembering all too well the last time we had been targetted against Brest under similar circumstances, and the split arse flying needed to get away from the barrage of fire, I prayed we wouldn't have to endure a repeat performance.

There was also a very different skipper in pole position on this occasion. Nearing the target area, we could clearly see the outlines of the two ships, or were they decoys? The whole of the dock area was a blaze of light, the glare of seemingly hundreds of searchlights and the usual blanket coverage of different coloured shells were filling the air. Hank sucked his teeth.

A lot of the area was filled with yellow smoke which slowly drifted across the centre of the aiming point. We began our timed bombing run, hoping to be able to keep straight and level. I knew it, I felt it in my water, I was going to do my praying act again. I knelt like a praying mantis, keeping my antenna well down. I hated bloody battleships and all who sailed in them. Hank's chewing rate increased tremendously. He muttered "Jesus" into his microphone. I put my foot on his shoulder for assurance.

"Left, left—steady," intoned the Navigator. "Bomb doors open."

We were being rattled again by shell splinters, it was a repeat performance. One orange light seemed to come right inside the aircraft. I was almost blinded by the glare, ducking automatically as tracer shells crossed over the top of the fuselage, rockets from both sides. Someone else was getting rattled.

"Nav. How much longer do I hold this course?" from a frightened skipper.

There followed a breathless reply of "Bombs away."

"Right hang on, I'm not going any further into this inferno. Turning port now. Give me a steer out to sea."

The answer came quickly. "Steer 270 and climb to 1500 feet."

"You OK under gunner?" said the pilot.

"Not sure, Commander, it feels like liquid running down my legs, could be blood, could be something else. By jeeze though it sure is cold back here. Time you guys had heated suits," replied Hank. We didn't have them, but that remark by our American observer was the forerunner of better things to come.

My thoughts as we slowly climbed away and set course for home was that I now knew so much about pocket battleships and how unsinkable they appeared to be, I might have been better off in the Navy. The Salmon and Gluckstein were not my favourite targets. We celebrated by firing the guns on the way home. It was a salute to me. It was my nineteenth birthday.

Neither Hank nor his colleague flew again on operations with the squadron. Someone realised Group could have broken all diplomatic protocol since America at this time was not in the war against the axis powers and consequently their nationals should not have been engaged in warlike acts against 'friendly' nations. Of course we were fortunate in 5 Group to have our share of volunteer Yanks flying with the RAF. They shared with us nothing but hatred for the Nazis. The two American airmen were quietly and quickly removed on to specialised gunnery courses.

In the spring, a young man's fancy turns to love. Jack Hunter completely out of the blue told us he was getting married. We were due for a week's leave, which now was granted every six weeks. I wondered whether to accept his invitation, or to spend my leave with my girlfriend down in deepest Gloucestershire. The decision was made for me. Jack Hunter was, to his great delight, posted to a fighter training unit, and the wedding was postponed. I went down to Stroud to stay with my girlfriend, and we became engaged.

The countryside around the Stroud valley is like another world, quiet, peaceful and beautiful. Here I could totally escape from the war. There was no war here, no nightly rumblings of aircraft, no line shoots, no saturation of airforce blue; complete rural peace. Young airmen weren't generally given to philosophising, nor did they think too much about the politics of war. For most of us time was too short, life had to be lived from day to day. Yet down here the frenetics were gone, slotted away for the period of your leave. The battle being fought in the air was swift, constant and deadly. By basic standards, nothing more than a supreme testing of dedicated individuals, modern day knights, who sought the elements kindred to the spirit of the air. Underneath the youthful exterior nevertheless there beat intense inward resolutions to do well not only for themselves, their comrades, but ultimately their country.

Each one of us listened to BBC radio news programmes, and when they announced that last night a force of RAF bombers attacked and destroyed military installations in Germany, and you were a small part of that attacking force, it entitled you to a twinge of satisfaction, a member of a productive and also a destructive team.

Seven days leave, especially when you are enjoying yourself, is not long enough. All good things as they say must come to an end, and as I said my goodbyes and boarded the train back to Stamford, I was at least feeling refreshed. Would I be fortunate to survive another six weeks of battle before my next leave? At least we were fighting our war from the green of good old England, thousands of my fellow servicemen would never see home again.

Chapter 8

The War itself was not exactly going our way in the spring of 1941, but at least the plans made by the Air Staff during the years prior to the beginning of hostilities were beginning to pay dividends. New aircraft and equipment were already on the horizon, replacements for the aged medium bombers.

The first minor crisis was to be told that my bin gunner, Taffy Richards, had gone missing. Not missing on operations, but absent without leave. Taffy eventually turned up unconcerned two days later and no way would he give anybody the reason why he was late. Naturally he was charged with absence and had to be punished. Punishment for aircrew for minor disciplinary and flying offences was a short spell at an aircrew punishment centre, with the posh title of 'Aircrew Refresher Course'.

There were two established centres, one at Brighton on the south coast and the other one at Sheffield in Yorkshire. The course itself was a posher idea of a glass house, involving a smartening up process.

The Brighton Centre was based in a local hotel on the seafront. Sheffield apparently was a much more sordid place. The staff who had been quickly cobbled together were unused to dealing with aircrew, all of whom outranked them anyway, and the so-called punishment was nothing more than a week's holiday. Brighton was favourite, and before too long, aircrew were actually volunteering for a quick dose of punishment, until the penny dropped, and Brighton quickly closed down.

Taffy came back from Brighton singing its praises, but in the meantime as a crew we had successfully completed another two operations. Both were relatively easy, no snags, smooth, and different.

Number one was to Geilenkerchen and the second one bombing submarine pens at St Nazaire on the French Atlantic coast. Taffy began to realise he would be sucking a hind tit by missing two trips, but he soon shrugged it off when I convinced the skipper to have him back. Taffy was now three trips adrift from the skipper.

My own tour of operations was beginning to go downhill. A promotion to Flight Sergeant was promulgated, making me the senior ranking member of the crew, and the end of my operational tour was in sight. A full tour of operations had not changed, it was still 30 missions or 200 hours operational flying.

Crew co-operation had improved considerably. We were getting to know one another's strengths and weaknesses. Taffy's was well known, nothing would ever change him. An insatiable gambler, but then we all gambled our existence every day. He still needed someone to keep him on the straight and narrow. That was my lot, I had more of an affinity with him than anyone else. It all needed tact and diplomacy, but Taffy was a likeable rogue.

Allan Kirkby had improved his flying skills by leaps and bounds. He was keen, dedicated, but his one small foible was his lack of crew togetherness. Most squadron crews were welded, spent their leisure time together, but our skipper could not bend. He was a tee-totaller, so that our wild nights out were generally headless. Mooning about the camp confines during periods of off-duty was too serious a proposition.

Sgts's Mess social life was one long round of entertainment. We were fortunate enough to have a fair sprinkling of Mess members with talents other than blasting hell out of Adolph.

The Mess was not exactly the place for born again Christians. My knowledge of dirty songs, most of which were parodies of well-known hymns, expanded immensely. There was without fail, seven nights a week, a ding-dong going on. Mostly we sang ourselves hoarse until the bar shutters clanged down, then it was Mess games, some extremely vicious, but enjoyed with great gusto. Copious quantities of beer were good lubricators.

'Mess games' was the time for drawing up battle lines. A battlefield with no place for the weak of heart. Sheer courage and bravado was the name of the game. Dutch courage indeed for some of the competitors, aided by more than the whiff of a bottle. There were some, always on the side lines, who thought we were out of our minds, a lot of silly buggers, exposing ourselves to broken heads. But they, nevertheless were always loud in voice, silly bloody aircrew. There was no lack of courage from well oiled flyers, tonight it was all a bloody game, tomorrow was another day when most of us would probably be strapped to a loaded bomber, where the stakes were even higher.

With two squadrons on the base, adversaries were tailor made, the honour of the squadron was at stake. The penguins generally watched the goings on from the side lines, allowing the respective squadron aircrews to beat the hell out of one another. With only one squadron, the groundcrew had to field a team. It was generally a one sided affair, when the poor old penguins took a beating. Age was against them, but the beatings were always taken with good grace.

The bar steward would have been detailed by the senior mess member present to leave out a couple of crates of beer, refreshment for thirsty warriors. The battle of the Ante room would generally begin with the most popular game, mess rugby. Let battle commence. The room would be cleared, furniture stacked at both ends and down each side of the room, leaving a clearly defined pitch down the centre. Furniture was a natural built-in hazard, some of which would be in splinters long before the night was out.

Two teams took the field, six a side initially. The ball, home made, compressed coggage formed loosely into a ball, stoutly tied with shoe laces. There were no rules, it was survival of the fittest, brute force, rough mauls, and savage scrums. The object was to try and get the ball over the furniture at the opponent's end of the ante room, by fair means or foul. The game had to be short, fifteen minutes each way, half an hour of cut and thrust, instant substitutes for injuries, and no shortage of eager replacements. The games always ended in a free for all, masses of heaving sweating bodies, tattered battledress and aching limbs.

Surprisingly really the brass didn't stop it. Issue an order banning all mess games, considering the injuries involved. Truth was the station Doc was generally leading the affray. On the spot healing. Comfort for the poor sods left at the bottom of the ruck, with more than the breath knocked out of them. Then there was High Cockleorum, or in a quieter vein, 'Are you there Moriati?' Both games could at times be equally as spirited and fiercely contested.

High Cockleorum sported two opposing teams; five players a side. One player, generally the biggest and the strongest, was the anchor man. His back firmly pressed against a wall on the side of the ante room. The other team members linked together line astern, bent over, heads and ears tucked under each other's rib cage, awaiting the slam on their backs from the first jumper of the opposition. He would vault as far up the chain as possible, hacking, bucking, twisting in an effort to collapse the chain. This was why all the squadron heavyweights were chosen. When either the link was broken, or a jumper would be dislodged, the teams would change over. Best out of three. I've seen more broken legs at Cockleorum than that.

By comparison 'Are you there Moriati?' was a breeze. A game for some of the older idiots. Two blindfolded players each suitably armed with a club of solid rolled-up newspapers, scuffling around the floor on hands, knees and bellies trying to beat the shit out of one another. Each one would call out "Are you there Moriati?" and, when getting a response would try to fix the opponent's position, to score a hit on any part of his anatomy. Naturally everybody wanted to get in on the act, spurred on by all and sundry, the ante room ended up like a bear pit, good clean fun.

When we had physically exhausted one another, it would be mess songs around a beer-sodden piano. A full repertoire of dirty and not so dirty songs delivered with the same amount of gusto. Never mind tomorrow, tomorrow was another day. Sadly, some of the merrymakers would by then be silenced, silent forever. For the survivors, they got the chop, had gone for a Burton, had his chips. Who the hell was Burton anyway? For us, short memories of comrades, we couldn't dwell too long, it invited the reaper. Soubriquets of silence. Tomorrow I prayed would never come.

It was always the same, the majority would eventually limp away to bed to snatch a few hours of unsettled sleep. Some, the insomniacs, would greet the dawn, slumped over a card table, enveloped in a blue haze playing poker, dealer's choice. Senile dementiates, ageing long before their time. Like grapes on the vine, once young blooming full of spirit, soon the first blush seeping away, leaving most withering on the bough. The politicians engineered this war, we, the airborne knights, picked up the gauntlet, riding out nightly on our winged chargers.

The Barons paid us regular visits, when the tempo increased. We on the other hand were limited to an occasional games evening, a misnomer for a good old piss-up or a Christmas exchange. Games evenings in general were more dangerous than operations, ranging from broken legs and arms to cracked skulls. You could bet your bottom dollar that if there wasn't a good poker school in session, Taffy would be in the thick of it. With his rich Welsh voice, he was always called upon for his party pieces. He came out of his shell and responded well. Richards was certainly a character, he would be remembered long after we had faded away. It was a tragedy when later on he was killed, while a game of poker saved my skin. Fate for me was kind again.

Jack Hunter now departed, we needed a new Co-Pilot Navigator to take his place. We were allocated a Baron, a Flying Officer, Radley College and Cranwell no less. Flying Officer Ron Young had, through a spell of sickness, lost his original crew and, now declared fit again, volunteered to take Jack's place.

Young had already completed half a tour of operations, so he was no raw recruit. Because of his time away in hospital, it had been decided not to allow him to pick up his own crew, but to put him back into the pot as a Navigator. Luck was on our side with our replacement. Young was an extremely good navigator, well-versed in up-to-date techniques. Not only had he made a thorough study of astro navigation, but he was an excellent mathematician, which made him an absolute ace in the art of dead reckoning. A rare bird indeed. Taffy and I thought he might bring the skipper out of his shell, considering their similar backgrounds. Alas young Kirkby was not for bending, and so the pair of us adopted our new blue blood and gently trained him in our ways.

For starters, Young and myself clubbed together and bought a motor car. Petrol was officially non existent, except for the chosen ones. Unofficially it could be 'come by'. All aircrew were issued with camp bicycles, large sit up and beg models, on which everyone careered around the station, and further afield to the local pubs. Just how many steeds went missing, scattered around the hedgerows of bomber bases, would be hard to quantify. No one ever appeared to worry though. Strange, when the time came to move away you could always find one to clear off your slop chit.

Later on when beer was in short supply, forays were mounted by outriders simply to find a pub with some ale. It was amazing how quickly the information was relayed back to base. Frying tonight was the cry, and masses of aircrew astride their trusty steeds set a direct course to the pub in question.

Getting there was easy, getting back home once the pub had been drunk dry was sometimes fraught with difficulty, with a large number of pilots parting company with their transports. We all played a game on the way back, the idea was to try and shoot down one another, bloody silly, bloody dangerous, but it made the journey back to camp more exciting.

Of course there were plenty of cars for sale. The problem was getting hold of the gravy to make them go. The cars were catalogued under the grandiose title of 'Committee of Adjustment' property. To be more specific, they were the personal effects of aircrews who had unfortunately either been killed in action, or had been declared missing on operations.

No one would ever buy one of these cars from either the station or the squadron on which he was serving. Not only was this considered *infra dig*, but was also reckoned to be one sure way of inviting the reaper. The sale of these cars did in most cases at least provide cash for the next of kin. A lot of them lay around gathering rust, and eventually if unsold they were given away as scrap metal.

Paddy Riley, a civilian on the camp who managed the Salvation Army canteen, had no supersititions about being shot down, and he was the benefactor who bought up at a ridiculously low price the majority of cars sold under C of A purchase terms. These cars were then carefully stored, and eventually became the seed corn from which Paddy became a millionaire. Out of death comes success in life.

Ron Young and myself invested the princely sum of eight pounds and bought a 1932 Rover sports car model. Getting the petrol to run it was an art in itself. The car had belonged to an Aussie pilot who got the chop on a sortie over the Ruhr. It was suitably fitted with rubber tubing, through which flowed the life blood from many a parked car. Doctors' cars were prime targets. We could now on occasions go further afield in search of a pub with some beer.

Our pride and joy came to an ignominious end one Saturday night, upside down and blocking the main road into camp. The crew, a mixed one; pilot, Wop AG and two ATS girls not even wounded in action.

The following day, bright and early, there followed an interview with the Station Commander. It was short sharp and to the point. "Get that bloody heap off my station by noon today without fail," he told me in no uncertain terms. Fortunately, someone knew a local garage owner who was looking for four wheels for a caravan. I sold him the wheels and the wreckage surrounding them for twelve quid, which gave us a profit of two quid each. Happy days!

We were beginning to be targetted against the towns in the Ruhr valley, night after night. Essen, Cologne, Duisburg and occasionally a run into Hamburg and the docks. I was beginning to get twitchy, closing in on that magical figure of 30 trips.

Number twenty-eight could have been my last if I had wanted to press it, since I had passed the two hundred hours operations mark. But I had already decided not to count the three sorties when we played the role of night fighter. Was I tempting fate?

The penultimate sortie was against the marshalling yards on a small town called Aachen. We expected it to be fairly easy, and we were right. It was a late take-off, crossing the Dutch coast in the dark, a short uneventful flight to the target and a reasonably quiet one back home.

One more to go Ginge, everyone knew. I was called Ginge because of my crop of bright red hair, with a crop of freckles to match. One way or another I was older than my nineteen years. X marked the spots on my course photograph where many of my colleagues had not been so lucky. There were precious few of us left, gradually being whittled down.

The last one was the one most of us feared. It had happened too many times, the chopper had come down. Small things stick in the memory. Taffy offered me his pre-flight eggs. I refused.

"Let's get this one over first Taff," I told him, "but thanks anyway. I don't really feel like eating."

Tonight Taffy would be up too, working as Wireless Operator. I would be in his place, sitting in the bin. I had prepared him for the rôle change. He didn't like it, but despite his reluctance, before long he would have to accept the added responsibility.

Frying tonight, Christ I hope not. I'd seen at least two squadron members who had been badly burned and survived. Shrunken eyes, emaciated noses and ears missing, they were lingering reminders of burning flesh. Doughy Baker's memory flooded back. If it had to come, please God make it quick. Why was I beginning to feel so damned morbid?

I was among friends. Those that weren't detailed to plaster the Reich in the early hours were as usual enjoying themselves. No thoughts of tomorrow, except that on return you could also join in. New faces at the briefing, sprogs due to be initiated. They were easy to pick out, they asked too many questions, spent far too long on simple things, and smoked incessantly. Some would learn quickly to become warriors of the air. Two crews would be snuffed out tonight in the prime of life, on a simple target like Aachen. Not by flak, but by night fighters, swift and sure, and blasted into a thousand exploding pieces. I saw it myself, almost felt the searing heat, wondered who it was, and then quickly dismissed it from my mind.

"Night fighters about skipper."

"OK gunners, keep a good look out."

"Target ahead. Can you see the incendiaries going down?" this from the Navigator. "Bomb doors open. Turn port two degrees. I'll give you a dog leg around the target area and we'll attack from the other side."

Good thinking, once we'd let our two thousand pounds of bombs go we were on our way home. Home, I was going to get married when my rest came up. Idle thinking—maybe I'll be posted somewhere near my wife-to-be in Gloucestershire.

They say home is where the heart is. My real home was soon to be blasted into a heap of rubble. I later often asked myself the question, why? There were no secret factories, but like us, the Germans used indescriminate bombing tactics. We patted ourselves on the back whenever we successfully returned, but the top brass knew that we were inflicting little real damage to the enemy's resources.

Things would have to change. New methods of pin-pointing a target would have to be devised. Navigation techniques would have to be quickly improved by using more sophisticated equipment.

The greatest minds were employed and set in motion, out of which would come the answers. Me, I was getting close to finishing a tour of operations. That was my own immediate goal. One more to do, and a well earned rest. I hoped that last one would be easy.

When it came, it was somewhat of an anti-climax. We were to drop small packets of tea to the Dutch. The tea had been presented by the peoples of the Dutch overseas colony of Batavia, and the packets were to be dropped over Rotterdam on the way to the primary target. This small gesture was in celebration of Queen Wilhelmina's birthday, each package carrying a suitably patriotic message, hoping to stir the Dutch people to greater resistance and sabotage activities.

The little tag on each one was inscribed in Dutch with the words 'Holland will rise again. Greetings from the Free Netherlands Indies, keep a good heart.' I wondered as I tossed handfuls of them into the slipstream, how many patriots would enjoy its flavour.

Later on, the Free French would request a similar coffee drop over the centre of Paris.

Having off-loaded the tea bags, we were to go on to bomb the harbour at Bremen. Bremen was a new entry in my log book. Bomber Command was beginning to concentrate more and more on shipping strikes, either against dockyards, submarine pens, or ports. The battle of the Atlantic was hotting up. Convoys were taking a hammering, the U-boats supported by long range Focke Wolfe aircraft. Battleships of the German navy were all beginning to inflict very heavy damage on the high seas. The blockade of Britain was on.

Tonight someone was on our side. For me, my last operation was completed without the slightest hitch. Congratulations all round were in order. The Mess staff gave me their own special award, a plateful of eggs and bacon. It went down well. All I needed now was a nice posting somewhere nearer to where my heart was, my adopted home in the South West.

Tomorrow all of us would be going on a well earned leave. For me it would be extra special. Laura and I were married by special licence in a small church at Uplands in Stroud. Absolute joy, two whole weeks' leave, and the honeymoon was to be provided free gratis, courtesy of Lord Nuffield.

Operational aircrews were allowed to take up to two weeks' leave once a year at either of two hotels, in Brighton or Borrowdale in the Lake District. The money was provided by a Nuffield fund. Laura and I decided to visit the Lake District, since we both enjoyed walking and pleasant countryside.

The Borrowdale Hotel, just outside Keswick, was all we could have wished for. The proprietors were two maiden ladies, sisters, both of whom adored the services, and the boys in blue in particular. They gave us nothing short of VIP treatment, considering their very young Flt. Sgt. guest and wife, far too thin, and in need of building up. We were treated to extra culinary delights that could have graced any royal table. The war was millions of miles away.

There were only six guests at the hotel, all honeymooners, all servicemen and their wives. One of the couples was an army major and his wife. He had been repatriated home from Germany for serious medical reasons, and was on borrowed time. None of us burned the midnight oil. After a long day walking the fells, followed by a sumptuous repast, stifled yawns signalled the end of another day. What a lovely way to spend a honeymoon. We both wished it would never end. But before my leave was over, a telegram arrived for me. I couldn't bear to open it, and left it to my wife. A small official form contained two pieces of information. My hopes for a posting to the south of England had been dashed, and tacked on the end was a cryptic congratulations telling me that I had been awarded the Distinguished Flying Medal, a hero at last! The citation should make interesting reading.

My next job kept me still in 5 Group, so it was back to Lincolnshire, to a posting at RAF Scampton. Posted to 5 Group Gunnery Training Flight was the simple order and a report date. This must be a newly established unit on an operational station. A gunnery flight. I was a little hurt since I considered myself as a Wireless Operator first and foremost and Air Gunnery very much a secondary duty. The small ribbon of the DFM would make up for any disappointment.

So I was to be an instructor. I was already thinking ahead, making plans, determined that Laura and myself would enjoy our marital status and live together. It was frowned upon by the authorities, but rules were meant for breaking and once I was settled into my new duties, the next priority was to look for somewhere to live.

Chapter 9

RAF Scampton was a busy station. Closer to Lincoln than Hemswell, it housed not only our tiny little unit, but also two famous bomber squadrons, numbers 49 and 83. Both squadrons flew Handley Page Hampdens. No 5 Group gunnery flight had a motley collection of aged aircraft, one Whitley, one Wellington, two Lysanders and finally two Martinets. The unit was established to give a very basic gunnery course to Sgt. engine fitters who were being recruited to become the first of a new breed of aircrew to be called Flight Engineers. They would replace one pilot in the new four engined aircraft, the Stirling, Halifax and Lancaster coming rapidly into service with Bomber Command squadrons. This was a day-to-day bread and butter job, coupled with research on aspects of air gunnery for improving airborne survival techniques. To this end, the gun turrets in the Whitley and the Wellington could be adapted for either guns or cine cameras. Live firing exercises used the Lysanders, acting as drogue towing aircraft, and for cine film exercises, the Martinets would simulate the role of attacking fighters.

It made me very proud to be part designer of a training aid titled the 'Shadowgraph Gunnery Trainer'. In essence all it amounted to was a chain driven machine on which were mounted scale models of a variety of enemy aircraft. These were capable of being moved backwards or forwards electrically towards or away from a light projected gun sight. Against the background of a large white screen, the student could stop the trainer by simply pressing a firing button. The idea was firstly to be able to recognise the silhouette of the enemy aircraft, and secondly to be able to judge distance and to open fire at various ranges, beginning at six hundred yards. It was simple but effective.

We were lucky, working a standard day, no operations to worry about. Work ended generally around 1700 hours, so that most evenings were our own. Naturally this was the time I began to miss my wife and so I decided to put in a big effort to find a place to live. My boss was very supportive. It didn't take too long, there was a vacant bedroom in a house on the outskirts of Newark, some twenty miles away. It was a long way to travel every day, but there were possibilities of pick ups, and I could always cycle. It was certainly better than having Laura hundreds of miles away.

At this time, women between certain age groups were either drafted into the womens' armed services, or required to volunteer for war work. It was easy enough to find my wife a job in a local factory making parts for ships of the Royal Navy. We moved into our sparsely furnished bedroom and Laura handed our ration books to the landlady, Ma Bullmer, who told us the rent was thirty shillings a week all found. Without pausing she also verbally presented us with a strict set of rules, from taking baths to using or misusing the electric light in the very tiny back bedroom. Never mind, we were at least together. Young love can surmount a lot of obstacles, even a more than fussy landlady. Ma Bullmer, we both quickly found out, was Hitler in skirts. Neither of us had met anyone like her before. She was a tyrant, the most domineering lady I had the bad luck to meet. No wonder she had a room to rent. Albert, her poor and obviously long-suffering husband, was five feet nothing of brow beaten skin and bone. Albert, the poor sod, worked twelve to fourteen hours a day, six days a week. I often wondered why he punished himself so much. The answer was simple to understand, at work he was at peace, at home he was at war.

Albert never spoke up, simply accepted his lot, and was doled out with pocket money on a Friday night like a small child being given a packet of sweets. One day hopefully Albert would turn, but in our time it never happened. Albert was a mental zombie, completely brain washed.

Ma Bullmer's two other adult children were not so different, both also completely brow beaten. Phyllis, the daughter, also worked on munitions. Arthur, the son, the older of the two, was a butcher. Phyllis would never aspire to anything more than the maiden stakes. She reminded me of a frightened mouse. We had of course been utterly spoiled by the treatment at the Borrowdale Hotel, but here everything found at our lodgings had been put through a standardisation programme.

Even during war time, to know exactly what meal would be served to me on my return from work each day including Sundays, was too much. Ma Bullmer had a logical mind, one which was locked on to a set of seven menus, day after day. Arthur the son produced for breakfast each day compressed sausages, rows of sawdust labelled sausage. Two would appear on my plate every morning with monotonous regularity. I refused to eat them after a couple of attempts, jokingly saying that if I ate any more, I would finish up shitting planks of wood. Arthur was not amused.

However the same pair, becoming greener and more shrivelled, appeared each morning on my breakfast plate. This was the battle of the bangers. Ma Bullmer obviously considered my rejection was an insult to Arthur's skill as a butcher.

On the seventh day, I consigned them to a fireplace, from which they were probably retrieved to poison next door's cat. Laura was given a long lecture in my absence on the sheer folly of wasting food. I had won the battle of the sausages, since they never appeared again.

We lived on fish and chips. Frying tonight had a completely different connotation, sometimes surreptitiously sneaking them into the bedroom, but knowing very little got by the nose of Ma Bullmer. "Don't you get enough to eat?" she would ask Laura when I had gone to work.

Dorothy Edwina Bullmer to give her her full name, reminded me of Charley's Aunt. Tall, large bosomed, always severely dressed, and with a huge bun at the back of her head. I always imagined her holding a daily seance with her cronies, who all seemed to be stamped from the same mould.

Ma Bullmer also cheated at cards. On Sunday afternoons without fail, the whole family, including relatives, played cards for money. This was the only real bit of relaxation the family enjoyed after a week's hard labour, in more ways than one. Occasionally I was inveigled into playing, and very quickly noticed that our dear landlady cheated. The game was always the same, five card Nap. Everyone knew what was going on, particularly when the kitty was interesting, but no one had the guts to come out with it, and that included me. My reasons for not doing so were purely of self interest. Trying as our mode of living was, at least we were together, and that made up for a lot of the bad times. Digs were also very hard to find. Laura and I were thankful for small mercies.

The small market town of Newark was the nearest watering hole. Newark, I reckoned, had three redeeming features, in order of precedence; one the local fish and chippie, two the tiny flea pit cinema they had the audacity to call a palace; and last but certainly not least, a brewery. Stock in trade for all three outlets was always good, so we could see two different pictures a week, have a good feed on fish and chips and finally wash it down with liquid refreshment.

As a Lancastrian, used to excellent fish and chips, I expected the best. The small chip shop I rated highly, good job really, since after Ma Bullmer's plain fare, we existed on its output. Newark suffered rigor mortis every night around ten o'clock, along with most of its permanent residents. We saw a lot of the town since the landlady discouraged her lodgers from staying in their box room, and as she put it, wasting electricity. A bath was by roster, and the 'three inches only' rule of tepid water did not make a bath enjoyable, more a survival test. Ma had painted a line rather like a plimsoll line around the inside of the bath, her way of doing her bit. We were charged an extra shilling for every bath, but since we were, like food, rationed to one a week, I made other arrangements to allow Laura the luxury or punishment of a double helping.

Nottingham on the other hand was the favourite place for a good blow out. Nottingham was sin city, all aircrew loved it. Occasionally we were lucky enough to have a free Saturday off together, and Laura and I would take an early train and enjoy the extra delights of a big city. Nottingham was alive, night and day. Some servicemen never got any further, and spent their entire leaves there. The city had everything, good pubs, atmosphere, cinemas, dance halls, and for servicemen away from home, an abundance of lovely girls. Nottingham girls were famous. They all seemed to earn high wages, and they were not averse to spreading money around. The girls, who mostly worked in the Player's tobacco factory, had very few inhibitions.

The local Palais De Dance on a Saturday night was the prime venue. Inside and outside it sometimes resembled a battlefield rather than a dance hall. The brown jobs with very little war to fight, still smarting over Dunkirk, were always spoiling for a scrap, venting their spleen on either the Navy or the Air Force. The brown jobs were out in force on Saturday nights.

Not quite the Ivor Novello type, I preferred to spend my leisure time with my wife, enjoying the shops, a good meal which was a rare treat, and a bit of culture thrown in, before catching the last train home.

I knew it couldn't last. The food of love was obviously fish and chips. "I think I'm pregnant," Laura announced one evening.

I gulped. "How do you know, are you sure?" What a stupid thing to say considering I was suddenly over the moon. A visit to the quack and Laura's diagnosis was confirmed. We had to make new plans for her to return home. No way would my unborn child have to endure any longer than necessary the torture of Ma Bullmer's cuisine. My wife would go back to the country to be molly-coddled by her family. Me, back to a celibate existence living again on camp, without the comfort and company of my darling wife.

Two quick decisions had to be made. Firstly, to give notice to the landlady that her favourite and only lodgers would soon be leaving, and secondly, I told Laura I intended to call her bluff and to pluck up enough courage to do it during next Sunday's card game. How would everyone react? Would the family support me in their condemnation that dear mother was a cheat, or would they slink away and express indignation by taking Ma's side? I wouldn't hold it against them if they did, after all we were only ships that pass in the night, they were long term prisoners.

I was beginning to look forward to Sunday afternoon, even partly enjoyed the lunch Ma dished up. The kitty in the middle of the table was a beauty, one of the biggest yet, when it became necessary to play my ace. Everybody around the table knew Ma Bullmer had had her usual sneak preview of the card to be taken up after a discard. She wasn't even slick enough to disguise it either. With the ace of hearts to be picked up, her Nap hand was a certainty. It had to be now. Looking Ma Bullmer straight in the eye I said, "You're up to your usual game of cheating, I see."

The effect was certainly electric, the atmosphere around the table explosive. Laura looked up from her knitting and dropped a stitch, giving me a 'Well done' look at the same time. Ma Bullmer had a fit of acute apoplexy, her pince-nez fell off her nose into the middle of the green baize tablecloth and broke into pieces. Albert, her husband slipped off his chair, struck his chin on the edge of the table, and almost knocked himself out. Phyllis broke into tears and almost fainted, while Arthur her brother rolled his eyes upwards and backwards, collapsing in a fit of splutters and coughs.

The best however was to come, the effect on her nearest and dearest crony. She immediately fell backwards off her chair, legs wide apart, showing a part of her anatomy which had not seen the light of day for many a long year. Making a heavy landing on top of the sleeping cat, the moggy promptly somersaulted onto the mantlepiece, scattering some treasured possessions into a thousand pieces.

Ma Bullmer was fuming. I was reminded of a line from a Mess song, *'She spit, she shit, she farted, You've got to be cruel to be kind'*. The game had ended with the finest of finishes, better than I had ever hoped for, and so had our association with Mrs Bulmer. Ma would never cheat again.

When the commotion had died down, Laura and myself were less than graciously requested to leave our lodgings post haste the following day. Preparations for this had already been made, and with fond farewells, I put Laura on the train to Stroud the following morning and went back to a room in the Sergeants' Mess.

It was shortly after this that the C.O. called me in for an interview.

He began, "Right Flight, two bits of news. Firstly you've been promoted to Warrant Officer, congratulations, and secondly I have decided to send you on a Gunnery Leader's course. If you pass the course with a good result, I want you commissioned, OK?"

The first bit of news was fantastic, I could count myself as one of the first Warrant Officer aircrew. This entitled me to wear officers' barathea uniform and of course be addressed as Sir by lower ranks. The thought of the Leaders' course did not excite me one little bit. After all I was primarily a Wireless Operator, a tradesman. However, *c'est la guerre*, if I made it and became a Baron it wouldn't matter.

The course lasted six weeks. It did not take long before I realised there was more to firing a gun than simply pulling a trigger. It was an eye opener. It was considered that selection alone for airmen aircrew was open sesame for commissioning. We were a mix of Officers and NCOs including American and commonwealth aircrew, most destined for higher things. The work was tough, mostly theoretical. Airmen like me were watched like hawks for attributes loosely called officer qualities, this was the leadership connotation. The supervision was extended to off-duty hours.

After all the air and ground examinations were over, I finished the course in third position of merit, and on return to my unit filled in my commissioning papers. My aspirations to become a Baron however were never to be realised. In retrospect, without the commonsense logic of my wife to advise me, I was lost. I probably and mistakenly assumed that as a Warrant Officer I was a king amongst men, but as Flying Officer I would be one of the lowest notches on the totem pole.

The upshot of my doubts was that I broke into the C.O.'s office after one too many beers, and, with earnest prompting from my fellow drinkers, tore up my commissioning papers. The papers I knew were lying in the boss's tray and had already been signed and approved. The following day I would have been a Flying Officer, it was as quick as that. The old man didn't say a thing about it, and my possible rise to baroncy was quietly forgotten. In my sober moments I had mixed feelings, but the wound was self inflicted.

Rumours of a very special squadron to be formed on the station, in addition to the two already resident, had been circulating for some time. New faces began appearing around the station, most of whom were experienced operators, all second tour wallahs. The majority of the pilots were Flight Lieutenants or Squadron Leaders, most sporting a row of fruit salad medal ribbons. Most had been drawn back into operational flying from a variety of staff and instructional duties. The ribbon of the DSO was beginning to be quite a common sight, and they didn't come up with the rations. A lot of the back end crew too were also second tourists.

Some operational squadrons at this time had been converted to a different aircraft, the Avro Manchester. The Manchester was a twin engined beast, nice to fly when it was serviceable, but if it lost one engine, it dropped out of the sky like a stone. It had the advantage of twin gun turrets, upper and rear, affording better all round protection than its predecessor, the Hampden. The Manchester had a short operational life, principally because of its severe limitations on one engine, not very nice on operations. It was however a reasonable test bed for the new four engined Lancaster, the fuselage of which was very similar. The new squadron was equipped with Lancasters.

5 Group collected another Victoria Cross. A daylight formation of aircraft raided Augsberg and were severely mauled. One crippled aircraft pressed on to the target and returned shot to pieces. The skipper was immediately awarded the country's highest decoration.

Our little non-operational unit had a hotch-potch of aircraft. They were aged throw outs; two Wellingtons, one Whitley, two Lysanders and two Martinets. The bombers were used for gunnery exercises, the turrets fitted either with guns or cameras. The Lysanders were used for drogue towing when live ammo was used. The Martinets were used to simulate fighters when cameras were used. With my new title of Gunnery Leader came greater responsibilities, amounting to the command of a small detachment. My mobile staff was an armourer, a photographer and a Sgt. Air Gunner. At this time we had researched a method of denying to the Luftwaffe fighters an easy target. A fighter is a fixed gun platform which the pilot had to aim at his adversary before pressing a gun tit. The unit had developed a manoeuvre which we called cork screwing. The idea was that once the attacking fighter had been assessed by either mid upper or rear gunner to be at approximately a range of six hundred yards, a range which fighters generally opened fire, the bomber aircraft would begin a gentle corkscrewing motion.

Either gunner would give the direct order "Corkscrew port" or "Starboard—go." This would of course depend from which of these directions the fighter was approaching. The pilot would then initially begin a gentle climb or dive to port, roll out to starboard and then continue the corkscrew action. The action would have the effect of upsetting the attackers point of aim in trying to follow the aircraft. At the same time, both bomber gunners would be able to concentrate their own fire power at the fighter, since neither had the added task of flying the aircraft. It worked, and we had lots of film to prove it. The only real blind spot was if the fighters attacked the bombers from underneath. This was another entirely different ball game. My little detachment were kept very busy. We were tasked with visiting every bomber squadron within the Group and flying with every crew in order to instruct them in the art of corkscrewing, amongst other gems of information on gunnery tactics.

The success of the instruction was paying dividends, the attrition rate was beginning to come down. Like topsy our parent unit was also beginning to grow in size and stature. Top brass were very interested, we had innumerable visits when staff officers flew with us to see if our expertise had any substance. It obviously had, hence Mohammed went to the mountain and my little detachment began to work its tail off.

It was a very worthwhile task. Flying with as many crews as

possible on each squadron and briefing, de-briefing and assessing all the fighter affiliation exercises was a wonderful way to spend a rest period. I flew not only with the aces, but new crews just beginning their war. Some were hairy crews who had chop written all over them. It didn't take long to get gut feelings about the ability of a skipper to handle both his aircraft and his crew. I knew as soon as the pilot opened his mouth on start-up checks whether he felt confident or otherwise. Some crews I knew wouldn't make it after roughly one hour's flying with them. Their discipline in the air was slap happy and it showed. This, coupled with poor handling technique, spelt doom. Mentally I had started to compile my own chop list. It was pretty good, but it could go no further. Some of the aces too couldn't quite get the hang of the right way to corkscrew, to allow their gunners the best of a stable platform. They flung the aircraft around far too violently, generally succeeding in making the rest of the crew airsick. Tact was needed here, ace pilots didn't like the idea of a jeep telling them what to do, but they soon realised that having two sick gunners was a liability rather than a credit. But at least the aces had experience on their side.

Changes were in the air. Our small unit had started to expand rapidly, we were obviously proving our worth. Two more pilots joined us, one Polish and the other English. Flt. Lt. Felixkapowski was the first of the Polish flyers to finish a tour of operations. He had converted to Wellington bombers, operating out of my old airfield at RAF Hemswell, and with his innate hatred of the Nazis had gone through a full tour of operations like a dose of salts.

We christened him Felix, cat-like he wasn't. Rumour had it he was a member of Polish aristocracy, no less than Count Von Felixkapowski and although Felix never advertised the fact, there was an aura of good living and presence about him that was hard to disguise. He had also been something big in the pre-war Polish airforce and in his finery, sported a chest full of decorations. Felix was small, gentle and shy. His very pale blue eyes twinkled like diamonds. Nothing but nothing ever seemed to ruffle him. He never complained, except of the fact he had been taken off operations against his will, and he mastered all the unit's aircraft after a quick training sortie. He flew the Wimpy with an ease which was awe inspiring, he was a pleasure to fly with.

Johnny Hurst, the other new arrival, was everybody's idea of a dashing young pilot. Good looking, tall athletic, blonde wavy hair, with a beautiful open smile. Johnny was always bursting with energy, a lot of which found its way to below his belt. Johnny was certainly a ladies' man, never went short of a bit of crumpet, never went short of partners at Mess dances. Like Felix, Johnny was also pissed off at being taken off operational flying, but he had been removed for entirely different reasons. The youngest of three brothers, all bomber pilots, both his elder brothers had been reported missing believed killed in action on operations against Germany. Unknown to Johnny his widowed mother, completely distraught with grief, had pleaded with Air Ministry to spare her remaining son from the same fate and Johnny had suddenly been transferred to instructional duties for a number of spurious reasons which didn't make sense. The tragedy was that both newcomers were to be killed on the unit. What a waste. Johnny and I fast became buddies and we tried to fly with each other as often as possible. We shared the same off-duty pursuits. Like myself, Johnny was a good sportsman, both of us had represented the station, Group and Command at soccer. We both loved a gamble, a good poker school. He was to become godfather to my firstborn.

We landed from a detail at a wet and windy Scampton just as dawn was breaking. As soon as I stepped into the briefing room to hand in my bits and pieces, code books, signals log, there was a shout from across the other side of the room. "Hey Ginger, congratulations, you're a father, a son, both doing well. We had a phone message about half an hour ago. Well done."

A son, both OK, I was so relieved. One thing was certain, I would sleep well in what was left of Sunday.

My son was born during the early hours of a Sunday morning, His entry into this world coincided with a heavy German air raid on Bristol, with the glow of the fires reflected strongly against a darkened sky. Delivery itself, to quote my wife, was consummately easy, like shelling peas. One strong push from Laura and our boy came into the world, against the background of death and destruction on the skyline. Doc Ryall, the family friend and doctor in attendance simply said, "Well done lass, you're built for babies," and in the same breath "by Jesus Bristol's copping it." As soon as the baby was born, both my in-laws stopped their flustering. No one could blame them, this was the first grandchild, and a lusty child to boot. My son and heir was born in the front bedroom, the only one in the small cottage which had the luxury of built-in light, one single gas mantle which fluttered and flickered throughout the long stages of labour. Doc Ryall was only called out just before final delivery. He hadn't long returned home from a Saturday night's thrash with my father-in-law. The pair of them were great bosom drinking pals, and both were still under the weather. There was a gas leak and it was noticeable. Laura told me Doc Ryall crawled around the bedroom on his hands and knees until he discovered it. "Get that fixed Vic as soon as possible," he said to my father-in-law. "We don't want anything happening to this beautiful grandson of yours, do we?"

The rest of the bedrooms in the house had built in blackout, candle power. Only Laura and myself occupied a small back bedroom. Candle power or not, I loved it. We would now have to make room for a cot.

Fate was once again in my corner the night Johnny Hurst died. The sortie to be flown was something special, a night fighter affiliation exercise in the aged Wellington, with a high powered bunch of gunners as students. The gunners that night were all Station Commanders, one from each of five operational stations. Each Group Captain would fire off a cine camera magazine from the rear turret against an attacking fighter, one of the Martinets. The exercise would give them the feel for corkscrewing, to be assessed on the ground after landing.

A gunnery instructor had been detailed, but as it was such a beautiful evening, I agreed to take his place. Meanwhile back in the Mess during the afternoon, I became involved in a good poker school. The upshot of it was that at the time I should have left to fly, I was so far ahead in the money stakes that Johnny convinced me I should stay in the game and he would stay with the original crew plan. One hour into the flight, the port wing fell off the Wimpy, the aircraft turned turtle and fell like a stone. There was no time for anyone to bale out, and everybody perished in the crash. Poor Johnny, his mother's deliberations had ended by being kind to be cruel.

Felix died like a true airman too, heroic to the bitter end, and bitter it was.

Bomber aircraft were becoming too vulnerable to attack by night fighters from immediately below, where both mid upper and rear gunners suffered blind spots. We were researching the installation of a mid under turret, a bucket-like affair, hydraulically operated only during flight when it could be lowered into position and manned by an extra crew member. At the same time, we were also looking into the possibility of improving the harmonisation of gun platforms with better gun sights and electrical fittings.

Felix's detail was to fly a Lysander with an airman in the back as the drogue operator. It was a sortie the unit had flown hundreds of times before without incident. Both aircraft, the Lysander and the bomber, rendezvoud over the North Sea gunnery range. The drogue was trailed and the aircraft gunners carried out a live firing exercise. Firing was concentrated from the newly-installed mid under turret, and special laying off techniques could be practiced. The gunner was the gunnery leader himself. The exercise went badly wrong. Instead of the drogue registering live hits, the Lysander itself was sprayed from stem to stern with lethal ammunition. Both Felix and his crewman suffered mortal wounds. Felix, a hero to the end, flew his aircraft back to base, landed perfectly, and died over the controls. He was hoping to save his comrade in the back. What he didn't know was that the drogue operator had been killed instantly with the first deadly rake of fire.

There was a sadness on the unit that day. Two gallant airmen lost by tragic mistakes. It presented also the C.O. with a huge dilemma. He wanted to award Felix a posthumous George Cross, but how do you write a citation when the killing is yours? The incident was quietly hushed up, but the memories will always linger on.

Felix was buried in the village cemetery with full military honours. No tears for Johnny, head in air.

After the birth of my son, I began to get itchy feet. Rubbing shoulders every day with operational aircrews, listening to their line shoots, their ups and downs, you are surrounded by an atmosphere which is always electric with every waking hour of every day. Yes I'd done my bit, but the thrill of looking forward to operational flying again was always there, it was hard to resist. Nothing specific was said by me to Laura about my twitches, but she could read me like a book, and in my letters home and my calls, telephone box to telephone box, I kept dropping hints that my rest period could not go on forever and very soon a posting back to a squadron was inevitable. She and I knew that as a family, the stakes were infinitely higher.

My logic was simple, it was better to return with an experienced crew of volunteers than to take pot luck of a posting to a newly formed squadron and join another sprog crew. The choice for good or bad would at least be mine to make.

Volunteers were never hard to find in 5 Group. There were lots of aircrew suffering the same withdrawal symptoms, wanting to be up the sharp end, rather than trying to instruct. I was lucky, two other instructors I met were having the same sort of qualms. One a pilot, the other a navigator, and together we could form the nucleus of another bomber crew.

Chapter 10

Squadron Leader Angus McLiesh Beattie, better known for some extraordinary reason as Big Tom, was the pilot. Scottish, describing himself as farming stock, but it would have been much more appropriate to say Scottish landowners of a very large estate. I soon learned his home address was the Castle of Feddes, a large windy edifice south of Aberdeen, thousands of acres which was now an Army training ground, and no doubt crawling with thousands of Sassenachs.

A better handle perhaps would have been Big Dick, an appendage he was particularly proud of. We had a saying not altogether complimentary, but perhaps with a little bit of jealousy, that anyone built like the skipper was donkey rigged, although none of us would have dared to say it to his face. In his more sober moments, the boss would quip that since he never had any toys as a baby, his mother would lift him out of the cot with it. Banter was for non-operational hours.

Big Tom was a different man with an aircraft strapped to his backside. He then became a disciplined, polished flyer. I found it hard to reconcile the fact he was a product of Stonyhurst College and Oxford. Oxford yes, but Stonyhurst I considered to be a training ground for monks of lesser brethren of the cloth. Big Tom was obviously an exception to the rule.

Funny how the drums beat, bringing the three of us together, all stationed miles apart. But the jungle telegraph had a fast beating pulse and the point of contact, like so many more important decisions, was made over a few pints of jungle juice in the snake pit in the fair city of Lincoln.

Tom Beattie convinced us he would like to stay in 5 Group and preferably join one of the squadrons based at either Waddington or

Scampton. We were easily convinced. Oh yes, the third member, possibly the most important, a good navigator. Tom O'Reilly looked like a leprechaun and at times smelled like he'd slept with one. Tommy had reached his zenith in the rank structure, and counted himself fortunate enough to have been allowed to retain his present rank of Flight Sgt. Presently helping to train navigators at a school of navigation, he couldn't get away fast enough. Tact and understanding were not Paddy's strong point. It was said he frightened his students to death, not because of his ability as a navigator, which was par excellence, but because of his lack of patience, a desirable feature of all good instructors.

The laird of Feddes pulled enough strings so fast that we were posted as the nucleus of a new crew to 49 Squadron, which by now had been moved from Scampton to a satellite airfield called Fiskerton. The three of us had hoped we might be posted to the mystery squadron being formed at Scampton and now named 617 squadron, but it was obvious that crews for that particular one were vetted very thoroughly and very carefully selected.

In my previous job, I had managed to fly with a number of crews now with 617 squadron and I had been very impressed with their airmanship. The pilots up front were all first class operators. A pity they were almost annihilated on their first operation. Whatever they had in store for them, they certainly got in plenty of practice. Most of it was hearsay in the bars, all low level flights over expanses of water, lakes in Wales, Scotland and the Lake District. A lot of the training required extremely accurate precision flying, with little margin for error. It soon became obvious why they were all the chosen ones.

Ourselves, we three citizens of the United Kingdom, Scottish pilot, Irish navigator and English wireless operator, were detached to a nearby heavy bomber conversion unit for a quick familiarisation course. My job was back to communications. There were new bits of equipment to master, particularly a piece of radar known as Fishpond. This gave off blips on a cathode ray tube of aircraft in the vicinity. It was suitably calibrated for range and direction. Staring at it during night flying made your eyes water.

There were rumours that it made you sterile, but later on I was able to disprove that claim.

We needed four more crew members, two air gunners, a bomb aimer and lastly a flight engineer. The boss hoped we would pick up a Taffy and make us a full UK bomber crew. The ginger beer (flight engineer) was a fellow Lancastrian. Nobby Clarke hailed from Manchester. Sgt. Edward Harold Clarke had volunteered for aircrew duties from the rank of Cpl. engine fitter. What Nobby didn't know about engines and ancilliaries wasn't worth knowing. He'd come up the hard way as an apprentice through Halton, the finest training anyone could wish for. He caressed the throttles on the four merlins like newly-laid eggs. His humour was as dry as dust, another good man on the team.

We awaited the arrival of the last three crew members with some trepidation. I prayed they would send us a Welshman, it would be a good omen. The two air gunners arrived next. The mid upper was Canadian from Newfoundland. The jokes about Newfies being as thick as two short planks was certainly borne out with Warrant Officer William Burley R.C.A.F., Burley by name and nature. What he lacked in grey matter, he made up in keenness and he proved to be a natural air gunner. He was a huge man, quick to fly off the handle, and a man to agree with, especially when he'd had a few beers—which was one of his two spare time hobbies. The other one was getting his end away as often as possible.

We nicknamed him Hank. He was from a small place in Newfoundland called Gander. He told me it was two shops, three houses and a rundown hotel, supporting a small commercial aerodrome. I couldn't help chuckling at the name of his birthplace Gander, how apt, since Hank at the drop of a hat would indulge in goosing the local lassies. Mind you, they all seemed to go a bundle on our mid upper. He had something going for him other than his Canadian accent. Hank had packed a lot in since leaving school, he'd tried trapping, hunting and fishing before joining the Air Force. He was a dab hand with a shotgun, a good man to protect the aircraft from bogeys making attacks from above.

It was chalk and cheese when the tail end Charlie reported in. Sgt.

Richard White, Chalky, was so tiny he even looked lost in the confines of a rear turret. Chalky was a local, a Lincolnshire poacher. If we all tended to be irreligious, he was the little man who read his bible every night.

One more crew member to go, the bomber aimer, and my prayers were finally answered. However before we had tamed him, there were times when most of us wished he'd gone to some other hole.

Pilot Officer Trevor Idris Williams was nothing like Taffy Richards. Williams came in like a prop forward, all push and shove. Before he arrived, I was top of the heap next to the skipper. Williams was still very wet behind the ears, and his manner was probably a foil to hide his lack of confidence. Far better if he had tried to assert his authority and his standing as a Baron quietly, and with time. But oh no, not dear Idris. The first day together as a crew, he blatantly tried to pull his rank on Hank Burley. Tact was not one of Hank's better points, and he immediately told Williams without batting an eye to "fuck off in fine pitch". There was a short lived threat of putting Hank under open arrest for insolence, but I took Williams to one side and asked him politely to think it over. What a start, this was no way to behave before we settled in as a crew. The boss would have to do something about his bomb aimer. Plt. Off. Williams was no great shakes either as a bomb aimer, he had already failed to make it as both pilot and navigator. As a retread he would need to do a lot more to impress his fellow crew members.

Paddy O'Reilly however wasn't going to let some bloody Welsh nit drop him in the shit, and for all our sakes, Paddy took Idris aside and under his wing began to smooth out some of his wrinkles on basic navigation, especially map reading.

And so another Bomber crew, one of Harris' boys, prepared to test our skills and stick our necks out against the enemy.

Chapter 11

What about the War? Aircrew survived in a very narrow point of reference. Our minds were fully concentrated on the land mass across the North Sea, that is where our battles were fought. Occasionally, but not very often, some of us would discuss war in its wider aspects, but most of us had little time to philosophise, life was too short, and philosophy was best left to abler and more settled minds.

The war in general however was not exactly going our way. Now into its fourth year, the sickly baby of Bomber Command was beginning to grow into a lusty infant. More and more squadrons of long range aircraft were thumping our enemies by night, with the American Air Force carrying out bigger and deeper penetration raids into Europe during the daylight hours. Round the clock saturation bombing was the name of the game.

The Yanks, poor sods, were taking a hammering. A fighter escort had not yet surfaced which afforded them full protection. Flying Fortresses were bristling with guns, but they were mercilessly attacked by waves of German fighters. We took our hats off to them. They were making it easier for us. Occasionally on the ground the Yanks strayed into our home territory, the pubs most frequented by Lincolnshire bomber crews. Infiltration had to be defended at all costs. There was no love lost on terra firma and the Americans quickly got the message to stay away from our preserves. We had a little ditty we used to sing whenever USAF crews were around. It went like this, "They're flying Flying Fortresses at forty thousand feet and they only drop a teeny weeny bomb. We're flying Avro Lancasters at zero zero feet and we drop a bloody great bomb." It was cruel, straight to the point, but usually taken in a spirit of esprit de corp.

There was a lovely story going the rounds about Clark Gable who apparently had volunteered as an Air Gunner and had taken part in a few daylight operations. Naturally someone as famous as Gable was fully expected to socialise at the top end of the cocktail circuit. The story goes that when politely asked by the lady of the manor to attend a party, he replied, "Lady, I came over here to fight a war."

RAF Fiskerton, a satellite aerodrome, was bursting at the seams. We joined the 49th light of foot at the beginning of April. Big Tom was instantly made C Flight Commander, and as his crew, we shared in his little bit of reflected Glory. People were always asking you in the Mess "Whose crew are you in?" It was a charade really with a lot of people, a prop to either boost their morale or in other respects shatter their nerves.

I used to surmise what life span an insurance actuary would have given bomber crews. Naturally no one would insure anybody during the war. What would historians and the statisticians write about it, if the war ended and we were survivors? It was considered extremely lucky to survive even one tour of operations, and two of us were now stretching the odds and embarking on a second tour. It was all in the lap of the Gods.

* * *

Aircraft have different smells. Blindfold I could have found my way around most of them. The Hampden was cold metallic, the Wimpy, wood skin and glue, and the Lancaster had a pungent odour of leaking hydraulic fluid. It leaked like a thin red line from numerous unions around the fuselage and it was sticky.

My position as Wireless Operator however was nice and snug. Protected by a solid step and armour plate, I was also the controller of the aircraft heating systems, ensuring I was always comfortable and warm. Pity the poor gunners in their plastic bubbles with the wind whistling in around the barrels of the four browning machine guns. Chalky White had the coldest position, although he rarely complained. Most of the time there were problems with the electrics down to the rear turret. Flying through heavy rain or snow, or even having the aircraft standing under similar conditions, generally set up a god damn howl on the intercom, making it difficult for contact with each other. As the Wireless Operator, it was my job to fix it, and quick. It was easy to isolate the offending intercom socket, and then attempt to dry it out. Sometimes my simple remedy didn't work, and it became necessary to isolate the offending helmet as well. Most of the time it affected the rear gunner's position. Sometimes poor Chalky spent many an hour without talking or listening to another soul. It was a dodgy practice, not to be recommended. Having a tail-end-Charlie out of contact could spell real trouble. The problem had to be resolved.

I designed a simple extension on a long lead from the mid-upper position, enabling any one of us to plug into a serviceable socket. It became a standard piece of equipment carried by all crews.

Operation number one as a crew, thirty-one for the skipper and myself, began against the armament works of Krupps at Essen in the Ruhr valley. Bomber Command was beginning to expand its lungs and we were told at briefing that over 350 aircraft would be on target, a big show. Mosquito aircraft, acting as pathfinders, would go in first and drop yellow target indicators in a line of approach, giving the bomber streams a flarepath as a good guide to the aiming point. The Mossies were using a device code named OBOE to pinpoint the way. In addition, there was a Lancaster pathfinder force dropping red and green coloured flares over a period of thirty minutes, more target indicators. Things were looking up. The main bomber force we were told would be attacking in three distinct waves, where timing was essential. The first wave would be aged Wellingtons bombing from 10,000 feet, then a small force of Stirlings from 15,000 feet and finally the largest force of Lancasters, five thousand feet higher at 20,000 feet. From my small smattering of German, Essen to me meant food. Tonight the Krauts would be getting their just desserts, manna with explosive and flaming centres.

As usual prior to departure from the Mess there was one hell of a party in full swing. Sleep had been impossible. I lay on my bed listening to the repertoire of songs wafting across wondering how number one would go. I decided to get up, and if you couldn't beat the racket you might as well join it. Parties viewed with a sober eye are not however entertaining. Mess piss ups usually degenerated into Mess games. Time to get the show on the road.

I felt like a mother hen gathering her brood of chickens. The apprehension surrounding an almost virgin crew was real enough, they would want some reassurance. The ace in the hole for us was the boss in charge. He knew the ropes and we were lucky. Taking off with a full bomb load aboard always rattled my eardrums. Full power on four Merlin engines with the skipper standing on the brakes, vibrated the airframe something awful. Brakes off, and a massive surge forward. I would never get used to it, sitting in the dark, strapped in, facing an array of wireless and radar equipment, and wondering if we would ever lift off safely. It was always a big sigh of relief when you felt the wheels leave the deck, and slowly but lumberingly climb away into the consummate darkness.

Tonight it was really dark, almost a deep purple sky, with April showers forecast ahead. Sitting in the belly, port side one small light above going through the usual checks, waiting for the green Verey light from the tower, the order to start engines. A white Verey would mean standby, a red one a scrub—the operation had been cancelled. I'd never yet seen a red Verey and probably never would. The bomb aimer saw it first, "Green light skipper."

"OK Eng, let's get on with it. Start up. Number two first."

"Roger skipper, starting number two," Nobby replied.

It was usual to start an inboard engine first to give us ancillary power to check and run radio and radar systems. Checks went like clockwork only dear old Idris had his finger in, nerves no doubt, he would eventually learn the hard way. Nobody had any snags, that was a good omen. Training was over, this was for real. Skipper to crew "Right let's go—praise the lord."

The aircraft taxied out in line astern, pitch black shapes against an equally dark horizon, each kite spewing sheets of sparks from deeply glowing exhaust manifolds. The boss was first to be airborne. Lift off, undercarriage up and locked, climbing power set on all four throbbing engines and we were on our way. Nobby had the donks very quickly fully synchronised. Some ginger beers could never quite get the knack of doing this. De-synchronised Merlin engines completely out of harmony were a very disconcerting sound indeed. We were blessed with a very good flight engineer.

First course set, out over the fishing port of Yarmouth, our first pinpoint before coasting out. Goodbye England for the next few hours. Down below all looked so peaceful and serene. The waves of aircraft were to stream in a loose formation, more like a gaggle over the North Sea. Time to tune my radio receiver to the Group Headquarters broadcast channel. Group broadcasts were transmitted at specific times in bomber code and I logged it and then decoded it. Tonight it was mostly nothing to report. Met. briefing earlier had promised us reasonable weather all the way to the target with the possibility of low cloud and showers over East Anglia for our return. Nothing much to worry about. But one tended to get cynical at times about good Met. briefings. They sometimes could turn out to be something entirely different. And tonight's trip was to prove to be no exception.

The weather quite suddenly clagged in half way across the briny. The aircraft began to gyrate like a cork in a rough sea. Air sickness had never worried me, but I came pretty close to it. Poor Chalky stuck out on the end in the rear turret where the turbulence must have been pretty fierce, was as sick as a dog. So was Idris up front in the nose in the bomb aimers position. All four new crew members honked their rings, sixpence half a crown, the smell was something awful. One consolation, the Luftwaffe would not be venturing too far in this crap either, so all we had to worry about was anti-aircraft fire. The skipper was having one hell of a job trying to keep this beast straight and level, it was all instrument flying. After six and a half hours more of this, he would be physically and mentally exhausted. No automatic pilot tonight, George could take a day off. This weather would sort out the men from the boys. Thank God we had a man in charge.

Crossing the Dutch coast by direct reckoning, we were still

labouring away trying to make twenty thousand feet. A few flashes of light lit up the sky below, and suddenly we were in and out of towering cumulus clouds. Flying through the tops of some was the worst sensation when the aircraft either continued soaring upwards, or hurtled nose down, depending on the draughts of air. Looking out at the port wing it soon became apparent we were rapidly picking up ice on the airframe leading edges. Occasionally it would break free and thump against the fuselage. Williams thought we'd been hit, but the calm voice of the skipper reassured us all there was nothing to worry about. The de-icing boots were working well, thank God.

The boss confessed to me later in his cups that he considered this first op. was a right bastard. The weather would no doubt have nastier things in store for us before we were much older.

Both the Mossies and the PFF had done a pretty good job of marking the target. The Lancaster force was far too early, we obviously had much stronger tail winds than had been predicted. Through the gaps in the clouds, large circles of fires could be seen on the ground. It looked like a good prang.

On the run into the target the engineer suddenly piped up "Don't like the look of the oil pressure on number three skipper, if it goes any higher we could have a fire."

"OK, keep an eye on it Eng. Open up the oil cooler shutters and if the temp goes into the red, I'll have to feather."

"Roger skipper."

"Bomb aimer here, left left, dead ahead bomb doors open."

"OK Bomb doors open."

"Can you see anything on Fishpond W/op?"

"Not a thing skipper."

"OK gunners we are running in. Nav give me a steer for home once the bombs have gone."

"Roger skipper, steer 240 magnetic."

"OK Nav, 240 set on. Bombs away."

The aircraft continued straight and level before turning to port. Number three engine had settled down, but Nobby wasn't entirely happy.

"Right, home my beauty. I can taste those eggs and bacon already. What's the ETA Nav at the coast?" asked the boss.

"Should cross over the enemy coast in about forty minutes. Jesus I could do with a fag. Two more hours to base," Paddy said.

"How we doing for fuel Eng?"

"OK skipper, I'll be cross feeding in about 30 minutes."

"Right Nobby, get your hands on this, about time you got the feel of the aircraft."

All four had recovered from air sickness and by now we were on the way home.

"Wop."

"Yes skipper."

"Pop down and have a natter with Chalky. See if he's still with us."

Chalky was glad to see me, he had become disconnected from his intercom socket. I plugged him in.

By this time we were over the North Sea and I'd got a very nice fix from three radio stations, which confirmed we were dead on track. It was such a comfort to have a good navigator who knew his equipment well. When we had settled in, I would have to badger Paddy to give me some instructions in the art of radar plotting.

Group were beginning to broadcast weather forecasts. After decoding the weather for base and passing it forward, all the skipper did was grunt "Not good." The weather for Fiskerton and for all of East Anglia was low cloud and rain, Met. had at least got that part right.

"Britch yourself up for a ZZ landing Wop."

"Ok skipper," I said.

The last one I saw carried out in anger, the aircraft finished up by flying straight into a hangar, not good. The thought of it broke me out into a cold sweat. What an opener this was turning out to be.

The message from the tower was short and to the point. "You can have one stab T for Tommy and if you don't make it, you are to divert to Leuchars."

"Scotland, Christ that's another hour's flying away. Have we got enough gravy Eng?" asked the boss.

"Going to be tight skipper," Nobby answered.

At least we've got the benefit of a full flare path if we ever pick it up. There would be no intruders around tonight. The ZZ landing went like a dream. We broke through the low cloud exactly right, almost lined up with the flare path. A quick jink to port, some fast throttle bending, and we went over the boundary fence spot on. The skipper greased it in. Some wag on the intercom said, "Are we down?"

Looking around the dispersal after shutting down the engines Nobby remarked, "We must be the first aircraft back." This was confirmed at de-briefing, most of the remainder of the squadron were scattered around the UK. Twenty one aircraft went missing, according to the BBC. Two crews got the chop from the squadron. They were both sprog crews. Group losses were a total of five crews. Bad weather had been the main factor for such high losses on what was considered to be an easy target.

By God that early breakfast was going to go down well. Chalky couldn't face his eggs and bacon, so Bill Burley and myself divided his ration between us. The party we had left behind in the Mess must have been a corker. The ante room was strewn with broken furniture and bodies and were still occupying the lovely old comfortable leather armchairs, out to the wide, like old dishevelled socks. I had one hell of a headache, and singing noises in my ears. With luck though I might get in a good solid eight hours' kip. It took a long time to switch my brain off.

I wondered what my wife and baby son would be doing at this ungodly hour. No doubt sleeping in all innocence whilst husband and father had struck another blow for England.

The weather was bad over the continent which meant we did not venture out again over the Reich for another two nights. Big Tom had pulled a few strings and borrowed a Tiger Moth, the basic pilot trainer. In between showers he gave us all a flying lesson, which every one of us thoroughly enjoyed. The boss mentioned to me that when I finished this tour of operations, he would strongly recommend me for pilot training. I liked his air of confidence. Not if I finished this tour, but when. "You have a natural aptitude young

Walker," he said. This was a boost to my ego indeed. It would have to be given earnest consideration at the right time—if the right time ever came.

Chapter 12

"Hey Ginge, you're famous," said one of my colleagues.

"I am aware of that, but do tell," I replied.

"Your name is mentioned in a new play about the Air Force called Flarepath. It's written by someone called Terence Rattigan. It's playing at the Apollo Theatre in London. I went to see it on my last leave, it's bloody good too." Pigeon holing the information. On my next leave, I would take Laura up to town to see it.

Later on we were to learn that the raid on Essen had been reasonably successful, damage to the armaments factory had been extensive. Unfortunately, a large hutted complex which housed hundreds of slave workers had also been obliterated by fire. Poor sods, they just couldn't win on either count. Frying tonight.

With two days standown, we were kept busy with lectures on a variety of subjects. I even gave one myself to an assortment of new boys. The lecture on escape and evasion found me hanging onto every word, it worried me at the end of the day. Pisceans are reputed to have strong intuitive feelings, and mine were twitching like mad. I began to read obsessively all I could lay my hands on about how not to finish up in the bag, how best to prepare to evade capture if we were lucky enough to be shot down and survive. I paid visits to the station library looking at pre-war travel books about continental Europe, particularly the terrain, customs etc. For some time I couldn't put the thoughts at the back of my mind. Mine was a classical case of second tour twitch already, aircrew called it ring trouble, sixpence half a crown.

Chalky invited me home to meet his folks. Mum and Dad White lived under the shadow of Lincoln cathedral, that magnificent edifice we knew so well. Their little terraced workman's cottage was in a cobbled walk up to the cathedral, quaint and tidy. Chalky's dad was a dead ringer for his son, except dad was the toothless variety. Picturing my rear gunner in thirty year's time, he would be a spitting image of his father. Pop White was a real artisan. His age old craft as a Master Mason was restoring the aged edifice in which the White family worshipped every Sunday. What a strange world we were all living in, dad helping to restore aged buildings with loving tenderness, his son helping to knock some of them down.

If I survived this war, I would attempt to do something, however small, to stop the power seekers from inflicting their sufferings and misery on the innocent multitudes of different nations. It was a big if. We were occasionally given bits of intelligence about the ruthlessness of the Wehrmacht towards the Russians, who really had their back to the wall. The news was not good.

At the end of a pleasant evening, Chalky confided in me that his parents were both amazed that someone so young as myself was not only married, but already had a son of my own. They were kind enough to invite my wife and I to spend a weekend with them. This was good news, and I immediately wrote to Laura to tell her all about it. God how I missed them both.

The squadron carried out three more trips on the trot. On the Sunday we bombed the Heinkel works at Rostock, a new name to put in my flying log book. Rostock sounded more like a Russian target, rather than a German one. It was plastered with incendiaries and high explosives with over 500 aircraft on target, including a number of specially selected crews from 83 squadron now designated as Pathfinders. 49 Squadron once shared Scampton with 83.

Paddy tried out a new radar system called GEE as a bombing aid. It was marginally fair, but much better as an aid to navigation. The town and works suffered severe damage, and as we pulled away from the target area, I remembered Bath the year before, fair retribution. The following day on the BBC news, it was mentioned that twelve aircraft had been lost, and another ninety-six gallant aircrew gone. The training of pilots was one area exercising the minds of the Air Staff. Inclusion of Flight Engineers and the automatic pilot had released one pilot from bomber crews. This meant that at least one crew member had to be given the rudiments of flying an aircraft, just in case he was needed. The boss decided it would be the bomb aimer, the Welsh wizard, but he was bloody hopeless at even flying straight and level, really cackhanded. Nobby christened him Diabolical. All of us prayed that the skipper would never be incapacitated, since George at times was very temperamental.

Monday night was Duisberg, second time around for me. The last time was easy, and I was hoping for a repeat performance. There was something to look forward to as well. The Boss promised us a free weekend in bonny Scotland. As a crew we were due for a long weekend pass. I remembered the boss lived in a castle. I'd never seen a castle before, except in films. My education was sadly lacking. Tonight we had been given an extra special task. This was to drop thousands of strips of metal foil. The boffins called it Window. The small strips of foil were supposed to saturate enemy radars.

Luftwaffe night fighters operating in pairs had been increasing all the time, tied in with control from the ground, and using some form of ground beaconing they could be successfully vectored onto bomber streams. It should be possible to misdirect them and Window helped, but we also employed spoofing, where aircraft on special operations carried operators fluent in German, who passed on spurious directions. The Krauts were obviously getting very worried too about the continuing bombardment of the industrial heart of Germany. I felt every gun and searchlight had been moved to the area. Things were certainly hotting up.

German night fighters were generally either the JU88 or the Messerschmitt 110. The latter looked like a Hampden at certain angles. German fighters usually opened fire from about 200 yards, but if we had picked them up before this range, we were corkscrewing like mad.

Duisberg was like Hamburg, an inland port, and our particular aiming point was the steel rolling mills in the town centre. The Ruhr was hit nine times during the month of April. Paddy glibly remarked, "All I need to do is to change the date on my navigation charts."

The boss agreed. "Yes, once we get to height I'll put George in and T for Tommy can find its own way to the target."

A new squadron had been formed on the outskirts of Newark. The squadron flying Halifaxes were crewed by Canadians. Burley Bill the mid upper now had some Newfie colleagues on tap. He casually mentioned he might be asking for a transfer, but the boss talked him out of it. It was bad news to split up a crew, and as a crew we were beginning to gel, with one exception, Diabolical. Paddy neatly summed him up, "He'll never make a bomb aimer whilst he's got a hole in his arse."

After a nice easy run, and a promise of eight hours kip, we were off again, this time to Wilhelmshaven. It would be a reasonably short flight, but I remembered the first daylight raid against the same target, when my first squadron were almost decimated. Eleven aircraft out of twelve were lost. Intelligence reports confirmed by photo recce from Mosquitos had shown a heavy build up of a large naval task force, including light and heavy battleships with destroyer escorts. The German navy were still reeking havoc against Atlantic convoys bringing in vital food supplies.

Wednesday afternoon, sports day, I played football for Bomber Command against the Royal Marines. Wednesday night was a different game of soldiers. Take off was late to allow us to return to base at first light. This would ease the landings, since the weather over the East coast would be marginal for our return.

There was as usual one hell of a hooley going on in the Mess, sleep after midnight was impossible. Mind you I was lucky, I had the privilege of a room to myself in the Mess, whereas the rest of the crew were billeted altogether in a hut of some twenty aircrew some distance away. But with all this mayhem night after night, I was beginning to seriously think about joining them. The maxim was true, live it up while you can, you're a long time dead. Most of the revellers were recent arrivals on the squadron, new boys, not yet operational, not yet blooded, enjoying themselves to the full whilst their virginity lasted.

Intelligence also briefed us about an increase in night fighter bases now taking place in Holland. This was preaching to the converted. It had been noticed that the number of aircraft being picked off over Holland and the North Sea, believing they were home and dry, had been rising. Vigilance was stretched all the time, nobody but nobody could afford to drop their guard any more. Christ, this war was becoming far too serious. Sleep was impossible, the racket from down below was strength five plus, so I decided to write a letter home and tell Laura how we were all looking forward to a weekend in the Scottish highlands.

The German navy at Wilhelmshaven were obviously caught by surprise. They were not expecting to be blasted to Kingdom come at four o'clock in the morning, and the trip was a piece of cake. A good diversionary raid over France and Western Germany also helped, and we went in and out with our bulk armour piercing bombs with the greatest of ease. George worked overtime on the way home, and the boss allowed himself the luxury of a quiet stroll as far as the spar. It was a very pleasant change to be able to stretch his legs. These were the trips we all appreciated.

About an hour out of Fiskerton, Nobby spread a bit of alarm and despondency by announcing quite as a matter of fact that we may have to feather an engine. The problem was the starboard outer which quite suddenly began to surge all over the place, possibly water in the jets, Nobby intimated. Engine surges are not nice to live with, watching the rev counters swing up and down. Nobby advised the boss it would be better to stop the damn thing, otherwise it could cause other structural damage to the airframe. Didn't like the sound of that, engine cowlings had been known to lift off and fly back into the fuselage, so the boss warned us all, and Nobby promptly feathered it.

There were no problems, we held height OK, but I told Group by sending off a quick emergency message. Base gave us priority to land, a straight in approach and landing, holding the other aircraft off, and the skipper greased it in with a whisper of rubber. Somebody wisecracked on the intercom that the skipper should land on three every time, since it improved his technique. Every landing you walked away from was a good one in my book. That was declared unanimous.

I could almost smell the heather. The boss borrowed the station Anson and sweet-talked the chiefie in the armoury to lend us a pair of shotguns and two boxes of cartridges. We stowed seven pairs of wellingtons and a weekend kit into the back of the aircraft and headed north to Bonny Scotland.

Chapter 13

The castle of Feddes had, believe it or not, its own small emergency landing strip. Looking down at it, set in rolling downs with the castle and grounds to one side, for me it was the Wizard of Oz come to life. After landing and off loading the gear, we tied the aircraft down for the weekend. The skipper introduced us all to his mother, and we were shown to our rooms. "Where's Pop?" he asked.

"Oh he's talking turkey with the Duke, he should be back soon," she answered.

"And Aileen?"

"Oh she's exercising the dogs."

"So you keep turkeys?" I asked the boss.

He laughed aloud. "No George, both my father and our neighbour the Duke are procelain buffs."

Looking around the castle, I could see why. There were cabinets full of exquisite pieces of colourful porcelain. I was told they were mostly 18th century, all of them from English factories, the majority from a factory at Worcester. Every alcove too on the lovely spiral staircase was choc-a-bloc with lovely pottery ornaments, some even earlier than the 18th century. Each room in the house was a joy to behold, furnished deliciously to expectation, luxury par excellence. We were all impressed.

The boss by way of explanation told us, "Mother and Dad have been tatting for years, it was one of their great joys. Dad is a member of the British Ceramic Circle and has written books on both Chelsea and early Worcester porcelain."

The skipper's father was an acknowledged expert. This was another world, considering most of the pots we owned at home were courtesy of F & W Woolworth. The academic interest meant little to me, but I could certainly appreciate the beauty of the wonderful items on display, furniture, books, pictures and pots; the war was forgotten. I mentioned some of the pieces of pot in the alcoves were broken.

"Oh yes, Dad will blame that on the cats, but in actual fact, between you and me George, Pops is slowly going blind. But whatever you do or say, don't get feeling sorry for him, he's had a wonderful life so far. Oh and by the way, before we leave he will want to give you a small token to remember him by, please accept graciously."

The boss's younger sister Aileen returned from her walk with the dogs, a pair of friendly springer spaniels. She was an absolute corker. I knew Bill and Paddy would both instantly fall in love with her, what a charmer. A barbeque had been planned in the courtyard during the evening. Oh what a lovely war!

The house stirred very early. Up at sparrowfart as the boss would say. The plot was to walk in the hills with the dogs for a day's sport. It was hoped we might bag the odd deer, rabbits and hares for a stock of meat. We occasionally used the shotguns at base for clay pigeon shooting, part of gunnery training. There was to be a small kitty on who would get the biggest bag. Bill Burley, mid upper gunner, was an odds on favourite. Stalking game is an art in itself, not as easy as it sounds, only the skipper and his sister had the hang of it. They were the pros, we were the amateurs. Aileen carried off the kitty, with a brace of hares and a large hind. None of us would forget this wonderful weekend, even the weather played its part, it was glorious.

True to form, before we departed, our delightful host offered each of us a small momento of our visit. Mine was a lovely medallion in black basalt made by Wedgwood. This I decided would be my lucky charm, my St Christopher, and I carried it tucked away in the inside pocket of my flying suit.

The weekend was over too soon, and on Sunday afternoon, with the family, the dogs, and the small household staff on the touchline to wave us all goodbye, we leapt into the air and back to Fiskerton. The dream was over. Mum had confessed to me before we left that her husband had thoroughly enjoyed our visit, and hoped we would do the same again for Hogmanay. The end of the year was a lifetime away, and a lot could happen to Bomber aircrews in a lifetime.

Something special had been planned for my first wedding anniversary on May day. The crew had organised a stag party at the local pub, but war waits for no man, and this anniversary was to be declared null and void for the time being. On the night of the first of May we were detailed to attack once again the Ruhr valley, this time it was Dusseldorf. The city of Dusseldorf was the commercial and administrative centre for the area. It also had huge interests in iron and steel mills, and these made important targets.

One little piece of personal news came my way to make up for the disappointment of the cancelled party, when the C.O. told me I had been selected to represent the Air Force at soccer against the Army on the following Wednesday afternoon. The game was scheduled to be played at Villa Park, the home of Aston Villa, and I was overjoyed.

On the battlefront, the name of the game had changed. Bomber crews had by now to bring back a photograph of the target. The rules were simple, no photograph, no trip recorded, no excuses. This was of course the expedient to stop anyone dropping his bombs away from the target area, shades of what was sometimes practiced in the earlier days. Lady luck was smiling on us. Once again the trip was a doddle. Were we beginning to get too lucky?

I went up to Brum for the game of football. During the game, in which I scored two goals, a large hairy first thumped me hard in the earhole during a goalmouth scrimmage, leaving me flat out unconscious for a couple of minutes. On my return to camp it was impossible to shake off a thumping big headache together with constant buzzing in the ears. The boss ordered me to go sick and see the Doc. After explaining the symptoms to the M.O. he immediately asked me if I had been flying with a cold.

"Negative," I told him.

"OK let's take a look, which lughole is the painful one?" he asked.

"The left one."

"Yes, old son, you've got a very nice tympanic perforation," he said.

"Christ doc, that sounds nasty. Give it to me straight, how long have I got to go?" I mentioned the thump in the ear at soccer.

"Ah I see, that explains it. Right Mr. Walker, go back to the Mess, pack some overnight kit and come back here. I'm keeping you in sick quarters under observation. You could be suffering too from concussion. I'll phone the squadron and let them know what's happening. Don't worry lad, you'll live," was his final comment.

I felt as sick as a pig. This could mean a couple of weeks on the ground, unfit to fly. On the darker side it could mean losing a crew, that would be the worst thing of all, all for the sake of a game of football.

The whole crew visited me in sickquarters, and Nobby reckoned I was swinging the lead. I mentioned my apprehension to the boss about the possibility of getting behind, not being allowed to fly with a torn lughole. He told me not to worry, if necessary the whole crew would carry on over the top until I had finished my thirty trips. They had already agreed to do this. Talk about good mates, and confidence, it made me feel so much better.

The following day, after evil smelling inhalation treatment from a long necked bottle which I'm sure had been used in the Crimean campaign, my headache and earache began to ease. When the Doc made his morning round, I told him I was now feeling fit.

He snorted, "I'll tell you when you're ready to be discharged young son. As a matter of fact, I've decided you might just as well heal yourself at home. I've given you a week's sick leave as of now, and hopefully the slight tear in your eardrum will have healed itself by then. Don't go swimming and don't get water in the ear. Have a nice quiet rest, OK?"

A week's leave. On the one hand it was lovely, on the other I was really sucking a hind tit. A well, *c'est la Guerre*.

What a lovely surprise Laura would get when I walked in unannounced at home this evening, and I would also be seeing my baby boy.

One thing we could fit in was a day in the smoke, a visit to the Apollo Theatre to take in the play 'Flarepath'. This was something new for both of us, a West End show. The play was based on a weekend in the lives of bomber aircrews, their wives and sweethearts. Most of the action takes place in the local hotel close to the aerodrome, which had obviously been fashioned by the author on the hotel close to RAF Hemswell in the early part of the war. It centred on one crew hoping for a weekend off with their loved onces. That was the plot, but it didn't exactly work out that way, with the crew at the last minute being detailed for operations.

With sounds off, the aircraft take off to bomb Germany. One of the aircraft is shot down shortly after take-off by an intruder, followed by a loud explosion as the bomb load goes off. Naturally the visitors are all on tenterhooks until the arrival of an officer informs them that A for Apple has been shot down and Ginger Walker had survived by baling out.

My wife and I at that moment both shed a tear. For me the laughter of the play beforehand had died. I couldn't help thinking of Doughy Baker dead, and the rest of my crew, survivors also, but crippled for life. The cockney gunner's wife played by Kathleen Harrison was magnificent, she stole the show. The aircrew songs too, sung in the Mess around an old piano, brought out memories.

> *"I don't want to join the Air Force, I don't want to go to war,*
> *I'd rather hang around Picadilly and the Strand, living on the*
> *earnings of a high born lady."*

Talking of high born ladies, there was no shortage of crumpet on the camp. Some of the Waafs considered keeping the aircrew well satisfied was an important part of their war effort. They were well organised. One of the female M.T. drivers on the squadron had been a fully paid up member of the ladies of easy virtue before joining up, and she made an excellent shop steward. Rumour had it she organised a daily roster. Anyway, Bill and Paddy never complained.

An extra leave was a real bonus, home comforts soon helped me to forget my duff earhole. The sheer joy of seeing my wife, and our baby son bouncing with health on government orange juice, was the finest medicine there was. There was also the small part I played in unmasking a German sympathiser.

My father-in-law for his sins was the local CID man, as well as a connection he had with MI6. The latter was kept very quiet, few people knew about it. Vic had a whiff that a stranger to the district living in an isolated cottage close to the airfield at Aston Down could be using an illegal radio set. We visited the cottage knowing the occupant would be at work. Having found the hidden radio equipment, I was asked to give a professional opinion on what it's capabilities could be. There was no doubt in my mind, it was a transmitter and receiver able to transmit by morse code as far away as Germany.

At a later date, and when it was absolutely clear what was going on, the man was nabbed and taken into custody. He confessed he was a supporter of Oswald Mosley and felt it was his right to work for the Fascist cause. Pop told me he was packed off very quickly to a camp for aliens on the Isle of Man.

Returning to camp was an ordeal in itself, the trains were always full to bursting point and very very slow. The ordeal was ameliorated by Vic taking me on a visit to Stroud brewery. Like most local bobbies, he had a secret ring on the brewery door. It was warm sitting around the vats, rows of Coppers helping themselves to a demi-john of beer. There was one pint glass, always full, passed around hand to hand. It had to be finished in one swig, and the dregs tossed over your left shoulder. I was poured onto the midnight train, drunk as a fart, with two quart bottles of beer and a packet of mother-in-law's beef sandwiches stowed in my greatcoat pockets. The beer and sandwiches went down a treat with my fellow travellers standing in a cold dark corridor.

Returning across country in the early hours could take one hell of a long time. This time was no exception. The train was already packed solid with servicemen and women most without hope of getting a seat. Settling down in the corridor, cold, cramped, the trip back to Lincoln would be a long and tiresome journey. Stroud best bitter though was a good sleeping draught, so it was head down for a few hours.

Unfortunately Jerry had other ideas, and Birmingham was being plastered by the Luftwaffe. The train ground to a halt about ten miles from the city. All the lights went out except for one blue light, and there we sat for a long time. Listening to the crump, crump of bombs and anti aircraft fire. Aircrew did not relish being on the other end of a bombing raid. The reaction from the swaddy next to me and his girl companion was to begin a very noisy knee trembler. I noticed he was a member of a famous Highland regiment, a point which made stand up jobs a lot easier. My eardrum must have been okay, hearing no longer impaired, the grunts of delight made me positively jealous. When the dirty deed was done he quietly chuckled, "If there was a chance of being blown to smithereens Sir, I might just as well die on the job." It was a long night. Eventually we were diverted around Brum, rumour had it that New Street Station had copped a direct hit.

Reporting sick on arrival, the Doc gave me the good news, the scar on my ear drum had healed perfectly and I was pronounced fit for flying again. The crew were all in bed sleeping off an operation carried out the night before, and, when I walked into the squadron, I learned that during my absence they had notched up another three trips. I was three behind. This was not good, it could mean having to finish off my tour with a sprog crew.

The adjutant handed me a tiny gold chevron which he told me was to be worn on the left sleeve and was called a wound stripe. We all knew that American airmen were awarded a medal, the Purple Heart, if they were similarly wounded in action, but the stories were legion that even if they got themselves a dose of VD it qualified. I was determined not to wear my wound stripe, and I never did.

Who the hell I wondered thought out these ideas? Who in fact was responsible when we were hospitalised for making us wear hospital blue? A bright blue badly fitting suit, white shirt, and vivid red tie. Every patient looked like a lost inmate of a looney bin. To make it worse, it was also walking out dress.

What twisted mentality coined the phrase 'Lack of Moral Fibre', LMF? Aircrews who were declared LMF were branded as cowards. The truth of it was they all needed help, not derision. They were the shell-shocked victims of the air.

There were no prizes for guessing who had stepped into my shoes for those three operations I had unfortunately missed. None other than my biggest and friendliest buddy, Arthur Paxton. Arthur was a floater, which meant he had no special crew. As Signals Leader he could please himself when he flew. His position was becoming something of an embarrassement to the Squadron Commander, since we now had a number of commissioned W/op AGs and at least two were Flight Lieutenants. Underneath, they didn't care too much at being subordinate to a Pilot Officer.

There was a way to solve the dilemma, and the old man had the common sense to use. P.O. Arthur Paxton DFM and bar was promoted to the acting rank of Flt. Lt. overnight, still retaining the post of Signals Leader. The boss and the rest of the crew were glad to see me back in harness. Me, well I was over the moon, I wouldn't have to change crews. Changing crews for any reason, mostly for sickness, was bad news for bomber aircrews. It was openly inviting the reaper, took a long time to settle down again. I would have to wait and see how it would resolve itself towards the end of the tour, when I would still be sucking a hind tit. As of now, slotting back into my position was great news. We still had a long haul ahead of us before that magic number 30 came up.

Chapter 14

On the last day of the month, we paid Cologne a visit. It was almost a year since Cologne had been the recipient of the first 1000 bomber raid, when some 1046 aircraft including over 300 from training groups had taken part in a massive raid on the city. A smaller raid was repeated at the beginning of June, but raids of this magnitude could not be sustained because of the adverse effect it was having on the training organisation. Nevertheless, O.T.U. crews continued to be used, but generally on diversionary sorties against close and easily recognised targets. When losses of training crews began to increase, they were suddenly stopped from taking part in operations against the enemy.

Saturation bombing of targets was now beginning to pay dividends. Photo recce showed up vast amounts of damage with large areas still on fire, the following day. The jackboot for the Boche was beginning to pinch badly. Targets in the Ruhr were severely hit on eleven nights during the month of May, and as a crew we were out on eight nights. Happy Valley was not exactly the best of addresses for those on the receiving end of our nightly forays.

Halfway through my second tour now, I was beginning to get end-of-tour happy. Not so our tame Welshman, Idris. He was beginning to act even more peculiarly; always something of a loner, he was now completely isolated. He was showing outward signs of going downhill fast, losing his rag, rubbing people up the wrong way. To give him some extra responsibility, the boss had made him Bomb Aimer Leader. He'd been promoted to Flying Officer too, but some are born to lead, others have leadership thrust upon them. Diabolical was in the second category. His quick temper got him into a lot of trouble. He went for Bill Burley again. A small incident easily forgotten, but not Idris, who started chewing Bill off across a crowded crewroom. Any Officer worth his salt would never dress down a Warrant Oficer when lower ranks were present, and Bill true to form quickly told Idris to "go and kiss my Royal Canadian arse."

"What did you say Burley?" retorted Williams. This prompted a quick barbed response from our mid upper gunner.

"Oh, you're going deaf as well as daft," answered Burley walking quickly out of earshot.

This was one feud that would never be settled. I began to worry about our bomb aimer, he was an outstanding candidate for a nervous breakdown.

Away from our own troubles, exciting events were on the horizon for one of 5 Group's special duties squadrons. It soon became clear why No. 617 squadron crews had been practising low level bombing, mostly over water, when on the night of 16th/17th May they pulled off one of the most magnificent and daring raids of the war so far, by blasting three dams over Germany and releasing millions of tons of water.

RAF Scampton collected its third Victoria Cross, awarded to the C.O. of the squadron, Wing Commander Guy Gibson. Looking back through my log book, I realised I had flown with him on two occasions, once in 1940 when he was Flt. Lt. at Upper Heyford, and once at Scampton during training. Gibson handled a Lancaster just like a night fighter and during a corkscrewing detail, I actually blacked out whilst standing in the astro dome.

A lot of 617 squadron crews perished that night, and shortly after the squadron, what was left of them, moved off to RAF Coningsby. They were never the same squadron again, their teeth had been pulled. Before the move, they were honoured by a visit from the King who personally presented medals to some of the surviving crews.

Life in the Sergeants' Mess was changing. The station, like most, was bursting at the seams with non-commissioned aircrew. They all needed feeding and food rationing was beginning to bite. No longer did we have the luxury of waitress service for meals, it was now survival of the quickest. Many times if you were slightly late for meals, the shutters would come down, everything was off. This was also true in the literal sense as well, a lot of times the food was really off, you could smell it long before you got to the Mess hall. Fish was not my favourite dish.

They were hungry days, some days missing most of the meals. Accommodation was poor as well. The majority of aircrew slept twenty or more to a hut, very sparsely furnished with a belching coke stove in the centre of the room. The floor covering, service brown linoleum mostly worn and cracked, was not exactly Ritz standards. During the winter the coke was rationed to each hut. The ration was never enough, and this led to the usual midnight forays raiding the dump to keep the fire going. Winter could be bloody cold in Lincolnshire.

Chalky said his parents were dying to meet my wife, and could I manage a weekend. I promised I'd give her a ring and make the arrangements. The first free weekend, Laura came up and she stayed in Lincoln with the Whites whilst I saw her in the evening. On Sunday night we were out again. Another fresh target, still in the Ruhr. God there must be somewhere else in Germany. If this war ever ended, what would the Ruhr valley look like?

We had just lifted off into the darkness where there was one god awful explosion down below. The brilliant flash lit up the whole of the sky. "Christ what was that?" It was rare to hear the boss swear. We headed off towards our coasting-out position, knowing full well that someone down below had bought it. Nobody said anything for a long time, until the flak started to stream up in the distance. The target was Wuppertal, a small town which housed power plants, gas and electricity stations. My radar set, Fishpond, went on the blink, extra care would have to be taken scanning the darkness for night fighters. It was easier for them. Once they picked up a bomber stream, there were lots of targets to have a go at.

Chalky picked up the bogey first. "Fighter, port quarter, range 600 yards."

"Have you got it mid upper?"

"Not yet skipper."

"I got the bastard. Corkscrew, port go."

"Right W/op, get up in the astro dome. Direct the fire if you can."

"I got him, range 400 yards, 3 o'clock high."

"Open fire, open fire."

Bill and Chalky opened up at the same time. The attacker was out on a limb, no way could he fix us in his sights. The streams of tracer were dead on target, both gunners had laid off beautifully, and this was one Hun who would be dying for the Fatherland. "He's on fire. Jesus he's exploded over the top of us." I hoped he would get out by parachute, but he was one fighter pilot who didn't have time.

"You can share that one between you gunners. Well done. Keep your eyes peeled, we've a long way to go," this from the boss. Christ, that was worth a noggin or two on return.

"Which half do you want Chalky?" quipped Burley.

"I'll have the Focke and you can have the Wolfe," the rear gunner replied. Chalky had a sense of humour after all.

The rest of the trip was an anti-climax. Paddy's radar had also gone on the blink so he had to work for his living. The new radar designed primarily as a bombing aid called H2S was beautiful, giving a mapping of the country below. A good navigational aid. We had certainly come a long way in a few short years. We were also carrying bigger and better bombs. They were called Cookies; as Bill Burley remarked, some biscuits.

The airfield was black for our return, so we were diverted into Waddington. The boss was told that the aerodrome had been blacked by one of our own cookies exploding on the runway. No. 3 aircraft had suffered a double engine failure on take-off, the flight engineer had quickly retracted the undercarriage and as the aircraft slithered along on its belly, the whole bomb load went off. Jesus Christ, what a way to go, the whole crew blown into smithereens.

It was the Squadron Commander and his crew, the most

experienced crew on the squadron, all second tourists. The reaper had played his ace again. The next day, the boss took over the squadron, dead man's shoes, instant promotion to Wing Commander. Group stood us down for twenty-four hours, so that the hard-pressed ground crews could remove the debris and at the same time prepare the aircraft for a maximum effort. That only meant one thing, a big one. The boss made one of his instant decisions. Two large coaches were laid on at short notice for an 'educational' visit to the bright lights of Nottingham. The skipper thought the squadron morale needed lifting, and he was dead right. Money-wise, I was well breeched, having won a few pounds playing a game of crap on the mess billiard table. It was a good excuse for a piss up, not that we needed excuses. Additionally, we could also celebrate the boss's instant promotion.

Guess who didn't turn out? Our tame bomber aimer. He was given an extra ten minutes to show up before the coaches left without him. Williams was beginning to worry us. Not only had he retreated into a shell, he was becoming religious to boot. Religion to a large extent had been declared obsolete by most bomber crews for the duration, after all we dropped bombs seven days a week, one day was like the next.

The party was a corker, a huge pub crawl taking in most of the favourite pubs. The Trip to Jerusalem, the Black Boy and many others all got a thrashing. Nobody let the boss down by misbehaving, the aircrew choirs were all in fine voice all the way home. The residents of Newark wondered just what had hit them as we breezed through on the Fosse Way back to Fiskerton, singing our heads off. Bill got off the coach, slapping the back of his neck with his open palm, loudly exclaiming, "I don't care if I do die George." Paddy's satisfied expression said it all, they both had made first base with two ladies of Sin City tonight. As an added bonus they were paid for their services with packets of Players cigarettes. Morale had increased by leaps and bounds.

There was another change of command that week, in the shape of a new Station Commander. Nobody cared too much for his surname, Group Captain Dea'th, pronounced death. Somebody quipped that perhaps the next mission would be a suicide one. Our joker was almost prophetic. The new Groupie was tall, iron grey hair, and a pilot sporting first world war ribbons. He also wore a deaf aid and spoke in stilted gasps. Rumour had it if he got bored with conversation, he simply switched his deaf aid off. On one occasion, a fellow officer pinched his batteries and his spare supply as well. He was a deaf as a doorpost for a whole week. It was not unusual to see him perched up a tree at night clutching a shotgun, blasting away at anything that moved. Station Commanders, on odd occasions, flew on operations. I prayed he wouldn't pick us.

The big one when it came was back on the milk run, Essen again. Paddy reckoned one of the top brass had had an awful holiday touring the area before the war. The brass certainly had a one track mind. We either concentrated on ports, submarine yards or armament factories. I was glad I didn't have any shares in Krupps.

After briefing, where the Group Captain made his mark, providing some light relief and a chuckle or two, Paddy told me he was worried about Williams. The Navigator and Bomb Aimer usually did their plotting together. Paddy said Idris seemed completely disinterested. I said, "Maybe he's in love."

"Who, Taffy? He still thinks its to piss out of." Nasty.

Seven men, strapped in, ready to go, bound by esprit de corp. "Skipper here, right check in, we're half-way home after this one." Good crew discipline.

We went through all the usual drills like clockwork. The boss was leading his new squadron for the first time, and he was number one to be airborne. Once again, the master bombers and pathfinding force had done their jobs well. The smoke and fires could be seen from a long way away. One Lancaster was being held by three searchlights. They showed it up well and the aircraft was being pounded by heavy flak. Bill and Chalky put in a burst at each of them, but to no avail. The poor sod was getting it in the neck. "Weave for Christ sake," I found myself muttering. Maybe the pilot had been hit. There were lots of aircraft going down in flames. That meant only one thing, night fighters were out in force. On the way in to the target, there was a sudden whoosh followed by a blast of cold air. We'd been hit. Paddy looked down towards the front turret. The front hatch had gone, and with it had gone Idris. "The silly bastard's baled out," Nobby said.

"Have a look W/op."

"OK skipper." I took my portable oxygen bottle, crawled forward and confirmed that Idris and the front hatch were both missing. Poor old Idris, he'd even forgotten to take his bloody parachute. I filled in as bomb aimer, just pressed the tit when the boss gave the word and jettisoned the lot. It was brass monkey weather all the way home. Now we knew what Chalky and Bill had to put up with most of the time we were airborne.

The boss found a letter from Idris in his pigeon hole. Diabolical said briefly he felt he could no longer go on killing innocent people, but in essence the message that came over loud and clear was he considered himself a failure. We tried all of us to help, but in the end he made his own disastrous decision. Fifteen more to go, forty eight ops under my belt, roll on. Not one of us wanted to eat, we all crept away too choked to enjoy our post flight meal.

Chapter 15

He breezed into the crew room, his forage cap on the back of his head, a smile to outdo a Cheshire cat, and an awful lot of swagger. "Hello dere, I'm your new bomb aimer, Wham by name Wham by nature." Winston Horatia Aloysius McKenzie wasn't kidding either. He was big, he was gangly and he was as black as the ace of spades.

Nobby Clark muttered, "Christ that's all we need. We won't be able to see him in the dark."

We christened him Sambo, he didn't seem to mind. He told us he was from Kingston, Jamaica, and his folks were in bananas. "Pity you didn't bring a boatload over with you," said Chalky. "We haven't seen a banana for years." Sambo's folks had hopefully grand designs for their offspring, and with all those Christian names, they were obviously hedging their bets. I thought, if nothing else he could strengthen the squadron cricket team.

Superstition raised its ugly head again. With a new crew member we had to go through that bloody awful cycle again, number one and number thirteen, Kelly's eye and unlucky for some. Sambo buttonholed Nobby. "Right boy, where's all the action around here?"

"You'll see plenty of action before you're much older, boy," Nobby replied with a hint of sarcasm. Sambo was persistent.

"Eh man, I meant night life, dolly birds. If my life is going to be short, it's going to be damn well sweet."

"Why don't you sit down and take the weight off your brains," Nobby snapped. He was getting wound up for some reasons.

"Come on man, answer my question." The new boy was like a terrier, stubborn.

"I told you Sambo, there's plenty of night life, the Berlin Follies, free fireworks display most nights. Don't be a prick all your life, take a day off occasionally," Nobby snapped again.

Someone in the corner of the crew room threw in an aside, "Hey boy, what part of Africa do you come from?"

Young Winston was beginning to get ratty. "I told you, I come from the sunshine isles, I'm no bloody witch doctor."

It was about time to step in and stop this banter in its tracks, it was all becoming too serious. "OK you lot, knock it off, and Sgt. McKenzie, whilst I'm talking my name is either George or Sir, not boy. I don't care which you use."

"Sorry Sir, I was just trying to be friendly."

"OK Winston, have you had an Intelligence briefing?"

"No Sir."

"OK, go down to Station Headquarters and make yourself known to the intelligence nark."

The tannoy spluttered intermittently into life, but we got the gist. There would be a concert in the station cinema at 2000 hours tonight. Winston left, and I tackled the engineer. "What was that all about Nobby, bit fierce with the new man weren't you?"

"Sorry George, but I can't stand twenty three fifty nines."

"Well I suggest in future you either bite your tongue or count up to ten and you'd better learn to like him for all our sakes. That doesn't mean you have to love him, OK?" The phone rang and I answered it. "Wing Co. here."

"George, did you hear the tannoy message?"

"Yes boss."

"Right, I want you to chaperone the concert party before and after the show. They will be entertained in the Sergeants' Mess, and the Station Commander will be in attendance, plus myself and two other officers, got it."

That told me two things. One, we had another night off, and secondly the travelling entertainers were all second raters. All the top ones were always entertained by the Barons.

With the demise of Idris, the boss began to give me the spiel about commissioning again. He plainly wanted another officer in his crew. I could see his point of view, and I told him I would discuss it with my wife. "You know George, you could be commissioned overnight, tomorrow a Flying Officer, it's as simple as that. Why are you so unsure?" He was right of course, if I wanted to stay in the Air Force once this war was over, it made sense to have a decent rank behind you. But before I said yes I had to talk it over with my darling wife, we were a team as well. I knew of course what she would say, she would be all for it.

Laura Kathleen Mountford, to give my beloved her full maiden name, was born in Belfast, the eldest daughter of Sgt. Victor Emmanual Mountford of the Royal Military Police. Vic my father-in-law had completed a horizontal shuffle from the Army to the local constabulary, and was now the same rank some twenty years later with Gloucestershire C.I.D. Vic had served with distinction within both arms of his public service.

My wife's maternal ancestors were Irish Protestant, seafaring from the North. My ancestry was Roman Catholic, feudal from the South, with a touch of Huegonots on my mothers side. The Mountfords, originally de Mountford, had come over with the Normans and settled in Gloucestershire to become country squires and farmers.

Laura and I had no hang ups about mixed marriages, or where our children would be educated. Myself, I had been saturated with religion during my youth, and having witnessed some of its darker side, had become a lapsed Catholic. It didn't stop me from praying however, an exercise I practiced regularly with each passing day.

Funny, I can never recall addressing my wife by her Christian name. Both of us always used endearing nicknames. My nickname for my wife was Preciouskins, Presh or Skins, and she always called me Presh. Vic, my father-in-law, behind my back referred to me as Whistling Rufus, later Young, and when my son, his grandson, was born, he was nicknamed Young Young.

His pet name for his daughter was Alias. I could never figure out the reason why. Vic Mountford was one of nature's gentlemen, a great character, and the sixth of seven brothers, all of whom had served with distinction in world war one, the Great War. Two ultimately paid the highest sacrifice, another was awarded the Military Cross and commissioned on the field of battle. The patriotism of the family was recognised by a personal telegram from the King himself, to my wife's grandmother, a telegram she treasured to her dying day. These personal touches need a mention because my Piscean intuition had been nagging away for some time and I had begun to get more and more twitched up about the possibilities of escape and evasion or even capture by the goons. This amounted to reading almost everything I could lay my hands on about the subject. I badgered the Intelligence narks to arrange talks from successful evaders, as more and more had made it back home. I recognised this as a blatant case of second tour twitch. I promised myself that if I completed this tour, never again would I volunteer for another thing. There were other good reasons too. If I was unlucky enough to finish up in the bag, I could by the use of code words, nicknames known only to my wife and myself, establish a genuine link, one which could have its advantages by passing and receiving information. It could also be useful for requesting articles or advice.

The morale booster of personal contact with squadron aircrew who had successfully evaded capture and returned to their units was far better than a dozen scripted talks by Intelligence Officers. I planned to discuss my plans with my wife on my next leave. It would require some earnest heart to heart, but it had to be done.

The new bomb aimer was to be initiated into the sixpence half a crown club with a short but violent trip to somewhere called Peenemunde on the coast. Intelligence were not saying much about the target itself, but it was obviously important. As far as we were concerned at briefing, it was an ammunition dump of some kind. Later the full facts of its awesome significance would be known. The production of a radically new and horrendous deadly weapon. Peenemunde was the testing ground.

The trip looked easy. "Piece of duff," Paddy said. "Straight in and out, no problem." Nice easy sea legs to and from the target, and good steady platform for Wham the bomb aimer to begin his operational tour. Everything, but everything about Sambo's first operation went pear shaped from the word go. Number one syndrome again, the reaper was beginning to stir. Our beloved aircraft which each of us had grown to love and know like the back of the hand, with all its foibles and smells, had other thoughts. It was going to misbehave itself and take a day off. Number three engine refused to start, and Nobby was completely perplexed. Since this donk provided power for important ancilliary equipment, it was a no go item. After about twenty minutes of pulling and pushing tits and knobs to no avail, even Nobby was completely nonplussed. "It's bloody Gremlins, boss," he said. "I don't understand it, I ran all these bloody engines up this afternoon, and they were all spot on. We've probably got a bloody Jonah on board." The flight engineer was wound up.

"Right you lot," interposed the skipper. "Outside, into the coach, we'll take the reserve aircraft—S for sugar."

"More like S for Sambo," piped in Nobby again. Nobby Clarke was beginning to get rattled, it was out of character. He never said another word until we climbed aboard the reserve kite. I didn't like it either. It was new, and I would miss the feel of my old equipment, I knew every spot on the dial. I knew all the little wrinkes, the Fishpond. I was beginning to get rattled too.

At the same time, it meant we would be the last one off, the last one to get airborne, with plenty of fireworks going on when we eventually got to the target. If we missed the stream, and we probably would, we'd be a lone ranger easy to pick off, sticking out like a spare prick at a wedding. Mind you all aircraft were supposed to be standard, but we knew this one was different. The boss expected a load of grumbles and he got them. Only Wham McKenzie who didn't know any better kept his mouth shut. Nevertheless he must have felt the hostility from Nobby Clarke, and I was beginning to feel sorry for the Bomb Aimer, Christ, I never felt so superstitious and the atmosphere inside that aircraft was not right. Nobby or Paddy would have put this bird unserviceable at the drop of a hat, except neither of them would ever dream of letting the boss down.

It had to be said though, this reserve aircraft was a bag of nails. It rattled every time Nobby ran an engine, and felt like every rivet was loose. There was a strange smell of newness about it once the heating was switched on. The brakes did not come on evenly and we skewered down the taxiway like a drunken man until the skipper had got it taped. S for Sugar wheezed its way down to the take-off point and lifted into the air like a ruptured crab. Maybe it didn't like us either. To fly it straight and level, the trims were all over the place. Once we had settled down, there was another strange smell, a smell of strong hot beverage. The intercom clicked on to a live microphone, "Bomb Aimer here, anyone for coffee and biscuits?" The new boy had scrounged a large hot flask of coffee and biscuits from somewhere and I'm sure he'd laced it with rum. That broke the atmosphere. Even Nobby grunted his appreciation. Both gunners thought it was their birthday. Hot sweet coffee served in situ.

Met. had promised patchy weather once we crossed the coast outbound, and this time they were almost right. The further north we flew, the thicker became the cumulus cloud. We bounced, we lurched, we snatched. Occasionally the whole of the fuselage glowed an eerie blue, St Elmo's fire ran all the way up the trailing aerial, all two hundred feet of it and danced around my left arm. I didn't like it. Nothing much was said by anyone, we simply buffetted along. Paddy had a reasonable picture on radar, so at least we were on track. "Pretty fierce headwinds skipper," Paddy piped.

"Lot stronger than forecast. Have you worked out an ETA for the enemy coast Nav?"

"Yes, more or less, we're going to be very late if these winds persist."

"OK Paddy, keep a good plot going, this bloody aircraft seems to be gobbling up the fuel. What's your last fuel check like Eng?"

"Going to have to come back on revs and boost skipper; and when we settle down, I will have to check for a possible fuel leak."

Christ that's all we wanted I thought, a nice cold douche in the North Sea. The boss told the gunners to keep a sharp look out, reminding us all of three hundred more other aircraft out there somewhere. Chalky answered, "Roger skipper, pretty murky back here, bloody cold too, the turret heating has packed up." Poor old Chalky, I felt really sorry for him. There was no doubt about it, being a tail end Charlie was one of the loneliest occupations in the world. There you were at the extreme end of the fuselage, a dark void between you and any other crew member. Mostly feeling very cold, sitting cramped in your small plastic bubble, facing four equally cold browning machine guns. When the turret was on the beam, the two small doors at your back rattled away like hell, unnervingly. At times the hydraulics would misbehave, leaving you stuck out in an unusual attitude. The rear runner would then have to manually rotate his turret. At least the mid upper could see the cockpit ahead. Chalky never complained.

"You OK Bomb Aimer?" asked the skipper.

"Feeling a little pale, man."

Christ that captured the imagination, Sambo turning white. I decoded a message for all aircraft of 4 group based in Yorkshire. This was something most unusual, they were instructed to jettison their bombs either on an alternative target, or over the North Sea. I wondered if 5 Group would pass the same message to us, but the frequency was quiet. 5 Group was not known for recalling its aircraft once they were on their way; the weather up ahead must be really shitty. Paddy said his radar was being saturated by all kinds of noise, and he suspected it was being jammed. It was impossible also to decipher any intelligence from my Fishpond, the screen was a mass of fuzz, so I switched it off. Group were now sending out coded messages forecasting very strong headwinds all the way into the target area; Jesus, we could have told them that ourselves a long time ago. The pounding against the fuselage of heavy hailstones, together with occasional large lumps of ice from the leading edges of the wings, were making it difficult for the boss to keep this bird straight and level. Shortly after this, we were struck by lightening, it almost blinded Nobby and the skipper. The strike, dead in front, cracked the windscreen which fortunately didn't blow out. We were now flying in the centre of a particularly vicious build up of storm clouds cumulo-nimbus, and we were taking on ice quite rapidly. Communications sounded like a whole fleet of two stroke motor bikes, building up from low popping noises and ending in a loud pitched screech. The cacophony of sound was something I'd never experienced before, it was frightening.

Poor Sambo, stuck in the nose, what a christening, and maybe the worst part was still to come. He was probably speechless with fright. If we were having a rough ride, it was twice as rough for Bill and Chalky, stuck out on a limb. At least we could see each other, small comfort, but comfort nevertheless. Pray God ease it up, it had gone on too long. Wish we had that bloody Met. man with us, he'd soon change his tune. "How we doing Nav, how much longer on this course?" from the boss. I sensed for the first time a note of real anxiety from the skipper.

"Another twenty minutes before we turn due east, pilot."

"OK Nav, thanks."

We popped out of the top of the weather like a cork in a bottle, and somebody muttered praise the Lord. We were going upwards and over in a most unusual attitude, but never mind, the sight of that moon and a tilted horizon was like manna from heaven. Paddy passed a quick revised track for the next turning point, and ahead and slightly to starboard there was a faint red dullish glow. That was where all the action was.

"OK crew, cut the cackle. Gunners keep your eyes peeled. Bomb Aimer set up your Mickey Mouse. Nav, anything on radar?"

"Yes skipper, I can now pick out the coastline. I should get a good pinpoint when we turn in. 093 is your next heading, I'll let you know when to turn."

"093 set Nav. W/op, get up into the astro dome, we might need an extra pair of eyes."

"OK pilot."

As I craned my neck, standing on tip toes, scanning the black night, cold, tired, thinking about the return journey and all that bloody awful weather to go back through, my mind wandered to much more pleasant surroundings and things. What wouldn't I give right now to be back in the Stroud valley with my wife and babe by my side? The thought of pushing a pram along a country lane, peaceful. The comfort of a warm cosy bed, with my son gently sleeping in the corner of the bedroom in his cot. No thoughts of war, peace perfect peace. The taste of the delights from my mother-in-law's table. She could produce a feast from basic ingredients, although in the country there were always little extras.

If I survived this war, I would make my home and earn my living close to those gentle rolling Cotswold hills. I could never go back to the North West with all its industry, that was gone forever. The countryside had fully converted me. Reality for the present however was astride a chariot of death and destruction, delivering one more package to induce permanent sleep to some of those on the receiving end. Some postman, some Airmail.

Paddy came through. "Turn on to 093 now skipper, twelve minutes to run to the target." We could see the markers going down. The Pathfinders were doing a good job of marking the target.

"Got the orange flares yet Bomb Aimer?"

"OK pilot I can see them, lot of light flak around."

"No, it's not too bad, seen a damn sight worse. Not a lot of searchlights either." Comforting reply from the boss for Sambo's sake. He was an ace.

"OK Bomb Aimer, take over. You're in command. Now give me a steer back to hit Northern Scotland, when we've dropped our load, I've no intention of flying back through all that God awful weather again. If necessary, I will land at Leuchars. OK Nav?"

"Roger skip." There was a sigh of relief all round.

"Engineer here, fuel consumption seems to have stabilised," Nobby said, "but this is a thirsty cow, we could be pushed to make it back to base. Can't see any signs of leaks anywhere."

"OK Nobby, we'll worry about that once we've left the target."

Two balls of fire suddenly erupted dead ahead. We could see the silhouette of a Stirling in flames, burning, burning. Get out, get out, praying for the sight of parachutes, but another fearful explosion spelt doom. The bomb load had exploded, nobody but nobody could have survived that.

The second ball of fire was gently spiralling towards the sea. It meant only one thing, night fighters. This was the real world, a battle of survival, machine against machine.

"Corkscrew port go, bogey at 3 o'clock, range 400 yards." Both gunners picked him up right away, and both opened fire at the same time. The twin engined JU88 skidded overhead, crossing over to starboard. We lost him against the dark side of the moon. As he peeled over the top in a climb, there was nothing to see. Had he gone underneath to exploit our blind spot? The boss continued corkscrewing, a gentle dive to starboard and then a roll over to port, but there was no sign of our bogey, we had lost each other.

Wham settled us down for the bombing run. "OK Bomb Aimer, bomb doors open. Are we OK on this heading?"

"OK skipper, steady steady, two port, steady, 30 seconds to run. Bombs gone, photo taken. One dead ahead, it's ours."

"OK crew, standby for steep turn to port. Nav give me a steer for home."

"Take up 265 degrees skipper, another 1000 feet will give us a better wind."

Shortly after leaving the target area, the starboard outer just coughed and died. I saw Nobby almost jump out of his skin, the sight of a donk suddenly winding itself down shook him to the core. "Number four gone skipper, must be fuel starvation."

"I can see that Eng, and feel it. It's windmilling like mad, feather it right away and cut out this drag."

"OK pilot."

I saw Nobby stab at the red feathering button, but the bloody propeller just kept on turning in coarse pitch. I could imagine Nobby cursing like hell under his breath, he never did want to get airborne in this bloody heap in the first splace. Pull the throttle on four back through the gate Nobby, I subconsciously urged him. It must have been telepathy, that was his next action. The engine went into fine pitch and stopped. Time for some quick decisions, a course for the nearest suitable airfield, try to maintain height for as long as possible on three engines. Get some bloody good bearings and fixes as soon as we left enemy airspace, just in case we had to fly back through all that shit on the way home. The boss told us to think seriously about ditching drills. Nobby was asked for fuel situation in tanks. We had to fly now for endurance. Nobby said the situation was OK, providing nothing else went haywire. One thing at least was in our favour, a good tail wind right up our chuff.

It was imperative now for me to establish good two-way contact with a ground station. This was an emergency situation.

Get on with the job in hand, some good MF D/F fixes. A quick call to the master station. No reply, not a bloody peep out of anybody. Oh no, not now when we really needed it. Everyone was relying on my professionalism and I was letting them down. Not much sound on the receiver either, just mush. The reason then twigged, I'd lost my trailing aerial, all bloody two hundred feet of it. I went for HF bearings, not fixes, and got some good Class A ones. Nobby was satisfied. We now had good two-way contact, just in case things suddenly deteriorated. "OK W/op, tell Group we are returning on three engines. I want a good diversion and weather report."

We droned on through a blackened night. Every now and then the starboard inner cut with a bang before picking up its revolutions again. I could imagine the sweat pouring off both the boss and Nobby, even though it was bloody cold. Bill and Chalky both remained as silent as the grave, both had stowed their parachutes for a quick getaway. I prayed, please keep going over the sea. Ditching in the North Sea was the supreme hazard, especially at night.

We entered cloud, and the noise factor increased. My ears had become attuned to thunder clouds, but we seemed OK for the present. Christ, where was Group with the reply to my request for a suitable diversion? I thought about them in their warm offices, sipping mugs of tea, filling in their chinagraph boards, wondering if my request was being actioned. Seven men at the mercy of the elements.

It took me some time to decode the reply in bomber code. This was not our night, every card was being stacked against us. Who had we offended? "Weather over the whole of the East coast looks bloody awful boss—it just says UNFIT whatever that means. We are diverted to Mildenhall, and something called FIDO will be in operation for our arrival."

"What the bloody 'ell is FIDO? A dog who talks you down? Some bloody secret weapon maybe. We won't know until we get within tower range on VHF. OK George, keep a good listening watch, this bloody aircraft doesn't like us at all. I'll scrap the bugger if I ever get it down in one piece. Anybody having problems with their oxygen?"

Funny, we hadn't heard from Sambo for some time. I'd better have a look and see what he was up to. The boss was obviously not getting his full whack of oxygen either, and neither was the Bomb Aimer, he wasn't getting any at all, and he'd quietly gone to sleep. I connected him up quickly to a portable oxygen bottle and he suddenly came back to the land of the living. Good job the boss had mentioned it, or Sambo would have joined his ancestors.

"Coasting in in ten minutes boss," from Paddy. "Mildenhall overhead in twenty minutes." Boy, those words sounded great, IFF was on, so they could plot a friendly from the ground.

"What's the range of Mildenhall Nav?"

"About sixty miles."

"OK thanks, I'll give Darkie a call in five minutes. Darkie Darkie this is George Apple Sierra One, do you read? Over."

"George Apple Sierra One this is Darkie, reading you strength three clear, go ahead, over."

"Darkie this is Sierra One request steer for Orange Nuts and present weather. Over."

"Steer 268 true—range four five miles. Weather ten tenths cloud at three hundred feet with mist and drizzle below. Wind gusting to forty miles per hour. Runway one one. Fido is switched on. Good luck. Contact Orange Nuts on tower frequency for radio descent. Roger Out."

Bloody hell, that's all we need, weather on the deck, a strange airfield, and the worst bloody aircraft I'd ever flown in. We would certainly need all the luck we could get tonight. I changed to the local frequency at Mildenhall and gave them a call. The tower confirmed the landing instructions, told us full emergency services were all standing by, and said we should pick up the glow of Fido from about ten miles or more.

"Fuel check skipper."

"OK Nobby, how's it looking?"

"I reckon we have enough for about half an hour."

"Right Nav, how long do you reckon for one good descent, that's all we can expect."

"I reckon from here we could be down in about fifteen minutes if we get a good controller on the ball."

"Right crew—skipper here, listen carefully. Chalky, Bill and Wham, you could all bale out over the top of the airfield, leaving the rest of us to try and get this beast down, or you could stay aboard, the decision is yours."

It was unanimous. They all decided to stay. Sambo picked up the glow from Fido first. It looked like the airfield was on fire, even through thick cloud.

The ground controller asked for a short transmission, and then confirmed he had us positioned. The boss flew a precise pattern with me interposing between the ground and the air. I felt a glow of confidence, the man on the ground was on the ball. We descended through the murk, the lower we got the brighter and stronger the glow from Fido—must be a St Bernard!

"OK Nobby, I'm on the final approach—six miles to run, undercarriage down."

"OK skipper, going down. Christ, we haven't got three greens." Could mean the undercarriage was not down and locked.

Bloody hell, everything was being stacked against us.

"Right W/op, have a quick look and see if both legs are down, and then come back up here and start pumping."

I checked the undercarriage on both sides. It looked OK, could be an electrical fault. "Both legs look down to me, skipper," I answered, but I began to manually pump, just in case one side was unlocked. We broke cloud at four hundred feet, with the runway lights dead ahead.

"All crew take up crash positions now. There won't be any overshoots—Praise the Lord," this from the boss.

I tightened my lap strap, hands clasped behind my head, legs hard against a stanchion and said a little prayer.

We slid in to a wet and misty airfield, felt and heard a quick kiss of rubber as the main wheels touched, and I sighed with relief. Thank God for Fido. It looked like both sides of the runway were on fire. This night however was not yet over. When you fly by the seat of your pants, you know when things are not right. "Crash, crash," from the boss. The starboard leg was not locked and we slewed around in a semi-circle, before coming to rest halfway down the airfield. "Abandon aircraft. Abandon aircraft." We were all out like shit off a shovel, and quickly assembled away from the aircraft. There was no fire, but all four propellers looked sick, and bent at the tips.

"Christ, you look pale Sambo," Nobby said. We all broke off into shaken laughter, spontaneously congratulating the skipper in turn for a good show.

He quietly said, "Any landing is a good one, if you can walk away."

I said "Amen to that boss."

This was number one for the Bomb Aimer, and the rest of us could count on one hand the end of a tour in sight. What a christening for Sgt. Winston Horatio Aloysius McKenzie. He would remember his first operation for a long time to come. The rest of us were on the home straight, maybe the remainder would be easy now this one was over.

The blood tub and the fire engine raced into sight, quickly followed by the Station Commander in his jeep.

"Well done chaps, I want you all to go to sick quarters for a check-up," the boss said, "And you can bury that bloody heap over there."

"We'll certainly have to shift it bloody quick, we've got a lot of pigeons coming home to roost," said the Station Commander. Funny, our two feathered beauties were clucking away like mad.

Apart from a few minor bruises, not one of us suffered any serious injury. My second belly flop, both of which I'd walked away from unscathed. Somebody was in my corner. The boss put in a quick call to base, and we repaired to our respective Messes to drown our sorrows. I wished I could have put in a call to my wife, but she would have been fast asleep, completely oblivious to the traumas played out tonight over Germany and down here in sleepy Suffolk. I was glad she didn't know the half that was going on. A sorrow shared was a sorrow halved—not so in our case.

The station was non-operational, awaiting transfer to the American Air Force. We were treated like heroes in the Mess; before too long, the booze was flowing and a good party was in full swing. I phoned the boss and invited him over to join us. He was over in a flash. The thrash ended in the early hours, in one glorious mutual admiration society, singing our heads off, the best anti-shock treatment there was. Nobody climbed into bed.

Nobby had done a superb job of engineering tonight, and I quietly congratulated him. All he said was "That's what they pay me for George." Typical Nobby, but a very professional performance. There were others who had the same ideas, and shortly afterwards Nobby was awarded the DFM and the boss collected a bar to his DFC. Incidentally, FIDO was designed to disperse fog and hopefully to also raise the cloud base, not by mirrors, but by a heat process.

The two awards called for a party, and we made it a good one, by one hell of a night out in Nottingham, sin city. A week's holiday in Bonny Scotland was also on the cards, families as well, once we got this tour over and done with. The suggestion was terrific, we all eagerly looked forward to it. All I could think of was my young baby son bundled in his lovely white baby suit, his face glowing with health. The sooner this tour was over the better. I was getting maudlin again.

Chapter 16

The skipper called me into his office, and we had a long chat. The upshot was that I was again presented with commissioning papers and told to fill them in at my leisure. They would have to wait until I had spoken with Arthur Paxton to find out how he adapted to becoming a Baron himself. Arthur was presently enjoying a well earned leave, and I would have to await his return.

Back at Mildenhall, S for Sugar was pushed well away from the landing runway and eventually it arrived back at base on three separate trailers, to be used as a Christmas Tree for spare parts, as and when required to service other sick aircraft.

The weekend following our own arrival, we were detailed as a crew to go up to an aerodrome near Manchester to the factory where they built the Avro Lancaster. There we were to pick up a replacement aircraft and having accepted it, fly it back to Fiskerton. Group had also made it a public relations exercise, the factory workers were to meet and entertain an operational aircrew, and the skipper asked to register our appreciation for the long hours they put in on our behalf.

Sambo was really looking forward to the visit. Paddy had been filling him in with stories about the lovely dolly birds he could expect to meet, and how in bursts of patriotism they would bend to our every wish; such gallant airmen. For the acceptance check, we had the company and the benefit of the factory test pilot. The boss called him Mutt, but he was certainly no mutt when it came to handling the Lancaster and putting it through its paces. His flying skills were sheer poetry in motion. As a crew, we had never consciously stalled an aircraft, it was frightening, even more so when Mutt calmly and methodically feathered each engine in turn, stopping fortunately with three feathered and one turning, to demonstrate how a Lancaster could safely maintain height on one engine. What a confidence builder that proved to be, since operational crews never feathered engines unless it was absolutely necessary. I think we could safely say we were the only crew to fly the Lancaster on only one engine. What a line shoot.

I decided to duck the social gatherings and to pay a nostalgic, and for me a harrowing, visit home. Home was a heap of rubble, so I paid my respects to my parents' last resting place, the cemetery at Cherry Tree. Why oh why did one single jerry landmine wipe out most of the road and the people who lived there? There were no important targets around us, the armaments factory was the other end of town. It was a most tragic event, never to be repeated throughout the war.

I turned away from the flattened houses, and remembered all the good times together, simply walking out into the countryside enjoying the surroundings. I wondered how many poor unfortunate German families were in the same boat. Strange too how father and son had both been wounded in action in physically the same places, fingers, leg and head. Pray God it would never happen to my son. Pray God too that unlike my father, I would survive.

My close friends at school, five of us, had all joined the services. I was the first, the rest went into the Army, Navy and Marines. Two had already been killed, one at Dunkirk, the other during training for the parachute regiment. The remaining two were serving overseas, in some far flung corner of the Empire. I don't suppose I would ever see them again, since I had no intention of ever returning to Lancashire.

We flew the new aircraft back, a much more knowledgeable crew, raring to get the next five sorties under our belts and a well earned rest, Sambo excepted. The Bomb Aimer slept most of the way, he had obviously had a very strenuous weekend socialising. He snored his socks off all the way back to base, other than that he was strangely quiet. The skipper after landing signed the aircraft diary prepare for B.O.A.S.A.P. This told the groundcrew to prepare the aircraft for Battle Order as soon as possible. Turrets needed rearming, Radar and wireless to be filled. Squadron and aircraft letter to be assigned. This was to be our aircraft for the next five sorties.

The skipper began to press me for my completed commissioning papers. I started to waffle, but he was not impressed. I still hadn't discussed it with my wife, or Paxton. It seemed a big step to take. Overnight of course you changed Mess, it happened so quickly. It was hard to explain why I was holding back, after all it was a natural progression from Warrant Officer to Flying Officer, and a privilege to boot, but it was my own private mental blockage.

The Bomb Aimer's quietness worried me. Something was amiss, it was out of character for him to behave in this way. "Anything wrong old lad?" I tackled him with when we were on our own.

He grunted "Why do you ask George?"

"Well it's not like you Sambo to be so damn silent. It's worrying me. C'mon now don't be shy, if there's something wrong get it off your chest. Don't let it fester."

"OK man, but keep it to yourself," he said. "I think I've got a dose of the clap." Sambo looked down at the floor, he couldn't look me straight in the eyes. "Every time I go for a piss, it's like pissing broken glass. I reckon that bloody mill girl handed me a decoration. VD and scar."

"Well you know what to do," I said. "You'll have to go and see the medicine man, and he'll mix you a potion. You're not the first bomb aimer to get a dose and you won't be the last. Go special sick right now, and you'll be back on the job within two days." Both of us managed a chuckle at that remark.

"Thanks George, I'll take your advice."

"And don't forget to pack your small kit, they'll keep you in for a couple of days."

Sambo missed the next two trips. The doc packed him off to the hospital at RAF Cranwell. Everybody knew he'd gone on a short map reading course to the college, a nice way of saying he'd got a dose of the clap. The boss was livid when he got the news from the medic but his anger was short lived, and he laughed his cock off when he saw the funny side of it. None of us felt over the moon losing a crew member. Aircrew superstitions lurked in every corner. Sixpence half a crown. Fortunately or unfortunately the squadron Bomb Aimer leader was spare, so he was quickly co-opted into getting airborne with us for the next two sorties.

There was no feeling of shame attached to getting yourself a dose. None of us subscribed to the view of Lady Astor that those servicemen who had the misfortune to pick up the pox should either be branded on the forehead, or should hang a sign around their necks like social lepers. Call it inverted snobbery, but at least Sambo had got his end away, we all said good luck to him.

Not that most people weren't careful, especially when rumour had it that the treatment was so horrendous. That the needle loaded with arsenic and pushed up the penis was as thick as a pencil. Gilbertian justice, the punishment fitted the crime.

The Bomb Aimer was back in two days, his huge face wreathed in smiles like the proverbial Cheshire cat. "You look like you've lost a penny and found a two bob bit," I said to him.

"Yeah man. I didn't have the pox George, something called non-specific VD. Can't remember the medical name for it. Doc said it was caused by straining too hard." We both had a good laugh.

Nobby when he heard the news was more vitriolic. "I always said his brains were in his prick," he said, and left it at that.

> *Cats on the roof tops, cats on the tiles,*
> *cats with syphillis, cats with piles.*
> *Cats with their arseholes wreathed in smiles,*
> *as they revel in the joys of fornication.*

This tour had dragged on almost a year, the end however was in sight. Three more to go and then a long leave, roll on. The skipper, Nobby, Chalky and Bill had all officially finished their tour, but true to their word, stuck by their decision to do that extra three for my benefit. I hoped their decision would not be a bad one.

Excitement reigned. There was a rumour flying around that the big boss, Bomber Harris, Butch to us, was to visit the station and give us all a talk on how the war was progressing. Also, what was expected of Bomber Command to achieve final victory.

We peasants could never quite understand why our supreme leader had never flown in one of his aircraft on operations. Maybe he considered Headquarters Bomber Command at High Wycombe was front line enough. The station was spruced up, even the aircraft were given a spit and polish. We were paraded and marched around for hours on end, something completely foreign to generally scruffy aircrews. The big day never happened, it was all a myth. We should have known better, since Harris rarely if ever visited his front line stations. It was probably a clever plot by the Station Commander to keep us on our toes. Butch Harris however could do no wrong.

For us, three battles had already been fought. We didn't really need anyone to tell us how we had fared. We had taken part in the battle of the Ruhr, followed by Hamburg, and then the awesome and dreadful battle of Berlin. Maybe one day like regiments of the Army we could nail these colours to the Bomber Command mast. Naturally as lower echelons we were not privy to the overall picture, except that all of us knew that a large number of friends and colleagues were either missing, killed or prisoners of war. These were pieces of the canvas that would never go away.

The American Air Force too had been taking a battering against targets considered vital to aircraft production. A fighter had yet to be produced with a long enough range to afford them full protection. It had been forecast that the Battle of Berlin would bring the Germans to their knees, possibly even to surrender. It never happened, the war was to grind on, and one wondered if it would ever end.

As the most experienced crew on the squadron for some time now, we had been chosen to fly at the head of the bomber stream. Paddy would make careful use of his H2S equipment to obtain fixes from which he would calculate the strength and direction of the upper winds. These would then be passed to me, quickly encoded, and then transmitted at intervals using a special procedure back to

Group. These were called 'Zephyr' broadcasts, and W/ops of all other crews would receive them, decode, and their navigators would use them.

The idea was to keep a bomber stream compact by assisting less experienced navigators in the art of finding winds. Theoretically the system was fine, should have worked, but at times due to a number of adverse factors like weather, jamming, and not all aircraft fitted with H2S, bomber streams were mostly scattered.

It would soon be my birthday again, twenty two years old, married with a family. This was my fifth winter of the war. The country itself was a floating arsenal, packed with troops of all nationalities from around the world. It could not be long before Hitler and his cronies got their just desserts in Europe. The Russians had long been pressing for the start of the second front. The news from inside Russia was good, their offensives were now beginning to make progress, and their defence in-depth policy, although very costly, was now making the Wehrmacht regret they had ever invaded Russia. The Americans too were doing very well in the Pacific against the Japanese, although in Burma the Nips were still advancing. I thought I'd give myself a birthday treat and take in a film in Lincoln. The film was 'Dangerous Moonlight' and the music, the Warsaw Concerto, was on everybody's lips. The time was the end of March 1944. Moonlight for us was indeed dangerous, and was now a fighter's rather than a bomber's moon. News from the home front was better too. Uncle Billy was a prisoner of war and Uncle Frank had declared his pacifism obsolete and had joined the Pioneer Corps to help his Russian comrades.

The boss called me into his office. "Frying tonight George. Hope they've picked somewhere nice and easy." It had to be somewhere in Germany, we had had targets associated with aircraft production together with Stuttgart and Frankfurt for most of the month.

Berlin had been hit on the 24th of the month. Rumour had it that a large number of crews had got the chop. We had been stood down for almost a week, maybe March would go out like a lamb. That question would soon be answered, and the answer when it came would be horrendous.

Take-off tonight was to be a late one. The aircraft were already bombed up for last night's target, which was cancelled. It was to be a maximum effort wherever it was. Bomb loads were changed to a much lighter load and more fuel was pumped in. It was obviously a long trip, and, with a quarter moon, not good.

Leave for some of the older hands was cancelled and some of the newer crews were stood down. There was the usual wild speculation. Hot poop from Group flowed from a variety of sources. Berlin again was the odds on favourite. We had this straight from the horse's mouth, the Waaf who drove the petrol bowser. The crew heard nothing more from the boss, since he had told us earlier we were definitely on the battle order tonight, so we sat around the crew room playing cards. Time to write a quick letter home, looking forward to that holiday in Scotland around April.

A first glance at the route on the board in the briefing room brought forth a few "Jesus Christs." "Bloody 'ell, that's a long way, and all those bloody dog's legs," somebody whispered. There was one long straight leg over Deutschland. Those few ungallants who had quietly gone sick beforehand knew a thing or two.

"Right gentlemen, settle down," from the boss. The buzz was enormous. The Station Commander mounted the rostrum, the silence was immediate. He spoke briefly and to the point, "Gentlemen, your target for tonight is Nuremburg."

"Heil bloody Hitler," Bill Burley muttered.

Nuremburg was one of Adolph's favourite cities. It had been compared with Bristol. Laura and I had pleasant memories of Bristol, before Jerry had reduced parts of it to rubble. Laura had gone to Bristol for a special course at the beginning of the war to learn how to use a comptometer. The two of us had simple memories of eating Welsh rarebit in Carwardines coffee house amidst a backdrop of bombed out buildings. Like many other towns and cities, it would need re-building when this lot was over. History was being flattened throughout Europe again.

One of the reasons why this tour had dragged on was that flying with the squadron C.O., he was only required to fly at least once a month. The boss in the main quietly disregarded this, and always flew on raids which were considered difficult. Tonight would turn out to be one of the most difficult trips to date. Additionally, we had been saddled with an extra crew member. No, not the Station Commander, thank God, but a young pilot who would act as a second dickie. This particular new arrival had talked his way into coming with us. He could be useful, help Sambo to open the brown packages of window. Like Sambo, he was in for one hell of a christening. What was so special about Nuremburg? Reading about it, it was just a medieval city, associated with toy making and the Nazi party. Why were the planners considering it important enough for maximum effort? Obviously they knew a lot more than we did. Intelligence had intimated that the making of toys had quickly changed over to war production. Perhaps another Nazi party rally was on the cards. At briefing, everyone was convinced of its importance, both for industry and transportation, but that long leg as straight as a die into the target sent a chill down the spines of the older hands. The newer crews were thankful it wasn't Berlin. They would all age considerably before the end of March.

A number of spoofs and diversionary raids had been planned to make things easier for the main force. It was to be a big effort, something in excess of seven hundred aircraft would be out tonight, but, whatever was preached by the hierarchy, nothing could dispel the smell of real fear. Long, long straight legs meant only one thing for the poor sods flying them, maximum night fighter activity. The Krauts had also one or two very nasty weapons up their sleeves. The moon was on their side, no longer a bomber's moon. Luftwaffe night fighters had developed new weapons for shooting down bombers from below without being seen. We called them scarecrows. The fighters' radar equipment for homing on to targets had improved considerably.

It was a fine night for take off. As usual, there was more than the normal complement of the hardy band of spectators waving us off. My mind drifted back to the early days, when it was still a game, deadly sometimes, but nevertheless still a game. My thoughts flashed back to a pair of silk cami-knickers, long tattered and torn, courtesy of the pocket Venus. Where was she now, still making headlines at the Windmill? The jousting was much more serious now.

Aircraft from the Northern groups started the show off. They were well on the way by now, and we would join the stream over the North Sea. For a lot of the knights the formal salutes, waves and cheers from the sidelines would also be their last rites.

The route out crossed the Wash, over Suffolk to the concentration point off the coast of Belgium. We coasted in before Paddy picked up the town of Ghent to port on H2S with the next turning point due south approximately two hundred miles later. We were streamed from 16,000 to 20,000 feet, with a moon which was still high in the sky. That awesome long leg before the next turning point into the target was beginning. Chalky White noticed it first.

"Skipper, rear gunner."

"Go ahead."

"I can see dozens of four engined vapour trails all around, they stand out like dogs' balls."

"Thanks Chalky, I've noticed it too. Gunners keep an extra good look out, we are sitting targets tonight." Bill and Chalky both acknowledged.

Bloody hell, the jerries wouldn't need their radar to home onto us, we were all dead giveaways. That was the start of the death knell. It all began just south of Aachen. The night fighters were in amongst us like a pack of angry wolves, snapping at our heels, biting off our tails. Aircraft were being hacked out of the sky, going down like ninepins. The diversionary raids had failed, the Germans had got it right. One crew in a Halifax had even forgotten to switch off their Nav lights, a dead ringer for the chop if something wasn't done about it. I quickly plugged in the Aldis lamp and from the astrodome flashed them a series of quick T's, whilst the boss switched on and off our own navigation lights. It worked. Bill and Chalky reported on a number of vapour trails going in the opposite direction. These would be the early return merchants aborting for variety of reasons, some genuine, some trivial, some simply frightened fartless.

My intuition was working overtime. This was going to be one

hell of a night before it finished. The battle zone was over sixty miles long, and the Luftwaffe were holding all the aces. Their planners had not been deterred by spoof raids, but had found the main stream completely out on a limb. This night was theirs, this night for them would pay off enormous dividends.

"Christ there goes another one," the mid upper said. It was too easy. When will our turn come? At this rate of attrition, the odds were stacked against us. What would be going through the minds of my four colleagues who had all officially finished their tour? How was our extra man, a very young officer taking it? What was going through his mind tonight? Would he think this was the norm, with aircraft going in all around him? I hope not, he would need reassuring if we returned successfully, that the Battle of Nuremburg was something special, something horrendous.

"Skipper here, Eng give me climbing boost and power, sod this for a game of soldiers. I'm getting out of the stream."

"OK skipper."

We slowly climbed out of the box, up through twenty thousand feet to an altitude of twenty-three thousand. Christ it was cold, even with full heat on. Poor Chalky and Bill, they must have felt like they were sitting on top of Everest, cramped in their tiny perspex bubbles.

"Everybody getting oxygen OK?" asked the skipper. We all replied in the affirmative. We could see for bloody miles and miles sitting astride some vast colosseum in the sky watching a crude gladitorial battle below, whilst ahead, Nuremburg and its surrounding countryside was already beginning to burn.

The visibility was so good we could have turned on to target long before the prescribed turning point. The skipper's decision had been dead right, but we all knew he would have agonised about having to make it. However tonight was the survival of the slickest and that extra height could mean the difference between life and death.

We bombed slightly late, adding to the conflagration down below. The homeward leg was uneventful. Chalky and Bill were both beginning to look like Father Christmas, icicles hanging from their oxygen masks, feeling like blocks of ice themselves. Who would be Air Gunners on a night like this? At last that bloody moon dipped below the horizon wrapping around us a cloak of darkness.

The homeward leg further south kept us away from the night fighters. We had been rattled by flak and could count our blessings no one had been wounded. RAF Fiskerton, flat, wet and misty, had never looked so beautiful, as once more the boss greased the aircraft in, and when Nobby pulled the throttles back those four Merlins like the rest of us crackled with relief. Christ those eggs and bacon would taste like caviar. Frying tonight.

Interrogation was a gloomy affair. Bomber Command had obviously taken the biggest beating of all times and the tension all around was fairly obvious. The grapevine estimate of losses was in excess of ninety aircraft. Everybody prayed these rumours would be scotched. The following day the overall losses even by BBC standards were enormous, over ninety-six aircraft and crews had gone for a Burton. Nearly seven hundred gallant airmen either killed, missing or now in the bag. Was a medieval city in Germany worth the price? Our extra body didn't think so. He decided to report special sick and was never seen again. Survival was his name of the game, lack of morale fibre had struck again. Who could blame him?

The squadron lost three crews, one crew in sight of a well earned rest, the other two crews raw, inexperienced, cut down in the prime of life. The boss stayed around to see his remaining shattered warriors home and then opened up the Mess bar and got pissed out of his mind. Tomorrow the remorse would all come flooding back, he had a lot of letters of sympathy to write. I phoned my telephone call box the following day to rendezvous once again with Laura. I disguised my feelings, daunting though they were. No way did I want anyone else fretting over my innermost thoughts. I assured Laura that it wouldn't be long before we could all relax.

There was no euphoria amongst the crews after Nuremburg. After an operational egg, the majority of survivors quietly crawled away to their pits feeling they had been whipped. I looked down the length of the Nissan hut at those seven empty bed spaces down at the bottom of the room, four on one side, three opposite. Tonight they would be undisturbed, sad empty reminders of young men snuffed out. Tomorrow, two of the station service policemen, so impersonal, would gather up all the personal effects of the missing crew, catalogue them such as they were, and put them into store to be claimed by loved ones sometime later.

Tommy Lightfoot and his crew had occupied those bed spaces only hours before. In the hut next door, it would have been even worse. Half the hut wiped out, a large slice of the two other crews. The Barons would have their share of losses too. Tommy and his crew were on the home stretch before Nuremburg, all making plans. Before the war, Tommy was a professional rugby player, played for Castleford, and was as tough as nails. The Air Force wanted him to be a Physical Training Officer, a P.T.O., but Tommy had other views—Pilot or nothing else. He used to joke, "Once I couldn't spell pilot, now I are one." They were one of the happiest crews on the squadron, they shared everything; money when it was short, beer, fags and women. They were all NCO's. Tommy was keeping the Queen Bee happy. It was frowned upon, but satisfying the erotic appetites of the head Waaf had its spin off for the rest of Tommy's crew. None of them ever went short of those little pleasures in life.

Sgt. Tony Blackett was the Navigator. A Londoner, he could play any tune called for on the piano. As a crew, they were an entertainment in themselves. From now on, the Mess would be like a grave. It didn't take too long before the beds were occupied again, a change of sheets was all it needed.

What mahogany Bomber Pilot had made the decision that bomber crews would have to complete thirty operations before qualifying for a well earned rest? Lightfoot and his crew had survived the Battle of the Ruhr and the Battle of Berlin. Berlin saw eight nights on the trot inflicting fearsome slaughter on both sides, battles which saw too young Pilot Officers catapulted to the rank and responsibility of Squadron Leader and Flight Commander overnight. The Battle of Berlin was for the brave. It was too easy to lay down rules and regulations from the comfort of a desk.

Recognition at last for Bill, Paddy and Chalky. Bill was awarded the DFC and both Paddy and Chalky the DFM. The citations were short and to the point. Gallantry in the face of the enemy. Sambo was now the odd man out. We could count ourselves as a highly decorated
crew. The boss was highly delighted, but then he would be, his recommendations had been approved.

In celebration, we bombed the city of Lincoln for the next two consecutive nights. The stories, the line shoots from rival crews, were a tonic. After Nuremburg, we all needed a laugh. A lot of the usual faces were missing, but we drowned our sorrows to the full. Surely there couldn't be another Nuremburg. Losses of that sort of magnitude were simply not sustainable. The sugar on the pill from above was thin and slightly sweet. "Nuremburg was a turning point," the prophets said. Saturation bombing was beginning to bite. Did Butch Harris sleep well in his Bomber Command cell, or did he have nightmares like the rest of us? We were not privy to his thoughts.

Two more trips to go. We were all on a high to get them over and done with.

Higher echelons had other ideas. The boss was called away as were most other squadron and Station Commanders. Nuremburg had obviously hurt. The German High Command had never stopped crowing. We were stood down for almost a week, it was unreal. Only the hard-pressed ground crews did any cheering, they had time to service sick aircraft.

Not so the aircrews. Nuremburg fever was still paramount, and withdrawal symptoms could be devastating. The fever had to be maintained. The boss said very little about his visit to the holy of holies, but we gathered it had not all been sweetness and light, but discussions had at least cleared the air. There were obviously mixed reactions from top brass to the raid on Nuremburg. Many would not have mounted it against Adolph's favourite watering hole. But someone's shoulders had to be broad enough to carry either the can or the bouquets. The broad concensus of opinion, particularly from the ones at the sharp end, was that it had been one big ghastly mistake all round, with scattered bombs and scattered bombers. History would have to make the final decision.

Chapter 17

At least something good had come out of the visit to Headquarters, the skipper was being groomed for stardom. He had been told he was to be given an acting rank of Group Captain in order to take over as Station Commander within the Group. It could spell problems for me. How would this instant elevation affect us as a crew? Station Commanders were generally not encouraged to fly on operations, and the posting was imminent. The simple expedient would have been for Nobby, Bill and Chalky to call it a day, and for myself and Wham to go on the crew spares roster. Naturally the idea did not appeal to either of us, least of all me, so near to finishing my second tour and possibly yet so far away. But in my heart of hearts, I knew they would all have something up their sleeves.

A crew conference was called. The decision was once again unanimous, they would fly me out, two more to go. When they told me, a lump appeared in my throat. This was what esprit de corp was all about, please God keep us all safe and happy. Surely my prayer would be answered.

After Nuremburg, closer relationships had been cemented between the older ground NCOs and aircrew equivalent ranks. There was always a small divide between some groundcrew, old sweats, who looked with jaundiced eyes on bouncy and undisciplined young aircrew. The losses over Nuremburg changed all that. Aircrew lived from day to day, they all deserved the best, and they were accepted for their courage and their bravery.

One person who had lost a lot of his bounce was Sambo the Bomb Aimer. The last trip had knocked most of the get up and go out of him. You had to feel sorry for him, pretty soon he was going to be out on a limb, a floater. Not nice. It was hard to have to change crews, so Sambo would be hoping these last two ops would be stretched out. Maybe that was the reason he had gone into his shell. Nobby didn't make it any easier. He still niggled away, mostly in fun. But the engineer had a warped sense of humour, and at times some of his asides were full of barb. We all outranked Sambo as well, since Paddy, Nobby and Chalky had all been promoted to Flt. Sgt.

However, one thing Sambo was up to was disturbing. He was servicing the camp bicycle. A girl with an insidious reputation. She was also the number one chop girl. Sgt. Alison Payne was pretty, friendly, an excellent member of the Mess, but needed little or no encouragement to drop her blackouts. She had instant hot pants. She also unfortunately had the reputation of putting the fickle finger of fate on whoever was fixing her up, and Wham was at present satisfying her insatiable demands. Talking to him about it would make matters worse, so all of us simply had to let it ride. It was niggling nevertheless.

For the penultimate trip, we were back on the milk run, back to the Ruhr valley, and back to Essen. The boss had now taken his promotion. He looked resplendent at briefing with scrambled egg on the peak of his cap and the extra ring on his tunic. He was every inch a Groupie. Whoever was lucky enough to get him as a Station Commander could count themselves very fortunate indeed.

Due to a minor administrative hiccup, Nobby, Bill, Paddy and Chalky had all got their next postings. They were all delighted with their next jobs. Bill the Canadian mid upper was going to be an Operations Officer at the nearest Canadian squadron, just down the road. Nobby the engineer was to be an instructor at an engineering school in Lancashire; he would make an excellent instructor. Paddy the navigator would be leaving bombers for Coastal Command duties on Sunderland flying boats based in Northern Ireland. Paddy was over the moon. Chalky was not leaving his beloved Lincolnshire, and his job as an instructor would be on a Lancaster finishing school. It had all worked out. The hand of the boss was easily recognisable. He loved his crew. I wondered if the pen would be mightier than the sword, and split up the crew early. Maybe I was being too selfish hanging on to the finest crew in the world.

Where would I finish up? Would I go on to bigger things, pilot training, commissioning, or would I be lucky enough to secure a posting south somewhere closer to my beloved family? The end of the lottery was around the corner. Number twenty-nine of my second tour, number fifty-nine in all was a piece of duff. Dead easy. Even the weather was on our side, nice layers of cumulus which broke up to give us a good clear run into the target, with a good photo job to prove it. Bill and Chalky could have slept this one out. It was so damned quiet to be eerie. No fighters, even the flak was lighter, and we were not even bothered by too many searchlights. Sambo perked up no end. The ghost of Nuremburg had been spirited away, maybe the spectre would never be seen again.

Interrogation was quick and quiet. Nothing much to report. It was early to bed. Dawn was beautiful, a splendid sunrise lighting the tops of fluffy cumulus clouds. Today would be warm, probably much too hot for sleeping. On such a beautiful morning the idea of bed was irrelevant. After my operational egg and bacon, I would get out my trusty steed and cycle around the country lanes. The boss was being pressed to take over his next command, and the new Squadron Commander was also eager to get his feet under the table. I felt I was a bit of a bloody nuisance, holding up so many people.

There was a long letter from home, together with a cutting from the local newspaper, the Stroud Gazette. Our young son had won the county bonny baby contest; no doubt he would break a few hearts later on. Laura was looking forward to my next leave. This one was the important one, one to savour, one in which we could all relax and enjoy every moment of it.

I rode in through the guardroom just as the rest of the station was beginning to come to life. Fiskerton was a satellite station, and like most satellites, put together in a hurry, some would say thrown together. It was basic, mostly Nissan huts, all having an air of being run down, clapped out. When it rained, it was mud and leaks. The quarters were cold, bloody cold in winter and bloody baking in summer. As a Warrant Officer, I was entitled to my own single room at the end of the hut. It too was basic, not a place to stay in and feel comfortable; it was simply a bedspace, somewhere to rest your head. Compared with this the permanent pre-war stations were like palaces, built with a bit of luxury in mind. The satellites were just the opposite.

My two hour bike ride, taking in the fresh morning air, had been completely invigorating. I fell into bed, between clean damp sheets, and slept like a log until late afternoon. Chalky woke me up and told me to get ready for a thrash in Lincoln. As a crew we hadn't yet celebrated the skipper's promotion to Groupie, and he was pushing the boat out. So the game was on.

The boss was unaware we had had a whip round and had bought him a small token of our esteen. The decision was to buy him a good Parker pen and pencil set, and by popular demand I was to present it to him with a few words of gratis for being such a hot shot skipper. I said I hoped it would be one small token on his way to Air Staff duties, and that one thicker stripe later on.

Lincoln as usual was buzzing, and most pubs were generally packed to the gills. The breweries had delivered the goods. Beer was a commodity, short in supply, which didn't hang around. There were far too many thirsty customers, most of whom wore Air Force blue. The boss had pulled a flanker and booked a back room in his favourite hostelry, The Snakepit. Four rings had plenty of clout, there weren't too many around.

Would Lincoln ever go back to being a quiet East Anglian town when this lot was over? Would the locals ever return to normality? At the present time they were saturated with thousands of boisterous members of the biggest flying club in the world. Flyers from every commonwealth country. They were bombarded with noise twenty-four hours a day, seven days a week, ringed with airfields all housing sentinels of death. A murder of crows.

The party had all the right ingredients to be a corker, all the right mix. The out and out pissheads, the squadron characters, and a sprinkling of barons who were always game for anything. The management gently threw us out before we drank the well completely dry. The game was on. I made a quick phone call to the Chairman of the Sergeants' Mess Committee, requesting he keep the Mess bar open; no problem. All of us, by fair means or foul, were hot to trot back to the Mess, to make it a night to remember, and it was. We drank, we sang ourselves hoarse and indulged in all the Mess games. Number 49th light of foot had itself a ball, and most of us had bruises to show for it. The boss was finally laid to rest, strewn with flowers and horizontally strapped to a bomb trolley. This was one thrash which would go down in the history of Bomber Command, and 5 Group in particular.

I crashed out for hours and hours, half waking to the distant drone of the tannoy system; it seemed to be saying something like all crews will report to the briefing room as soon as possible. I must be dreaming, so I rolled over, to be awakened by a thumping on my bedroom door which brought me back to reality. "Wakey wakey sir, rise and shine. Get your arse over to briefing on the double. Your time is up." Little did my knocker-up know how prophetic his word would be.

With one exception, as a crew we were like zombies at briefing. The boss looked like he'd been a tee totaller all his life. I thought, I must remember to ask him what his cure for a hangover is.

"Right, settle down gentlemen. Can't hear myself think," this from Groupie De'ath. The target map was uncovered by the intelligence nark. It looked like a gift for my last one. Christ not even into Deutschland, just over the channel and into occupied France. Somebody was looking after my interest. I couldn't wait for the man to tell us where. Come on, come on, where is this piece of cake target? My last trip and they'd picked me a beaut.

"Quiet please. Gentlemen your target for tonight is the aircraft factory at Le Creusot in occupied France." We went through all the rigmarole. I was in a dream, half taking everything in. Most of this trip would be over friendly territory, I couldn't have asked for a better one as a finisher.

There had to be a sting in the tail, this was just too easy. We were to bomb at dusk, following on from a massive daylight raid by American Flying Fortresses. At least they would soak up the Luftwaffe fighters before we went in. Hopeful thinking.

A quick pre-flight meal, and down to the aircraft. We all took our last piss over the main wheels, some ritual, and climbed aboard. It was a glorious evening, a clear blue sky, warm and sultry, making us sweat with every small exertion. Bill and Chalky were the coolest, both cramped into their tiny bubbles of death.

Everything checked out fine. Paddy would have an easy navigation ride tonight, plenty of pinpoints provided by Sambo's map reading. The boss and Nobby were happy with the four Merlins and all the ancilliaries. We sat, awaiting the green Verey light from the aerodrome tower. The usual crowd of erks and Waafs had gathered to wave us off.

"Okay Nobby, brakes off, taxiing."

"OK skipper."

We gently rolled forward, the boss checked the brakes, and we moved forward again. We were number one. I looked back from the Astrodome at the squadron behind us. A long line of sleek black Lancasters nose to tail, spewing puffs of smoke and sparks from exhaust manifolds. A dozen aircraft, almost one hundred men riding out to war.

The duty pilot flashed us a green on his aldis lamp, saluted the boss, and we rolled gently away. Tonight we were carrying high explosive and lots of incendiaries. No streaming for this one, climb out over England to twenty thousand feet, before coasting out over Land's End. Bomb singly and then back home. Frying tonight, my last operational egg.

The boss had George in most of the way across England, and everyone had a long look at good old blighty below. The Cotswolds looked like one glorious patchwork quilt. I blew a kiss as we passed over the Stroud valley. Maybe I would be a gardener if I survived. I took a delight in seeing things grow, and here we were heading for another night of destruction.

"Coasting out in ten, skipper," from Paddy.

"OK crew, check in, starting with guns."

Everybody checked in and took up action stations. Bill and Chalky each fired a quick burst as soon as we crossed the coast. I gave my feathered friends a piece of chocolate each, and both clucked with delight. George, the auto pilot, was taken out, Sambo lay prone in his bombing position and Nobby did his last fuel check before target. Le Creusot here we come.

We crossed the enemy coast in daylight. Light tracer floated away to starboard. These guns were fortunately not radar controlled, and were out in both direction and height.

There was nothing on Fishpond, maybe the Yanks had exhausted the fighters. I prayed they would stay grounded. Group was coming through loud and clear on the radio, but we didn't need the computed winds for this one, it was pretty straightforward. The target was illuminated from a good ten miles away. USAF had done a great job and their fires were still burning. The factory itself was like a large block schematic, silhouetted against the dusk, covering quite a large area. I wondered about the labour force down below. Would they be slave workers, or conscripted Frenchmen overseered by their German masters? This was no maximum effort, but we were about to plaster it good and hard.

"Bomb doors open. Stay on this course for now. Lovely view from here," Sambo piped up. Markers went down and he could see the Mosquitos circling the target. The searchlights surrounding the factory were now on, silver lanes of light stabbing frantically across the sky, probing, probing, trying to brighten up any target.

"Give 'em a quick burst, gunners," the skipper said. Two of them were instantly blacked out. The pungent smell of cordite drifted forward, and lingered in the cockpit.

"Running in, skipper. Steady, steady, steady, bombs away, bombs gone." The aircraft lifted slowly away, still flying straight ahead, crossing over the target area. "Wizard prang, skipper," said the Bomb Aimer.

"Well done, crew. Home for an early breakfast. Turning sharp port now. Nav, give me a steer for home."

"OK skipper. Come round on to zero one five for the next ten minutes."

"Zero one five it is."

Chapter 18

Not one of us saw the sting in the tail. Whatever hit us was swift, sure and deadly. I looked around back down the fuselage and saw only thick acrid smoke. There was no response on the intercom from either Bill or Chalky, the wires were dead. "Chutes on crew, I have no control over the aircraft, the elevators must have been shot away." We were flying like a sickened porpoise, losing height, and then gaining some by Nobby using the throttles, but it couldn't last.

I volunteered to crawl back to the rear of the aircraft to see what had happened at the back end. With a chute on it was awkward. I didn't get far. It was hopeless, the heat and exploding ammunition made it an impossible task. Bill and Chalky must have taken the full impact of whatever had hit us. By the time I reached the spar on the way back to the front end, I was nearly exhausted from lack of oxygen and lungs full of dense black smoke. There was a savage electrical fire creeping and popping its way towards us, gobbling up the inside of the fuselage like a farmer burning stubble.

Sambo, Paddy and Nobby had all gone, blown away in the wind. The boss and myself were on our own. "Sorry skipper," I mouthed. "It's all my bloody fault."

"Can it George, we've just been bloody unlucky. Now let's get out before this bloody thing explodes. The best of British, see you back at base."

Leaving the kite from the front hatch, door already gone, I saw the aircraft disappear quickly overhead. It was cold, very cold. Oscillating like mad on the end of my shroud lines I was feeling very sick. It was me. I was the bloody Jonah. The last one syndrome had taken its toll. The reaper had played his ace.

Reaching up and pulling sharply down with both hands, the

violent oscillations started to slow down and I began to try and take stock of the ground below me. Guilty feelings again. Yes it was me. I had wrecked a crew. Poor Gunners Bill and Chalky. They could have both got out, but after seeing the awful mess at the back end of the aircraft, I knew instinctively they were both dead. Pray to God they knew little about it.

The front enders, the rest of us, stood more than a better chance of survival. At best we could successfully evade capture, at worst finish up in the bag. What about Wham, how would he get on? He would stand out like a sore thumb, but maybe with luck three of them would be together to bolster up each other's courage. The boss, like me, would be on his own. Not that I wanted at this time a bar to the membership of the Caterpillar Club, that was one momento I could have well done without.

Terra firma looked far from inviting, a blanket coverage of tall trees. I hit the canopy of the wood with a thump, and there I dangled. The sudden jerk knocked all the stuffing out of me. I was suspended trying to catch my breath, helpless swinging gently almost upside down. The crashing and snapping of twigs and branches was loud enough to awaken the dead. I couldn't stay too long swaying about like a drunken trapeze artist. Besides being bloody painful, I was a sitting duck. There was another problem, I was unable to judge how far it was down to mother earth. My right leg was painful. If it was broken, that was the end of any thoughts of evasion. Blood was pouring from cuts on my face. Make a move, make a move, the first rule of survival. The parachute harness was cutting into my groin and shoulders. Carefully I released the quick release box, sliding gently out of it, making sure I grabbed a stout branch with my left hand at the same time. So far so good. With care I disentangled the chute from the branches, slowly lowering it and myself to the ground.

I was in the middle of a wood, the ground cover large ferns and bracken. It was as silent as the grave. It was all so bloody morbid. Stripping off the top of my flying boots to make them look like an ordinary pair of boots, I removed my badges of rank and, together with my parachute, buried the lot under a large bush. I suddenly felt very, very tired, drained of all energy. But the temptation to go to sleep had to be resisted. Rule number one, rule number one, I repeated to myself, get away from the scene as quickly as possible. Put some distance between yourself and the crashed aircraft, was a prime rule for escape and evasion. Walking was painful, but I was too geed up to let it worry me.

There was still a lot of darkness on my side, hours of it. Had the Group ground wireless operator received my belated May-day call? There wasn't much time, just enough to give my callsign and baling out, before clamping down the morse key. With luck, somebody might have been in our corner, able to fix our position, and pass the information on. Somebody could have spotted our parachute canopies. I knew though it was pissing against the wind, yet hope springs eternal.

I must have walked for about two hours, staggered might have been a better description. This was some big wood, probably a forest, I had landed in. Try to remember more or less where we were when we were hit. Was I walking in the right direction? My immediate plan of action was to aim towards the coast and try to get across the channel. I kept telling myself how lucky I was to be in occupied France and not in Germany. My leg was very painful. Walking any further was impossible. I dozed off, and awoke with a start, shivering like mad, not with cold, but shaking with fear. It was all so bloody quiet, nothing seemed to be stirring at all. I thought I heard the distant sound of motor vehicles, but it was probably all in the mind.

The perfume of the pines was beautiful and strangely familiar. I was back in the Stroud valley, walking the hills. How would my darling wife react when that bloody awful telegram arrived? Air Ministry regret to announce etc. etc. etc. The second bloody time. The first time left nothing to the imagination, blunt, cruel officialese—Killed in action, and yet Laura refused to believe it. How could penguins make such awful mistakes. Why oh why did it have to happen to me? Why didn't I just give up on bloody number fifty-seven? I was perfectly within my rights to do so. No, not me, I had to tempt fate. Maybe I should have swallowed my pride, instead I put at risk six other brave comrades, all superb guys. A lot of aircrews were superstitious and most carried their lucky charms. Once more the reaper had reared his ugly head and some of my greatest friends could have bitten the dust.

As I lay huddled up, my earnest hope was that Bill and Chalky had made it. Stirred again, but I knew it was an impossibility. Neither of them would have had time to leave their gun turrets, strap on a parachute, and bale out. Bill, the mid upper, would have the hardest task, he would have had to jettison a door. I was pretty sure it was still intact. I consoled myself with the fact that at least five of us could be roaming the French countryside; where there's life, there's hope. Sambo would have his problems, but with luck they could be picked up by friends. My left leg had borne the brunt of my hitting the tree tops, the wounded left knee was still tender, especially under the knee cap, and after this spell of rough walking, was very badly swollen with fluid.

A rest up during the daylight hours was imperative. What walking had to be done, had to be done at night. Any thoughts of a brew up or hot soup from the survival pack was out of the question. A fire was out too, the bracken underfoot was tinder dry. A piece of chocolate would have to stave off my hunger. Water was my prime need, my mouth was so dry. So to slake my thirst, I pulled a button off my trousers and sucked it. It worked.

Escape and evasion exercises were enjoyable. Once I managed to return to camp without being captured, but this was for real and I was quite honestly shit scared. Nothing concentrates the mind more than real fear. I needed to think, needed a plan of some sort. Lying propped up against a tree, the sun streaming through the trees, warm to the back, and the taste of thick chocolate in my mouth, it was all like a dream. What was it the old gypsy fortune teller had told me one night in Blackpool? A few pints of beer too many and I was coaxed into parting with a quid to have my fortune told. She began by saying, "You will travel far." How right she was. "You will also be happily married and have six kids." Five more to go. I was certainly happily married. Finally she said. "And you will be very rich." How do you measure riches? A lot had happened to me during the last four years. Mine was meeting some of the finest young men England had to offer. Real friends, some had already made the ultimate sacrifice so that others would live. These were riches indeed.

We were given superficial briefings on the organisations inside Occupied Europe, established not only as sabotage and resistance fighters, but at the same time engaged in helping allied airmen to evade the Boche. I sat there under the tree piecing bits of it together, trying to remember important details of what had been said. How would I recognise members of the organisation, even if they ever turned up? Maybe it was pure wishful thinking on my part. It all seemed so simple back at base. In reality, here, tired, wounded and all alone it was all a different kettle of fish. Could I even recognise them? How to make an approach? What to say on meeting up, if I ever did? My decision was simply to say RAF aviator, parley vous Anglais. Nice and short. Later, I could produce my dog tags strung around my neck. On the other hand if the Germans picked me up, I would know exactly what to say, name rank and number, and nothing else.

I dozed off again, waking after about two hours. My left leg was throbbing away like mad, very painful. It needed bathing, a cold compress would ease the swelling, but there was no water.

It was going to be extremely difficult trying to make progress with a crook leg. One thing that would help would be a stout stick, and there were plenty of these lying around. It was amazing just what was packed into personal survival packs. The small compass and the silk map were important items. After studying the map, my decision was to walk on a compass bearing of North East in order to make towards the channel coast. Late evening, dame fortune was on my side and it rained, a short sharp shower. It slaked my thirst and give me my wet compress, easing the throbbing in my leg, but the bruising looked very nasty indeed.

I felt relatively safe and secure, still plenty of daylight left, so I dozed off again, there was nothing better to do. As I opened my eyes, intuition told me something was wrong. There were shapes, dark sinister shapes around me. Startled, I looked up into the barrel of a short sub machine gun, which prodded me sharply and painfully in the chest. The message on the other hand was easy to understand, get up, get up, and be quick about it. I didn't need a second prodding, rising quickly and painfully to my feet. Nothing was said, so I murmured weakly "RAF aviator." This was answered by another sharp prod in the back and a signal for me to move. I stumbled, crying out with pain, pointing at my left leg, but sympathy was not their strong suit. There appeared to be four people, four darkened shapes. None of them wore any kind of uniform, that was in my favour, except what looked like bandoliers of ammunition and hand grenades. My luck could be in, they could be members of the Maquis.

Have another try to establish contact I told myself. "Parley vous Anglais Monsieur? Je aviator Anglais." The response was still negative, only a quick grunt from one of the quartet. Conservation of energy was important so I shut up. Every ounce of it would be necessary. The going was going to be very hard. We must have been walking for about two hours before my leg finally gave way, and stumbling, I collapsed into a heap. One of the four took pity on me and examined briefly my leg. There followed a short discussion during which I discerned that the one who had done the examining was female.

She spoke softly to me, "Avez vous identification?"

"Oui Madam," I replied attempting to show her my dog tags dangling around my neck. She seemed assured. Thank God, a breakthrough at last, these were friends. I was safe for a while. Roughly one hour later we broke clear of the trees and made towards an isolated house on the skyline. She spoke again, this time in English, English with a delightful accent. "Sorry we were so rough with you, but we must be sure. The Boche are bastards." I told her how I came to be in that place, and, full of questions, asked for a news of my other crew members. Nothing had been heard, but she promised to make some enquiries.

After a meal of soup, farmhouse style, followed by a hunk of bread and cheese, I was taken to the attic and a bed of straw in a palliasse was provided. Tomorrow they promised me a visit would be made by a doctor, to look at my bruising. Sleep came easy, I sensed I was amongst friends, and was absolutely clapped out. True to the promise, the following day the doctor arrived. A quick diagnosis of my injuries, and he produced bandages and a dry powder to cover the worst of my bruises and torn flesh. The fluid on my knee was something else. It had to be drained off without using any sort of local anaesthetic. It was a very painful business.

During the day, there was much coming and going, with me the object of much curiosity. Most of the conversation was carried on by gestures, French was not my strong suit. I was glad to see Madame again. Her name was Helene and it was plain to see she was the controller of the group. There was no new information to add to my questions about the crew, except unofficially she had heard that at least three British aircrew had been captured by local German forces. One, probably the boss, was still on the run. If anybody could evade capture it was the skipper, he was a natural. I prayed he would have mother luck on his side.

What did excite Helene was the fact that I was a fully trained Wireless Operator. She told me they had recently lost their radio operator who had been picked up by the Germans and summarily executed. To them it was a major loss. It soon became apparent that once on my feet, she had designs for making use of my expertise. She intended I should earn my keep, that was the message coming through to me loud and clear.

Whatever was in the powder provided by the doctor was magical. The soreness died down and the bruising healed very quickly, and after two days I was able to walk quite well. From the different visitors to the farmhouse I estimated the group was about ten strong. They all looked like peas in a pod, with the exception of Helene, of course. She was small, dark, olive skinned with twinkling green eyes, and energy to match. She was never still, always giving orders, which her male companions never questioned. I was beginning to feel curious about the plans she had for me. How soon would I be moved on? I now felt fit enough to travel. After all, for me, I wanted to be filtered down the line as an evader. Whatever the Group's activities were, it was obvious they were a professional team, they oozed it. The men all looked like desperate desperados, each one capable of cutting your throat without batting an eye.

Later on when Helene addressed me as George, I knew that something nasty was around the corner, informality was not her normal method of approach. She was blunt and straight to the point, "We need your expertise tonight, George."

"How? Why?" I asked.

"Tonight you will send a message by morse code to London—and you will also receive the reply. It is very important." Helene continued, "At the same time you will sign off with a term of endearment known only to you and your wife. There are two reasons for this, one, we want a further check on you, and secondly, if you're right, it will let your wife know you are alive and for the present safe." I didn't like the sound of that.

My uniform was taken away to be burnt, replacing it with mufti. When fully dressed, I was reminded of an onion seller, especially when later I was given a sit up and beg bicycle. At least I was at home on this. Helene and I started our journey at dusk. Once we hit the road, we cycled on for about forty minutes before pulling onto a large building. The smell told me that it was a brewery. Once inside, we quickly made our way to the top floor and out onto a flat roof. The wireless gear was all set up, guarded by two members of the group. No time was wasted, we had a schedule to keep. Helene gave me two callsigns, mine and the contact station, together with a long message in code groups of five letters. There was no answer to my initial call, which I repeated. The reply the second time was simply the letter R in morse followed by the station's identity and then the letter 'K', meaning carry on. I started to send the text of the message at about 18 wmp, when interrupted by a series of dots. The interruption was followed by a Z code signal meaning send a little slower. I knew than I was connected into a military network. The full message was transmitted without any further interruption at about 12 wpm and I signed off with the signature 'skins'. It seemed like hours before the reply came back. This time there was a different hand on the key at the other end. It rattled through at a much faster speed, the text all in French, ending with a signature Alias.

The significance of that signature did not dawn on me immediately, Alias was my wife's nickname from her father. Contact had been established between my darling wife and myself, even though we were hundreds of miles of hostile territory apart. Laura would know I was alive and not in enemy hands. Helene was bubbling with joy, and so was I.

Chapter 19

Helene's joy didn't exactly make me jump. "You are to work with us George," she said, "as our Wireless Operator," when we had returned to our safe house.

"Who said so?" I asked.

"London," was her reply. "It was in the message n'est pas?"

"For how long?"

She shrugged her tiny shoulders. "C'est la guerre," was all she would say.

Time softens the blow, the blow that I was not as yet to join a line to take me home. The rest of the month of May went by like a dose of salts. We were busy as a group, mainly minor acts of sabotage, arson and harassing the enemy. Each job was different, a new place each time to hole up in whilst transmitting information. We lived dangerously and I was beginning to enjoy it. The only time my stomach turned over was the time we were down one of the local sewers after blowing up and de-railing an ammunition train. The smell was nauseating, although Helene had provided small masks of gauze material soaked in cheap perfume to minimise the stench. I hadn't seen huge rats at such close quarters since my schooldays. I used to throw stones at them as they left the old grain mill to take a nightly swim. The mill was on the bank of the local canal, and as boys we swam in it as well. Greenwoods Flour Mill was a safe refuge for large black water rats. It was good sport trying to kill them.

One of the group who worked as a sewerage man pointed to the largest of the pack and said to me, "Mange très bon, oui?" God forbid it would ever come to that.

The hardest pill for me to swallow came at the end of the month. Helene briefed me we were to rendezvous in the early hours of Sunday morning with a visitor. A visitor from home, from

England, who would be arriving by air. The landing strip some ten miles away was an old disused racecourse. The aircraft was scheduled to land at approximately 0200 hours. We gave ourselves plenty of time to set everything up and await his safe arrival.

Four makeshift goosenecks were positioned, two at the beginning of the landing run, twenty-five feet apart, and the other two some hundred yards away to mark the centre of the makeshift grass landing strip. It would be essential for the aircraft to have a strong undercarriage as the ground was undulating in parts. With time to kill, the wireless was set up, slinging the aerial between two trees, so that everything would be good and ready. Identification was simple enough, I would transmit the letter T in morse on my torch, and the aircraft would reply with the letter R on his downward identity light. Challenge and reply. We were also provided with a special frequency for contact with London. The throaty sound of a low flying aircraft could be heard almost two minutes before estimated time of arrival. Helene signalled the ground party to light the flares, just before the aircraft joined the circuit, and after exchanging signals, it quickly landed. One figure quickly dismounted from the rear cockpit. The aircraft, a single engine Lysander, turned through 180 degrees, opened up the taps and roared away. It was all over in just five minutes. In less than two hours, the pilot and his craft would be home, the pilot enjoying a hearty English breakfast no doubt. I felt sick, and questioned Helene on our return why I couldn't have occupied the rear cockpit and returned home to blighty.

She kissed me gently on the cheek, "Don't worry cheri, your turn will come, but not yet, have patience," she whispered. I couldn't argue, at least I stood a chance of getting home, not like the rest of the crew, if they were all in the bag.

"What about the visitor?" I enquired.

"You do not need to know, so put it out of your mind—she has gone."

I remembered the addition to the signature of the message in answer to mine, it was Luv. My friendly operator in London was also female and she was good at her job too.

At the beginning of June, the weather was hot and sultry, clear skies with morning mists. There was a buzz in the air too, Helene and members of the group seemed a little more tensed up than normal. The local Wehrmacht it seemed were preparing either for a large exercise in the area, or possibly moving off. Information was filtering back from a number of sources. The radio nets we listened to were full of messages, most of which meant nothing to me, but as a trained operator, a large increase in radio traffic was significant. Something big was brewing. During the first week of the month, we pulled off our most daring coup so far by attacking a moving column of trucks and men. The road had been mined beforehand and the task of detonating them was mine. It was exciting and very productive. The ambush was well executed, beautifully carried out, and inflicted major destruction on the enemy. Afterwards, we laid low for forty-eight hours in the local caves. Unfortunately, the reprisals by the Boche were savage. They took revenge on innocent civilians, and a number of women and children paid the price. This was the bitter pill the Resistance forces had to swallow.

Fresh supplies of ammunition were needed quickly by the group, and so a message was coded up requesting an air drop. The reply was in the affirmative, together with the phrase 'Lorraine has been struck'. The phrase meant nothing to me, Helene however immediately threw her arms around me and there were tears running down her cheeks. She shouted aloud, again and again, "The Allies have landed, the Allies have landed." Her tears were tears of joy. The date was the sixth of June, the year 1944. The invasion had begun. It was also true that the Wehrmacht in the local area were on the move. Helene briefed us that there was one excellent way of putting a spoke in their wheel. An army needed fuel, and a sabotage action by the group could deny it to them. The fuel dump close to the main camp was always heavily guarded, patrolled by guards with dogs. This operation would be our biggest one to date, but if we pulled it off successfully, the most important. My suggestion to call in an air strike was ignored because it was simply not logical. Speed of execution was paramount, and no doubt with a second front now established, every single aircraft would be needed in support of it.

The enemy camp itself was in a valley surrounded by low hills on all sides. The answer to the problem of how best to attack it was in the geography of the area. We would mortar it from four different positions, a cross fire. The time when the Boche troops were most vulnerable was when most of them would be fast asleep. A quick reconnaissance during the day gave us the appropriate firing ranges and the best manning positions. Eight men would form the weapons team, one to load, and the other to fire. Myself and Helene would act as look-outs. She prayed the mortars would work as this was the first time they had been used. Each mortar shell was decorated with the Cross of Lorraine in white chalk, as a symbolic gesture. The message 'Lorraine has struck' now made sense, it was the symbol of the Free French forces.

Blackened up, and a night also thankfully as black as ink, we silently crept away. Just over an hour later everyone was in position. The camp was still well lit, and we could hear music and singing. This was contrary to our hopes, but I whispered to Helene, "The bastards are obviously having a farewell party, let's make it one to remember." It had been arranged that the mortar teams would fire the first shells at 0100 hours, each team carrying two shells each. There would be no room for mistakes, every round would have to be on target. One shell in the right place, could, with luck, ignite the whole of the petrol dump.

Helene squeezed my hand. She was warm and inviting lying so close together. "Now," she hissed softly. The four mortars could have been electronically synchronised, each one smashing into the centre of the dump, separated by a whoosh and a bang. We didn't need a second dose, but the Boche got it. Nevertheless, it was a lovely sight, flames and explosions, followed by more bigger and better bangs. Figures silhouetted against the flames were all caught up in a ring of fire. "Let's go," Helene whispered, slinking away and going our separate ways. Helene was to go back to the house before searches were made, and I was to join the group in another section of the caves. It was a night to remember.

Retribution by the Boche the following day was again swift and brutal. Thirty people were taken out and shot, presumably one for each dead German. The fuel dump was completely destroyed. Its destruction in the end would probably save lives. Two days later I crept back into the farmhouse. It had been visited, but Helene had convinced the enemy she had nothing to hide. More news of the invasion was beginning to trickle down. It was good. Beach heads had been secured, the Germans being completely taken by surprise at where the invasion forces had landed.

Rumour had it that the town of Caen had been captured by the British. Maybe it would be all over by Christmas. People were saying the same thing years ago, and here I was almost five years later, learning French the hard way.

Lying here on my bed of straw, staring into the rafters, listening to the bird song outside, the war could have been a hundred light years away. The warm smell of freshly baked bread filtered upwards, bringing back again vivid memories of my childhood. I was in my grandmother's cottage. In front of a lovely blazing fire sat a huge brown and cream earthenware bowl of rising dough, covered by a clean white crisp tea towel. Soon loaves would be baking in the oven, from dough lovingly patted into small open tins. The smell of freshly baking bread was all around. The flames warm and comforting from the fire were casting flickering shadows across a semi-darkened room. The creaking of a huge wooden rocking chair in which grandma sat, completed the picture. Before I left for home, she would give me a thick jam butty, a door stop of freshly baked bread, warm, with the butter running down my fingers.

Mam's questioning on reaching home was always the same. "Why are you so late? Been to see your Gran?"

"Yes."

"Suppose you're now full up with bread and jam?"

Sadder memories flooded in. The day I called when the rocking chair was still, only to find Grandma sitting in it dead, suddenly and swiftly from a massive heart attack. I can still see her face, serene and peaceful, no pain, with a little river of saliva bubbling from the side of her mouth. It was a long time before I went near that cottage again. Not long after that Granda died as well, his heart plainly broken.

I had a visitor that night to share my bed of straw. It was Helene. She came to me not out of love, not out of sorrow, or pity, but, although she never mentioned it, to ease my physical well being. She was my biological necessity, my surrogate wife. Maybe it was the warm balmy night, or the freshly baked bread, washed down with rough red wine. Whatever it was she satisfied my needs. As I spilled my pent up feelings into her warm slender body, I found out what I had long suspected, Helene was a virgin. She left as quickly as she had come, no words of endearment, pure entente cordiale. It was never mentioned again.

Her folks, both good peasant stock, were like chalk and cheese. Poppa, as she lovingly called him, was Gallic all over. Small and hard, he rarely smiled, you couldn't blame him. His deep set almost black eyes never really looked at me with any kind of rapport. He never wasted words on me. I was an intruder, an added danger to his family life, bad news too for his daughter who he adored. Only once did he speak to me at length. The gist of his conversation was that La Belle France was just a carcass to be ravaged and raped by friend and foe alike. Helene and her mother were both annoyed with him, reminding him that we were also making sacrifices once again to liberate France. He never spoke to me again.

Mother was large, plump and rosy. Mama, like daughter, was perpetual motion, always on the go, lovingly caring for her assortment of animals and pets. Besides Helene, her only child, her children were flocks of hens, ducks and geese. In our terms, the farm was a smallholding, half a dozen cows, but mostly poultry. Mama even sold fresh eggs to the Boche, which must have hurt. On the other hand, it stopped them probing too deeply.

The Germans eventually left, leaving a vacuum behind. There was no enemy within the local area that we could continue to harass and attack. To coincide with the departure of the Wehrmacht, London gave us our biggest airdrop, no less than a full Dakota load, and all for us. The drop was enormous, guns, ammunition, food which included coffee, and someone important we were to meet later.

The important human cargo was an agent, code name Orange, another woman. When we met and were introduced, she told us her remit was to co-ordinate the activities of all the small groups operating independently like ours into one large organised body. I was astonished to learn that as many as 7000 resistance workers could be brought closer together to give the Germans a much bigger headache. It was important that the Wehrmacht were kept on their toes, attempting to counteract the sabotage, killing and fire raising that the resistance movement was inflicting upon them. It was now also doubly important to the Allies that thousands of the enemy were kept away from the battle areas, tied down looking after us. The slackened pressure on the group and for me in particular was encouraging. Prior to this, days had been long and boring, restricted to the inside of the house. Even though I had excellent forged papers, it was not considered safe to step outside during daylight hours. These restrictions could now be lifted. My little bit of extra freedom allowed me access to the nearest village, always accompanied, and I began to get my bearings.

Chapter 20

The little farmhouse was about ten miles south of the small town of Le Blanc in the district of Touraine. Helene told me it was approximately 100 miles south of Paris, and Poitiers to the west was the nearest town of any size. She also confided in me that the Maquis had set up an escape route for aircrew from Brussels in Belgium, down through Paris, Tours, Limoges and towards Biarritz, before crossing the Pyrenees into Spain. That was the kind of news I wanted to hear. It was a bloody long walk, but the sooner it was started, the better. Of course it was always possible that the combined forces of the Allies might just liberate us before the long march became necessary.

The deserted enemy camp was not left empty for too long, it was much too strategically placed for the Hun not to make further use of it. The occupying troops appeared to be even younger, young boys working up to be cannonfodder. They didn't really stand too much of a chance against seasoned resistance fighters and our hit and run tactics melting away into the night meant they were totally confined to camp, prisoners of their own making. News from home was improving all the time, the Krauts were being pushed back in all directions.

The summer was moving on too. I had now been part of the resistance for almost three whole months. It was time to pester Helene again to allow me to become a real evader before I began feeling very sorry for myself.

The celebration of Bastille Day was not to be allowed to pass unheeded. Orange had planned one of the biggest concerted efforts, hitting enemy formations stretching from the Massif almost to the town of Nantes. The Luftwaffe had a small airfield on the outskirts of Chinon. That was to be our target. The group planned to use the river Creuse nearby and sail most of the way under cover of darkness, rather than the ten of us striking across country. The plan was to leave the river about five miles from the perimeter of the airfield and to set up our final positions in undergrowth roughly two hundred yards outside the airfield fence. Night flying was still in progress when the first of our mortar shells went down. Direct hits were scored on the intersection of both runways. One aircraft was definitely destroyed, others could have been damaged. I felt sorry for the aircrew who must have been killed, wiped out without firing a shot in anger. Return to base was just as easy, the Germans had no stomach for pursuing us. Helene never came to my bed again in way of celebration. She confessed she enjoyed losing her virginity, but she could not allow herself to commit any more mortal sins of the flesh. My guilty conscience remained brand new.

Tremendous news, good and not so good, coming down the pipeline. The Boche had been completely smashed in Normandy. Caen had unfortunately been reduced to rubble by Allied bombers inflicting heavy casualties on Canadian troops as well as the enemy. The Germans were being pushed back across the river Seine and unofficially Paris had been liberated. If that was so, the heart of France was pulsing again.

For our part, we continued to develop hit and run tactics on the marching columns of enemy troops being drawn into defence of the homeland.

News also that French troops, Free French forces, had landed in the south to take on the Germans and their stronger divisions around Marseilles.

At the end of July, for me the news was even better. News I had been hoping to receive. I was to be put into the escape line and make my way south to Spain and home. Helene was both happy and sad when she broke the news to me, maybe I was their good luck talisman. "Orange has decided now is the time for you to begin your journey back, before the weather breaks across the mountains," she told me. Home for Christmas, I must keep my fingers crossed. Farewells were short, promises, promises to meet again when the war was over if we survived. Tears all round, even

Helene's father had to brush away a small one at my departure.

My first contact with the Comete escape line was to be made at Orleans. There I was to join a party of two other evaders, both airmen, one American and one English. Both of them had already walked from Brussels. The American Air Gunner had been shot down over Northern France. He had been badly burned before baling out, but the French doctors had done a remarkable job of patching him up. Like most Americans, he had an infectious sense of humour and an unpronounceable surname, Eskalwolski, so I left it at Joe. I sincerely hoped he would never have to be drawn into conversation with any dubious characters en route, for his few words of French had a distinct Brooklyn accent.

The third member of the party like me, was RAF, an Air Gunner from a light bomber squadron supporting the invasion forces. The Boston aircraft he was flying in had been hit and crashed behind the enemy lines. He was the sole survivor of the crash, his remaining two crew members had both been fatally wounded. He left the aircraft with nothing more than a few minor bruises and cuts, and an aching back. Before the long march had finished, he was to become a pain in the arse. Sgt. Laurence Valentine was small, Jewish, and born well within the sound of Bow bells. He reminded me of a spiv, the connotation given to wide boys, generally from the east end of London, and Valentine was its personification.

Physically, he reminded me in many ways of Taffy, my second Air Gunner, dear old Taffy. Both of them were chain smokers. Valentine would have sold his mother for a cigarette. That was one thing in his favour, his ability to scrounge almost anything, mostly for purely personal reasons. We were five in the party, the two French guides later changing at regular intervals. It reminded me of the classic western Wells Fargo. The guides, Gaston and Henri, were peas out of the same pod, medium build, swarthy, but both immensely strong. Neither of them said too much. We had the feeling they were doing us a great favour, either of them would have been happier killing Germans. I gathered from Gaston that we were now at the most dangerous stage of evasion. The terrain ahead was too open and travelling would be dicey. I kissed my little piece of black basalt, my St. Christopher, for luck. We were all probably going to need it over the next 500 kilometres. It sounded so easy, said quickly, like one of those useless pearls of knowledge learned at school; the distance from John O'Groats to Land's End; some people actually enjoyed walking it.

We travelled light, a small rucksack each containing the basic essentials, dried food and water, a change of socks, toothbrush and a piece of soap, plus a small hand towel. With luck on our side, we could live off the land. We were among friends, that was important. Both the guides had weapons. Gaston would go well ahead spying out the land, and Henri would cover the rear, the three of us walking together Indian file. Laurie said we usually covered about twenty miles a day, mostly during the hours of darkness. It seemed a long way. If all went to plan, we could be at the base of the Pyrenees in about three weeks. There was a distinct possibility we could be home for Christmas.

"*Georges, allez vite.*" We were on our way. Joe, Laurie and myself looked like the poor relations from a second rate circus. We had used mother earth, mixed with spit, to blacken or rather brown our unshaven faces. After a while, it would tighten and itch like mad, a practice soon to be ignored. We passed silently through a number of villages, Henri at times issuing curt directions. Occasionally my mind wandered away to greener pastures. What wouldn't I give for a long cool mug of local Gloucester cider? I passed away the miles mentally doodling with each village we skirted, recalling one at home. A simple exercise, but it took away some of the pain of aching muscles.

The measured distance the guides had set us was about 20 kilometres, and we covered it with time to spare before it became too light. The three of us collapsed in a heap, too tired to think about anything but sleep. Valentine had by fair means or foul purloined half a dozen eggs along the way. Henri left an IOU, maybe one day he would redeem it. I ate my egg raw, like a bombay oyster minus the Worcester sauce. We had pitched up in a barn and it was warm and dry. Off the ground covered in dry straw, the three of us slept soundly. Henri kept guard below whilst Gaston went into the local village for food and information. He relieved Henri some hours later. The local contact at Beaugency had passed on the positions and approximate numbers of enemy troops to be avoided on the next leg of the journey. They were confined to small pockets, since it had appeared the major Wehrmacht forces had moved either north or south to strengthen the campaign against invading troops.

Everyone was wide awake, preparing to move on, when the huge barn door creaked, opening slightly ajar. Gaston moved in silently, his forefinger vertically across his closed lips. His half closed eyes said the rest—quiet, danger. None of us moved except Gaston who crouched ready in a corner, pistol in hand, cocked for action. The German shepherd dog followed him in almost immediately, head down, moving from side to side sniffing the floor as he padded towards us. Head suddenly cocked upwards, the dog saw Gaston. The sniff turned to a savage growl, foaming lips showing bared white fangs. Head up, the dog ran, his face crinkled with fury, teeth exposed by a curled top lip. Gaston stood his ground as the dog leapt. Taking the animal's front legs, one in each hand, he moved them outwards and upwards with the speed of light. There was a short painful whine as the carcass hit the floor, its heart and lungs punctured. Gaston dragged the body still twitching across the floor, covering it quickly with a block of straw. He spoke then for the first time, only one word "Boche," but the message was clear enough, we must be on our way immediately.

Henri went first. The three of us watched him through a crack in the door, weaving his way across open ground, killing ground, towards a small copse on the horizon. Gaston meanwhile guarded the rear of the barn. I followed next, heart in mouth, keeping a low profile, heading towards the same patch of trees, and reaching them without trouble. Laurie and Joe followed suit, and the four of us lay low to await the arrival of Gaston. We heard the German soldier calling and whistling for his dog, "Herman, Herman." How long would it take him to find its dead ruptured body? Not too long after visiting the barn, the signs of the struggle were too plain to see. Come on Gaston, we must be on our way, getting well clear of the area was paramount.

There was no sign of our brave guide, and Henri was plainly worried. He intimated we would give him another five minutes and then we must start walking. If there were troops and dogs in the area around us, hanging around was dangerous, and it was still daylight. The plan was to walk along the river bank, the river Loire which flowed south towards Tours. Hopefully, Gaston would eventually rendezvous with us. He would not think twice about killing the dog handler as well. That would certainly put all the enemy units in our vicinity on full alert.

Suddenly and without any warning, everyone stiffened. Someone was approaching from the opposite direction. Henri slipped the safety catch off his pistol. My heart was pounding away, we were scared stiff. Laurie was sure we were about to be captured, complete fear showed in his eyes. No one moved as the sound came nearer, nearer. The boxwood around us crackled and broke. There was utter relief when Gaston came into view. Sizing up the situation, he had left the barn by the back and by a detour, had come around the other way, behind us.

The adrenalin stopped pumping and we moved rapidly off in single file, stopping again outside a small town called Blois. There in a wooded area we had a brew up before tackling the next leg taking us south west towards Tours. Gaston and Henri told us they would be leaving us at Tours, having first of all settled us in a safe house. The safe house turned out to be a large chateau on the outskirts of the town, where the three of us kipped down in what had been the stables. There we stayed for the next three days, almost under the noses of visiting German officers. We had time to chat, time to find out something about each other. Joe the yank told us he had only been in England six months, based at Watton in Norfolk. He reminisced mostly about how he loved the city of Norwich, and how he spent his off-duty hours, mostly doing the rounds of the local pubs, something completely new and exciting to a Brooklyner from New York. The only thing I knew about Norwich was the local football team, nicknamed the Canaries, because they played in yellow shirts. Joe knew something about canaries too, especially the two legged songsters. He confided in me he had wasted no time in laying one of the Norfolk dumplings, and shortly before his last flight, she had told him she believed she was pregnant. Joe would make an excellent father.

It had taken us almost a week to cover roughly sixty miles, and the weather was becoming colder. The thoughts of having to cross the mountains during winter, even with expert guides, was a daunting prospect. The highest hill I had ever climbed was Pendle in the Pennines. The only reason most people climbed that was to visit the pub on the top of it.

The lady of the house introduced herself as Monique. There was a wonderful charisma about her. She oozed top drawer, and seemed little concerned about the enormous risks she was taking, sheltering Allied airmen on the run. We learned not from her, but from one of her servants, that her husband was the C.O. of a Free French squadron flying Spitfires, operating from England, and that her son was flying Typhoons. Monique was also a titled lady, the wife of a Baron. The Baroness survived by playing a double game. Her locally produced fruit and vegetables were sold to the German garrison at Poiters, the monies helped to sustain not only the household and herself, but her section of the Comete line. Like many a French patriot who had dealings with the Boche, fragments of information that she collected helped to fill in the bigger picture. The Baroness paid us a visit during the evening of the second day. She was plainly very agitated. We feared the worst. Valentine almost collapsing. It appeared that four members of an American crew sheltering in a neighbour's farmhouse had been betrayed. Not by the farmer or any of his family but by one of his associates whom he had trusted implicitly.

We gathered that this traitor had wormed his way into the escapers' confidence by assuring them that if they wrote short letters home, he would see that they would reach their loved ones. The Germans were still offering large rewards to anyone providing information on evading aircrews. "This Judas has taken their money," snarled Monique. And the four Americans had been captured. The poor farmer, one of her tenants, had been shipped off to Germany, where it was assumed he would be shot.

Joe asked her if sheltering us was worth the risk? There was no doubt or hesitation in her reply. "You are helping to liberate us, the least we can do is to help to liberate you," she replied. She warned us. "You must not leave the stables. Stay inside until we are ready to leave. But I can assure you that our traitor will be punished," she said. Before we left we were told that Monique's son had been declared missing on a train busting operation on the German border. That was one brave family.

For the four of us, Shank's pony was to be rested. We were to ride into Poiters, tucked in the back of one of our hostess' trucks. Monique drove it herself, making it absolutely certain we would be undetected, or even stopped and questioned on the way. About halfway between a place called Chatellerault and Poiters, we disembarked from the truck and were met by our next guide. His name was Jacques. We rested up until it became dark in a vault of a graveyard in the village cemetery.

Before we began the next section of the journey, the weather broke. For the next 35 kilometres it rained and it poured, and we squelched our way onwards, a sodden quartet. We were surrounded by thunderstorms, heavy rain, and shafts of lightning, purple brightness which lit up the countryside around us. It was hard going, carrying all the extra weight of sodden clothing. Valentine grumbled for most of the way, until Joe finally told him to belt up in no uncertain manner. If it was tough on us, it must have been murder for Joe, his burns were sore and weeping.

Eventually Jaques signalled we would rest up. We were in the middle of a wood. At least no one else would be out on a night like this. We were four lifeless shadows, cold, hungry and drenched through to our bones. The rain was incessant, beating down through the canopy of leaves, Drip, drip, it never stopped. I suppose we could be thankful the rain was warmish, not like the cold biting stuff that swept across the Pennines. Memories again. My grandmother chiding, "ee lad, come in an warm theesen by the fire, you'll catch thee death o' cowd. You're sopping wet through." I looked across at the guide, suddenly thinking of the tune we learned at school, *Frère Jacque, Frère Jacque*. It was true, he was a real brother in arms. In reality, Jacques was old enough to be my father. What was going through his mind?

Joe and Laurie were both slumped against a tree, eyes closed and faces drawn with exhaustion. The pair of them had by now been walking for a hell of a long way, living rough for most of the time, with pent up feelings, wondering what awaited them around the next corner, and it was beginning to show. The Yank had guts, his burns had started to give him problems, and his face and hands looked raw angry and bleeding. The burns on the covered part of his body were continually chaffed and had begun to ulcerate. It must have been sheer agony, though he rarely complained. Joe was a fighter. If he made it back to Norfolk, how would his dumpling react? Valentine, on the other had, was a born whinger. He exercised the right to moan for most of the time, an Englishman's right to moan he would say. Fortunately, Jaques understood very little English, otherwise he might have come to the conclusion he was wasting his valuable time.

I'd been surmising about what Valentine did for a living before the war. I guessed he probably was mixed up in something possibly shady, extracting money from people in some way or another. I was right too. He was the son of a pawnbroker, with shops in the East End of London. He fitted the bill exactly. Valentine was learning the business before volunteering for aircrew. I only knew of one other Jew, in Bomber Command, a Pilot, who had won the VC. Lying against that tree like a drowned rat, Valentine certainly hadn't got golden balls. Aircrew applied that term to someone who was lucky, someone who led a charmed life. For the life of me I could never understand how it equated with a pawnbroker's sign. It was said that your life flashed before you before you passed off this mortal coil. I hoped it wasn't true, I was beginning to wander down memory lane again as we had time on our hands.

Chapter 21

Blackburn like most other towns, had more than its fair share of pawnshops. There seemed to be one on every street corner. The popshops formed an important slice of a survival kit for working class families. Looking down at the pair of trousers given to me be Monique, they reminded me of my first new suit. It cost thirty shillings from Burtons—the thirty shilling tailors. That suit spent more time in the popshop than on my back. It went in on Mondays and mostly came out on Fridays.

The nearest pawnshop was at the bottom of Mary Ann Street. For the majority of people the popshop was the last resort. For the neighbourhood we lived in, it was for almost everybody the first resort. Popshops flourished, they were the people's banks. They provided the lifeline with the necessities of life Monday through Saturday. Food for empty bellies, coal for warmth, money for the gas. Light and cooking. Pledges were usually redeemed on Friday nights, pay nights. There were times though when my best suit stayed in over the weekend. Money was short, tempers at the time were long. But it was soon forgotten, and Mam was forgiven. But it meant staying in for the weekend since I didn't have anything else to wear other than my post office messenger uniform, which was the job I was doing at that time. It seemed such a long long time ago.

Mary Ann and Mary Ellen streets ran in parallel to where we lived in Devonport Road. The street names themselves conjured up some of the worst housing conditions anywhere in town. Cramped dark back-to-back houses, no bathrooms, except portable tin ones hung on a nail in the scullery. Outside lavatories and inside smells. Most of the houses were infested with bugs, fleas and large ugly cockroaches. It was a lost cause trying to rid them. They had taken over. Although it wasn't for the want of trying.

The long dark winter nights, when the gas mantles were first lit, were the worst time and I always hated it. A black legion of cockroaches would scuttle across the brown lino floors to disappear through chinks in the skirting boards. To catch some of them traps would be laid, saucers of beer. The following morning they would be full with pink corregated bloated bodies full of mild ale and floating upside down. A sight which always turned my stomach over. Cockroach disposal, was, like washing pots, a daily breakfast chore.

Most of my relatives lived like matchstick families in either Mary Ann or Mary Ellen Street. There were lots of Walkers, they were prolific in adding to the human race. Half way down Mary Ann Street was McCluskeys, the grocers. Paddy McCluskey's shop was like one huge jigsaw puzzle, assorted packages of food all mixed in with hardware, dried goods and bundles of pungent firewood. Firewood at a penny a bundle was one of the best sellers, until even that was too expensive, and rolled up pieces of newspaper were used instead. Even before I was old enough to go to school, I would be allowed to go down to the shop most mornings, clutching two pennies in my hand to buy my own breakfast, an egg and a parkin biscuit. No wonder they called me Ginger.

McCluskey himself must have been a saint. He needed to have worked a few miracles in order to survive Mary Ann Street, since most of his customers shopped daily on the credit principle known as strapping. Eat now, pay later—generally much later.

Just off Mary Ellen Street was the Ragged School. The Ragged School for Boys. Its title was no misnomer. It was unbelievably true, since most of the school's pupils had the arse out of their trousers and the toes out of their clogs. The Ragged School though did one thing once a year which the staff were justly proud of. One day during the long summer holidays, the staff ran a day's excursion by train to Blackpool. A day out at the seaside, it was better than getting a new pair of clogs. Getting hold of one of the extra tickets was a real prize. A whole day by the sea, an apple, an orange, a bar of chocolate and a train ride to boot. It was just like having Christmas twice a year.Mam didn't even mind changing my religion for twenty four hours just to get a ticket, although in the end, the Roman Catholics seemed to outnumber the Baptists on the train every year. What price religion?

The tiny pawnshop with the name I. Solomons in faded gold paint over the door lintel was well used by the residents of both streets. The owner was endearingly known by his surfeit of customers as Iky Moses, whilst the few who knew him better called him Old Solly. The little shop with only one window was always dark inside. The two gas mantles inside were very rarely lit, Iky was a firm believer in saving money. There was always a permanent smell of lamp oil, which Iky also sold, mixed with a strong aroma of moth balls. The smell which lingered was a dead give away, embarrassing if you had a date over the weekend, trying to mask the smell. "Suit bin in eh George?" Behind rails covered by cheap curtains, hung rows of clothing, suits, men's and women's, overcoats and dresses. Each article of clothing was neatly tagged with half a pawn ticket pinned with a huge safety pin.

Sometimes on special occasions like funerals and weddings, my suit would be redeemed before Friday night, but I generally only needed it for the weekend. Iky spoke in monosyllables, usually numbers. He was sparse with everything, money as well as conversation, which he kept to a bare minimum. All he needed was the other half of your pawn ticket and he would go straight to the article in question. You paid your money, and he handed over your property. Piles of brown paper parcels, large and small, all stacked together on slatted shelves, almost to ceiling level since space was at a premium. What little treasures did they all conceal? Where Iky had to climb the ladder, his thin bent over body wheezed with every step. People popped most things, sheets, blankets, eiderdowns, jewellery, watches, rings, gold and silver chains, sovereigns and half sovereigns. Solly, at the end of the day, would lock all his smaller and valuable items away in a large wall safe at the back of the shop. My suit cost half a crown to redeem, which meant sixpence profit for Iky. Not bad I suppose for a week's storage. Most of the residents of the streets around took advantage of Iky's fitted wardrobes, it was after all a cheap form of storage.

At the top end of Mary Ann Street on opposite corners were the pub and the chip shop. They were just as important in the art of frugal living as the pawnshop, links in the chain of pure existence. The pub, The Australian Inn, was a leftover from the first world war, the Great War. It had been adopted by soldiers from down under, and the name had been retained by the brewery. It was big brash and noisy, especially every weekend when the customers were mostly my relatives, a weekly gathering of the clan. A gathering also meant a mixed bag of offsprings, cousins all, and we would play a variety of games outside the front of the pub, regularly fuelled with bottles of pop, crisps and hot meat and potato pies.

Friday nights were always fish and chip nights, pay nights. No meat was ever eaten on Fridays by any of the Walkers. Good Catholics don't eat meat on Fridays. It was probably the extent of the majority of the clan towards the faith. The best Catholic without any doubt was mam, and she had been converted. At least we went to Mass every Sunday, for me a choir boy, it was three times on Sunday and twice more during the week.

Saturday nights the clan let its hair down, determined to be skint before the grind of Monday morning came around again. Money burned a hole in the pocket, had to be spread around. As children we played our games outside the pub, listening occasionally to the sounds of revelry going on inside. Saturday night was a bandio, a time to forget all sorrows, a time to enjoy! A bandio was an excuse for the clan to swill away the meagre earnings sweated for during the rest of the week. Six and a half days of blood, toil and sweat pissed up against the wall on a Saturday night, it never changed. A communal relief valve, they let off steam once a week for a few glorious hours.

Mam drew in the crowds on Saturday nights. The Australian Inn would be packed to the gills. She had a beautiful voice, Blackburn's own Gracie Fields. Give us a song Alice was a popular request, and she would oblige with a fine imitation of Gracie. Listening to her sing, I would have mixed feelings, embarrassment and pride all in one. Mam certainly sang for her supper. The landlord recognising a good thing, even paid her to entertain his customers. Mam sang for the joy of it.

On Saturday nights too, always on time at nine o'clock, the hot meat and potato pie man would arrive. He carried his goodies on a large wooden tray lined with clean greaseproof papers. The tray finely balanced on his head. Everybody looked forward to the arrival of the prater pie man his wares were delicious. The tiny lady wearing the serge and red uniform of the Salvation Army, the SAL DOS selling her copies of the War Cry always appeared at the same time. Synchronised sustenance for both the body and the soul. The clan were doubly generous, but I don't suppose they ever read her paper, except to use it to hold a hot meat and potato pie.

Eventually when the landlord finally ejected the last of my boisterous relatives off the premises, pie eyed and happy, they would all repair without fail across the road to grannie's house. There having loaded up with crates of bottled beer, they would carry on singing drinking and arguing until the early hours of Sunday morning. By then most of us children would be all fast asleep.

The arguments were always the same. To us kids mostly disturbing, frightening at times. Arguments against capitalism, religion, the state, exploitation of the workers. Uncle Frank was the shit stirrer. A born red, he knew how to raise the temperature. How to steer an argument. How to get my father going, which didn't take much. Grannie Walker always had a large skillet of stew gently simmering on the kitchen range, and between songs and arguments the lot would be polished off.

Grannie Walker, my paternal grandmother, was a force to be reckoned with. An early widow, her husband had died very soon after leaving the south of Ireland following the potato famine, leaving his wife to bring up a large family on her own. Grannie Walker was tiny, like a small bird, but she ran her brood with a rod of iron. She was a stayer, of good Irish stock, and she could sup with the best of them, a noted special expertise with the clan. Where the hell she put it all was a mystery.

My grandmothers were so entirely opposites. Grandma Sutcliffe was huge, a big woman in every respect, yet extremely shy and quiet, a confirmed teetotaler who rarely went further afield than the shop on the corner. Her small back garden was always well tended, and a riot of colour during the spring and summer. She was happy cleaning, baking and crocheting, as well as looking after half a dozen scrawny pullets who scratched a living at the bottom of her garden. Grannie Walker was never quiet. She buzzed like an angry bee most of the time, her blue Irish eyes mischievous and twinkling. It was hard to believe she had produced from her tiny frame ten lusty children, all to adulthood, without too much help from a sickly and dying husband.

What a lot of aunts and uncles to be sure, although I never knew them all. My granny trotted off to the local every night without fail armed with a quart sized jug, filling it to the brim with her favourite tipple, milk stout. Her elixir of life.

The postage stamp back garden was always an untidy mess. The only things that grew there were the mountains of empty beer bottles, sculptures of Saturday night fevers, awaiting return to the Australian Inn. She was always on the go, and never seemed to be ill, never had time. The only thing in common my grannies shared was a love of their grandchildren. Grannie Walker was always good for a silver threepenny bit, and Grandma Sutcliffe believed her jam butties were just as good. Both were now long gone, the quiet one violently, suddenly of a massive heart attack; the busy noisy one, peacefully and in her sleep, following one of Saturday night's bandio.

Hometown want to wander down your backstreets. See your tumbledown old shack streets. Not for me. My horizons were far wider, even at an early age. For me the grass was far greener on the other side of the street. Blackburn was dead. A desert. It wasn't all below the line. Some places I would miss. One of them would be Ewood Park. The home of Blackburn Rovers. The Rovers were one of the few teams who were founder members of the football league. Founded during the reign of Queen Victoria, older than my father.

Football for me was a passion. My bedroom walls were covered with large coloured photographs of famous players, courtesy of the Hotspur comic. Every Saturday was a day of magic during the season. School match in the morning, and the Rovers in the afternoon. The thrill of those blue and whites coming out of the tunnel and on to the pitch was enormous. For any schoolboy to play on that hallowed turf was considered the epitome of success. Every year on Pancake Tuesday, Ewood Park echoed to the cheering of thousands of school children. Shrove Tuesday was the day when the finals of the schools knock out competition were decided. Junior and Senior teams. I played there on two occasions. Pure magic.

My other favourite venue was Blackburn market. The town was very proud of its market, and it had every right to be. The market square itself was enormous. A huge cobblestone patchwork of tiny stalls, erected early in the morning and struck late at night. In between, flaunting the wares, anything from a pin to a pineapple. A miasma of colour, sounds and smells. Pure open air theatre for its customers. The players were not all itinerants. Some were permanents rooted in the tradition of market trading. The fruiterers and the greengrocers had their own small lock up warehouses on the periphery of the square. These they would transform on market days into shop windows of pure design and colour in order to tempt the myriads of patrons.

Potatoes from the lush soil of Ormskirk. Fresh crisp vegetables from the Fylde. Fruits of every shape and colour. Baskets of big brown newly laid eggs. Cheeses from the farms in the Ribble valley. Sausages from Clitheroe, and strings of big shiny black puddings from as far away as Bury. Street theatre to titillate the juices, stretch the imagination. Pure lasting lessons of social history.

To complement the open market there were two indoor ones. One housed the butchers, the bakers, florists, silks and satins, the other was fish and fishmongers of every shape and size. Money was the only commodity in short supply.

There was homespun entertainment too. Buskers, jugglers, conjurors, tramps, they all vegetated onto the market circuit. Some were characters never to be forgotten. Strong Dick, an escapologist, who with audience participation had himself tied up in chains and padlocks and then stuffed into a large brown sack. Dick was slightly around the bend. There were plenty of times when some wide boy would make sure there would be no quick escape, Dick would writhe around for hours before someone would feel sorry for him and secure his release.

Poor Strong Dick. He once decided to walk around the world. The publicity for his stunt in the local rag was big. Hundreds of people turned up to wish him God speed. Last seen shrouded in mist on Darwen moors, some ten miles away asking somebody the quickest way to China.

Billy Buttons the local tramp was another character, a walking sideshow. Completely covered from head to foot in buttons. There was even one on the bulb of his corn cob pipe. Rumour had it he had been an eminent surgeon in the Army during the Great War. The experience had turned his head. A riot of activity which on occasions had overtones. This was when Mosley and his blackshirts would hold a meeting. These demonstrations always ended up with punch ups galore.

But for me the market came into its own at Easter. The huge square would be covered with a fun fair. Rides of every size and description. The big boats in tandem. The Cake Walk, Ghost Train, Swirl, Electric cars, Cocks and Hens, Hobby horses. They were all there. Sideshows and hawkers of every kind. For a week it was all pure magic roundabout. One of my favourite sideshows was the boxing booth. Lean hungry professionals awaiting the mugs to step into the ring with them. Stay on your feet for three one minute rounds and win £5 the barker would cajole. When the beer did the talking, Dutch courage, the local heroes spurred on by the crowd would volunteer and pick his man. There were few who came away with the prize other than a few coppers thrown into the ring around their prostrate bodies revived with smelling salts. The professionals used the booths on the route to the top as champions. There was always the fear that Dad would be among the faces of the challengers. He fancied himself as a boxer. He taught me the rudiments, a straight left, the uppercut and how to protect your chin, but in all honesty he couldn't punch his way out of a paper bag. However a dozen oysters (a shilling) from Kennedy's Oyster bar washed down with a few pints of Guinness from Yates Wine Lodge next door had more than an aphrodisiacal effect. These were lean and hungry times. The festival of Easter could be uplifting in more ways than one. A lad could leave Blackburn, but Blackburn would never leave a lad.

Chapter 22

Shortly after midnight, the thunderstorms had rumbled away and Jacques said we must continue. Still following the course of the river and skirting the small town of Ruffec, the aim was to get as close to Angoleme before daybreak. Jacques had told us that he would leave us in the next safe house and return later by train back to Tours. For me it was roughly half-way house, for Laurie and Joe three quarters of the journey completed before we tackled the Pyrenees and real safety.

Of course the Spaniards were not necessarily friendly either. Stories of aircrew spending months in Spanish gaols were well known. However, the line had now been running successfully for a long time and the other end across the border should be well organised by now. The sooner we reached the shelter of a neutral country, the better. Joe was beginning to get worse. He was starting to break out in angry looking boils on his body, as well as nasty and large painful abscesses under both armpits. He was plainly run down, and would soon need urgent medical attention.

What would any one of us give for a hot bath, a change of clean clothing and a decent hot meal? My knowledge of the geography ahead was scant to say the least. I knew the Pyrenees went right across country from the Atlantic to the Mediterranean, forming a natural barrier some 250 miles long between France and Spain. Somewhere in the back of my memory I also knew they were about 5 miles wide, but not so fearsome as to have to cross the Alps. Jacques had assured us that the climb would not be too difficult. I only hoped he was right, there was still a long way to go before we got our climbing boots on.

Either one of us could easily have modelled as a scarecrow, we were all so thin and gaunt. What we needed was a lift, something or someone, anything to raise our spirits. It came in the shape of a rough newsheet produced by local Maquis. The news of the war was all good. Jerry was on the run squeezed on all sides. The Ruskies were advancing in the East and we were also moving forward in France. There was again that faint glimmer of optimism, hope almost, that the war in Europe could be over by Christmas, a time for peace. What a wonderful Christmas box that would be. The Boche had been offered nothing short of total surrender, and up and down France the resistance movement was expanding rapidly. For three of us there was still a long way to go, maybe the most difficult parts were still to come. We quietly slipped into another safe house on the edge of town. Another safe house run again by a woman. What would we do without them? Our hostess was middle-aged, spoke excellent English, and assured us we were in good hands. Code name Angelique, she gave the impression she was more the fire and brimstone type. She allowed us to listen to the BBC broadcasts which were all full of inuendoes and coded messages of all descriptions. Angelique listened in particular to one religious programme during which the chaplain was quite obviously passing important information together with his blessings. Angelique told us the news was all good, once she had made sense of the religious offerings. Listening to home bucked us up no end.

There was however one dark cloud on the horizon, Joe's condition was beginning to be a cause of some real concern, and Angelique decided a doctor should pay him a visit as soon as possible. We never stayed in any place too long, generally never longer than seventy two hours, the short rest would do Joe some good perhaps.

The doctor turned up the following day and gave Joe a really thorough examination. "What's the verdict?" I asked Joe once the doctor had left us. His face said it all.

"Holy shit house mouse," was all he could say.

"Can't be that bad Joe, can it?" I replied. "What's the problem?"

"I'm too much of a liability to go on, that's the god awful problem—so I'm extending my holiday and staying here for a while," he grunted. "Christ, I've come all this god damn way and some Frog quack knocks it all on the head, tells me I'm not up to it."

"It's probably for the best Joe," I waffled. "You'll make it, you'll see. I'll see you later in Norwich."

"Yeah, yeah," was all Joe could manage.

Later in confidence Angelique told me that the doctor considered Joe would probably suffer from severe frostbite if he attempted to cross the mountains in his present condition. She also told me that the hills and the approaches were still heavily guarded and crossing the rivers and streams was a real hazard in itself. "Don't worry George—we will get your friend home, better safe than sorry. We cannot afford to risk any compatriots—I have it on the grapevine that at least four American airmen are in the pipeline, so Joe won't be lonely for too long," she concluded. Valentine said little or nothing about the change in plans, non commital. I was beginning to worry about him too, he was not exactly the best companion for the final leg.

We reckoned we still had about 150 miles to go to the base of the hills. The walking, Angelique told us, was reasonably easy, level countryside ahead following the course of the river before the waters started to flow across our route. The three days of rest, with the luxury of a hot bath, hot food, and a comfortable bed, was a real tonic. We must have been feeling better, both itching to be away and on the road. Lying on my bed staring into space, my thoughts kept returning to the lovely old watercolour hanging on the opposite wall, a scene of rustic charm. The picture was a family scene—kids, dogs and parents, all enjoying a picnic on a river bank. Not that we had too many family picnics, but the clan Walker was certainly one big family.

I was saturated as a child with aunts and uncles. This excess of relatives was thrust upon me at weekly intervals.

For instance, I had two Uncle Bills, both so completely different, the differences so distinct that even as a child it was noticeable. Uncle Billy Walker and Uncle Billy Barstow. Billy Walker, small, dapper, and short tempered, was as smart as a new pin. Billy Walker had lifted himself out of the rut by his boot straps courtesy of the local territorial army. A part-time soldier, he had taken to soldiering like a fish to water, a terrier who had made his mark. Billy Walker was now a Sgt. Major and like most small men with power to his elbow, a terror to boot. One of my favourite uncles, not because he was always generous, but because most of the clan respected him, he had made something of himself, and he was as straight as a die. Uncle Billy was always good for a silver sixpence too.

Not so Uncle Barstow. Ungraciously known all the time in conversation only as Aunt Nellie's husband, he was a total outsider, almost completely ignored. Not that he did anything to improve the situation. Uncle Barstow was a pariah. Fat and grossly overweight, his large bloated face matched his equally large sweaty podgy hands. Always uncomfortable in company, his presence was tainted with a strong lingering smell of a mixture of body odour and snuff, cheap mentholatum snuff which stained everything below his nostrils with ribbons of dirty brown. Uncle Barstow was easily bottom of the popularity stakes. He was also mean, even though he probably had more money at his disposal than the rest of the clan altogether. Uncle Billy Barstow was his own man, who ran a dubious back street business as a bookmaker, complete with a small army of bookie's runners. These were characters who spent their days standing on street corners furtively taking bets on tacky bits of paper, betting slips, and putting them and the money into little black bags. Some of them were out and out rogues, much to the chagrin of Uncle Bill. Not that he was fond of settling winning bets, he hated losing as much as dipping his hand into his pocket to buy a round of beer. Uncle Barstow was a sponger, maybe in truth he was careful with his brass, but poor Aunt Nellie bore the brunt of his meanness week after week with a silence worthy of a saint. The clan never fully forgave her for marrying a Prod. That was the biggest strike against him.

Auntie Nellie was my favourite auntie. Plump and rosy, she had a beaming smile, one which lit up her entire face, disguising the pain caused by all the snide remarks about her husband. There was a hidden sadness too beyond her small twinkling deep brown eyes, one of which was slightly deformed, almost closed, giving her face an almost permanent wink. The sadness was caused by the sudden death of their only pride and joy, my cousin Jimmy. It had always been a complete mystery why her only child had suddenly died. The clan always discussed it in whispers, the reason referred to as Uncle Barstow's nose. I was always puzzled, why should a sore nose cause someone to die? In my teens, the answer to the riddle became suddenly crystal clear. My mean Uncle Barstow was suffering from syphillis before making Auntie Nellie pregnant. Later she became sterile and an early widow.

Aunt Mary was the eldest member of the clan. Auntie Mary was a tyrant , certainly not a lady to be crossed. She ran her house and her large family raw and bleeding. The image of her mother in most ways, her once flaming red hair was now streaked with pepper and salt. Uncle Nick, her long-suffering husband, had long ago surrendered, subdued into absolute silence, completely and fully impotent. Poor old Uncle Nick, one of life's walking disasters. He had already one foot in the grave having lost a leg during the Battle of the Somme. Unkindly labelled gas gangrene, he hadn't worked for years, subsisting on his meagre war pension, topped up with small ungracious handouts from an endless variety of means tests.

Auntie Mary in her cups could be vicious, and like Uncle Frank, enjoyed a good argument. Uncle Nick was also known as Uncle Peg Leg. Hammered by life, his wife, and terrible wounds suffered whilst he slept in a trench somewhere in Flanders, he had been drained of conversation. His wife was one shrew that would never be tamed. She piled on the agony, giving him a dog's life. Nick stomped around like a sloth with his wooden leg, coughing and spitting most of the time, his existence being consciously shrivelled away. In a perverse way, he was proud of being gassed, proud of losing a leg, he'd done his bit for England even though his patriotism had marked his card for a miserable aftermath and an early grave. He could do nothing right. Mum told me so quite often. "Oh him, he does nothing but cadge, hasn't done a decent day's work in his life, a born sponger." Saturday nights saw him slouched in his favourite corner, his pint pot always being topped up until finally his head would fall on his chest and he became lost to the world for the rest of the infighting. "Nick's gone." Auntie Mary would spit, and he would then be totally ignored until it was time to drag him home. I was still quite young when Uncle Nick booked his plot in the Cemetery at Cherry Tree, finally gone to his better 'ole.

The clan gave him a passing out day the like of which had not been seen for a long time down Mary Ann Street. A day of mourning, never. The outward signs were there, a cortège of four shiny black horses, and a brace of funeral cars. The street was having a field day, only the bunting was missing.

Buried on a Saturday, the wake carried on until the early hours of Monday morning, through mountains of potted meat sandwiches, pigs' trotters, and scrawny chickens whose early demise from grubbing in Auntie Mary's garden had been suddenly precipitated. Cow heels, black puddings, and mountains of broth, they were all consumed, washed down by the contents of one brewery. The clan did nothing by halves, and the street would talk about it for years to come. Uncle Nick was given a send off he would have been proud of.

Auntie Mary finally said it all, "Creeping Jesus, he would have enjoyed it." She couldn't wait to get her hands on his pension books. Matty Brown's, the brewery, even sent a wreath—they could well afford it.

By contrast, the rest of the clan were insignificant, the second division of hangers on, who sat and nodded like tired back benchers to the never ending same old arguments, no matter how they were disguised. Yes, most Saturday nights swilling and spilling over in early Sunday mornings were a bandio.

My mother's brother and sisters were characterless human beings compared with the clan. Uncle George was rarely ever seen. He was serving abroad most of the time with the Army somewhere in Egypt.

I could only remember seeing him once. A lean polished soldier, all muscles and tattoos, anxious to get back to the sunshine and away from the cold grey clammy wet of Lancashire as soon as possible. Aunties May and Violet reminded me always of instant playbacks of Olive Oil, Popeye's lean and hungry girlfriend. They were all lookalikes, frightened shadows, and grey translucent bags of bones. None of them ever ventured into clan territory, which they considered brutal, and consequently I rarely saw them.

Uncle Frank was my father's youngest brother. Tall, good looking, a cock of the North, he spent most of his wages on clothes, sartorial elegance in a sea of hand-me-downs.

Frank Walker was a shit stirrer, he revelled in it. He started all the late night arguments, timed to perfection, and ably assisted by Auntie Mary. It was easy to wind up my aged Aunt, and she was a dab hand at steering the argument into something entirely different. When the air was blue, Uncle Frank would then quietly slip away. It was a long time before he was eventually rumbled. Four Uncles—a soldier, a sponger, a cadger and a lecher. Two more I never knew were only faded sepia photographs, lost forever in a place called Galliopoli, but discussed with every Saturday's binge, so that I felt I knew them very well indeed. The kindled patriotism always mixed with tears.

Very few of the clan made early morning Mass on Sunday. The majority, strong in their religious convictions when the beer was flowing, collapsed like good lapsed Catholics into a sodden sleep and snored away their mortal sins.

It was absolution by relays. You always felt cleaner if you attended early morning Mass. The last Mass was for the sleepers in. Straight out of church, into the pub across the road, hair of the dog. *You won't go to heaven when you die Mary Anne when you die, when you die, when you die Mary Ann.* A ditty we used to sing in the school playground. Mam would go to heaven, she was the best catlick of them all.

For us, the children, it was different. Committing a mortal sin by not attending Mass and having to confess it before all your classmates on a Monday morning, was too unbearable. It was a long time before I too became a lapsed Catholic.

Like a lot of families of our ilk, we always seemed to be moving house during my early childhood. We flitted around like gypsies. I never fully understood the reasons why, but each time we flitted away, once doing a moonlight flit, there would be a bust up between Mam and Dad. Looking back the reasons were simple enough, it all came down to money, or to be nearer the truth, the lack of it. There were always plenty of unfurnished houses to let, so there was little problem about finding a roof over your head. Nevertheless, it was very embarrassing even for one so young, I felt we were social lepers. Once we suffered the indignity of being evicted when the bum bailiffs moved in. Dad was hard to live with for a long time afterwards. Most families like us scraped by from one week to the next, most of the time from one day to the next. "Have you paid the rent this week Alice?" Dad would regularly enquire. Mam would reassure him by producing the rent book. It was long time before he cottoned on to the fact that Mam had two, one for the landlord, the other for Dad's eyes only. It was not that Mam was deceitful, but money was so short, she had to get her priorities right, and the rent man was low on the totem pole. The weeks she missed paying the rent went on settling up the bills at the grocers strapped up the week before. Life was one of continual tick, a never never land, and I often wondered if Mam would ever get straight. Some of the houses I was glad to see the back of. Dark damp sinister flea pits, ridden with disease, they were frightening places. One in particular had a black history, mentioned in whispers, it was either a murder or a suicide which had been committed within its bug pocked walls.

The last house, Devonport Road, was a real step up. It was a palace, clean and bright, with a garden and a cellar. We were static here for years, able to put down roots, with no mention of flitting, except for the flit powder kept down the cellar just in case.

Of all the days of the week, Sunday was my favourite. A day of rest for Dad, no letters or parcels to deliver. He could have his long lie in, recovering from Saturday night's fever. When he eventually surfaced washed and shaved Dad would take us all for a walk to the local park. "I'll get them from under your feet Alice before dinner," he would say to Mam busy in the kitchen.

Mam was no dab hand at cooking. Not exactly cordon blue more Gordon Bennet with the accent on Gordon. Dad said she was trained at the holocaust school, everything burned to a crisp. I was unaware food could taste any different for a long time.

One Christmas, never to be forgotten, we rose to Duck. Mam left the giblets inside wrapped in brown paper all through cooking. Dad said it was Duck a la papier mache. We laughed our way through the festive season. Mind you Mam's cooking equipment was very limited indeed. Two frying pans, one jug, and a varied assortment of ancient knives and forks. The very old gas cooker was a trial in itself. Mam once remarked, even if she wanted to commit suicide by putting her head in the gas oven, the damn thing would let her down. So we couldn't be too critical of her culinary skills.

If Sunday was my favourite day, after tea was my favourite time. Dad told us stories. He was an excellent story teller. Always something different. For me his vivid memories of his war were the most exciting, and at times very scary. His recollections of going over the top, bayonets fixed, were meat and drink to an over active young mind.

And now history had been repeating itself. We too had been going over the top, night after night. Berlin, Happy Valley, Nuremburg, they were our battles of the Somme, our Paschendale, our Ypres, as we drove deeper and deeper into the underbelly of the same merciless enemy.

It was time again for the three of us to be on our way again.

The next target to aim for was the small town of Libourne which was slightly north east of Bordeaux, the one place I knew well, it was down in red ink in my flying book. The Germans had built submarine pens there and during my first tour of operations, we had laid mines outside the entrance to the harbour. It all seemed so long ago.

Our next guide was a total surprise. Female, young—no older than sixteen, and beautiful as well. A very pleasant surprise indeed. Angelique told me even for one so young she was something of a heroine within the local resistance. Apparently, together with her even younger sister, they had taken part in a number of daring escapades including the major sabotage of a large number of tank transporters shortly after the start of the second front. The denial of a division's tanks in Normandy was a godsend to the invasion troops. Toting her six shooter on her hip, I was reminded of Annie Oakley. Let's hope she didn't have to prove the point.

Her name was Christine, and she was certainly different. She kept up a running commentary, obviously with the intention of improving her English. Even Valentine came out of his shell and began to perk up a little. One thing was certain though, she certainly hated the Boche. We we soon to find out why, she had good reason since her father had been executed some months before as part of a snap reprisal by the Germans. Our cover story was now changed slightly. We were brother, sister and companion making our way to the Dordogne to pick grapes. Christine herself bubbled all the time like fine champagne.

One day when this lot was over, I would come back here and walk this trail again, without the fear of being captured. The countryside was glorious, perfumed by gorse, juniper and olive trees. The vines were plump with clusters of fruit, this could certainly be a good year in all respects. The locals had a lot to be proud about. After all, Acquitaine and Catalonia close at hand were once empires themselves, with territories stretching as far away as Greece. Memory lane once again, bits of general knowledge gleaned during my schooldays were drifting back. How the local farmers stuffed their geese with truffles to make the finest pate. At the time, to me French food, frog's legs and snails were all far too disgusting. Outlandish eating habits apart, right now Laurie and myself needed our little French Miss to see us through to the base of the mountains. She regaled us with stories of how we would survive once we reached the foot hills and the mountains beyond. She carefully showed the pair of us how to set traps for hares, foxes and even wild boar. Christine was a veritable mine of information, a walking survival kit. I questioned her how for one so young she was so close to the soil. All she did was tap her nose, "Papa was my tutor George—he was par excellence. One day I will pass it all on to my son just like you will n'est pas?"

"Amen to that," I replied.

All specific idea of time was lost, the nights were drawing in and it was getting decidedly cooler. July had gone, and we were now well into August. If everything worked out as planned, Christmas at home was still possible. If we walked about 35 kilometres a night, and rested up during the day, we could be around Bayonne by the end of the month. Well laid plans were unfortunately often changed quite rapidly. Our rate of progress almost came to a full stop and we covered only twenty kilometres stretched out over three days and nights. There were good reasons for this happening; firstly the country was so open that cover was becoming sparse, and secondly and perhaps more important, the roads were crawling with enemy troops. We observed them on a number of occasions from our hideaway, convoys all going north east, even on minor roads, and we were very strictly limited to night walking. Christine disappeared from time to time for short forays ahead. She brought back scraps of information and food. The Boche were becoming very trigger happy, they smelled defeat staring them in the face, and everyone was a potential saboteur. They were brutal to anyone in the way, no more prisoners. Extra care was definitely needed, we didn't want to throw it all away at this stage. Most of the time we lay hidden away awaiting Christine's return. Valentine was poor company, he had begun his whining again, all mostly self pity. He saved it all up for when the two of us were alone. Valentine was like a Jekyll and Hyde character, his mood was different when Christine was around, but she had sussed him out quite quickly. "Your friend Lauri," she would say to me, "he is like a spoiled child." I would apologise for him, saying he was very tired. She knew better though, one old head on such young and pretty shoulders.

Periods of enforced rest give way to day dreams. What wouldn't I give for a lump of freshly baked bread garnished with a generous wedge of Double Gloucester cheese and pickled onions, washed down with a sparkling pint of Cotswold ale? My thoughts slipped back further, back to school. Whitsuntide school processions, followed by a sports day, with a brass band in attendance. The best part of the day was yet to come, Mam's big meat and potato pies, big enough to feed an army of hungry relatives. Prater pie doos they were called, and here we were stuck in a hole in the ground wondering where the next meal was coming from. The maxim was right—belly empty subject food, belly full subject cunt.

Valentine awoke first, shaking me vigorously by the shoulder. I'd been in a deep sleep, forgetting for those glorious moments where we were. When I calmed down, I asked him what was worrying him. "She's gone George," his voice was trembling. "She's left us, pissed off, we're finished."

"Calm down for Christ sakes," I said. "She won't be away long—go back to sleep."

"But she's left us a note, and I don't like the look of it—here." He handed me the piece of paper on which Christine said she could be away for some time. We were told to stay put and on no account to wander away. How long was longer than usual? Maybe Valentine had a point. We would have to sweat it out.

After forty eight hours, there was still no sign of Christine, and I was beginning to expect the worst. Maybe she had been picked up, maybe she had been shot. Very soon a decision would have to be made, we couldn't stay here much longer. I knew the decision would rest with me alone, Valentine had by this time become a maudlin nonentity. His constant blubbering was sickening, over and over again he ranted on, "If I survive this, I will get myself invalided out—no way will they ever get me into an aeroplane again." I agreed with him wholeheartedly, he was a dead loss, one great big liability. Never a thought for what could have happened to our brave and courageous guide, he was only thinking about his own wretched hide.

In no uncertain terms, Valentine was told we could do one of two things; one, both of us move and hope to be picked up by friendly forces, or two, I would recce on my own and return for him later. No way would he agree to be left on his own, so I set a deadline to move on as soon as it was dark. So near and yet so far. To be on our own was the last thing we needed, I was very apprehensive about the outcome without help. Let's hope we didn't run into any trigger happy soldiers.

It was obviously me who had the golden balls. We were on the point of moving on, when wonders of wonders, Christine suddenly appeared. I could have taken her in my arms and kissed her. "Where have you been? What happened? Are you OK? We were both so worried." It all tumbled out.

"I have been making love—my boyfriend lives very close by." She was so unconcerned. There was no answer to that, I was completely deflated. She continued, "We have to change our plans and our tactics. Libourne is out—the safe house has been blown." Christine's plan was now for us to strike out further west, towards a place called Bergerac. The reason was that a large concentration of mechanised troops were moving out of Bordeaux and across country to the Dordogne. We would have the benefit of higher ground until we crossed the river Garonne. Bayonne was also out too, so we would now attempt to cross the Pyrenees from a base camp at Pau. The news from the war front was also good, but on the debit side, the Germans were now launching an unmanned flying missile against London powered by a rocket, a flying bomb.

Somewhere in the back of my mind was a target called Peenemunde. Was this the launching pad? Christine said they were all aimed at south east England, and when the buzzing stopped, it meant they were on the way down. Londoners had christened them buzz bombs.

Bergerac was reached by the last week in August. It was early Sunday morning and the locals were preparing for early mass. The billet was a doctor's house, so we were in good hands. It was bliss to be able to soak my feet, although by now they had become hardened after so much tramping. Christine intended to stay with us all the way. That was a relief, with roughly another eighty odd miles to go. Both of us were declared reasonably fit, despite the trials and tribulations we had been through. Our host was cock a hoop about the progress of the war. The Nazis were getting their just desserts. The doctor's prognosis was that there would be no need for a Comete line soon, before too long it could be open house. That was the best piece of news in a long time, and even Valentine managed a smile.

Belly full at last, a real bed to stretch out in, clean sheets, and a drop of good wine, sufficient to induce a sound sleep. Pity it was only a one night stand. We would pick up our original trail at Marmande. The doctor considered it might be safe enough to cycle the rest of the way. The vote was unanimous, it would take the strain off our feet, and harden up some other part of the anatomy for a change. Three bikes were quickly produced. I expected Valentine to say he would need at least a day's practice, but like Christine and myself, he was pleased not to be hiking for a while. The doctor told us his brother had escaped to England with the Air Force, and like Monique's husband, was flying Spitfires operationally somewhere on the south coast. We promised to contact him if we made it back home safely, perhaps the Baron was his Commanding Officer.

At last we were beginning to make real progress again. Cycling was much easier, the only snag about having to take to the roads was one of sudden exposure around every corner. Christine as usual led the way. The rhythm of her slim strong nut brown legs, sensuous, made me more than envious of her Maquis boyfriend. The line from a Mess ditty came to mind, watching her up ahead, *and the cheeks of her arse went chuff chuff chuff.* It seemed appropriate.

The next safe house at Marmande was not too far away, when the incident happened. I should have known, my Piscean intuition had been twitching for some time. Rounding a bend in the road, we were suddenly confronted by three enemy soldiers. At least we were evenly matched. They seemed even more frightened than we were. Christine sized up the situation very quickly and she made the first decisive move. She literally snarled the words *"Hande hoche, hande hoche"* her pistol already at the aim and pointed at the leading soldier. The reaction was unbelievable, up went three pairs of hands, absolute fear registering on each of their faces, they were all so young, mere boys. *"Sie ist meine Kreigie,"* was Christine's next instruction. *"Ja ja ja,"* they answered in unison, like lambs to the slaughter.

"What did you say to them?" I asked her.

"They are my prisoners, that's what I told them, they understand. We must get rid of them as soon as possible—George take the pistol, sit them down and guard them. They will not run away—they are already deserting." I noticed they carried no weapons. Christine was off. She told me she was going to fetch help as quickly as possible, and for us to march them towards Marmande. She intended to rendezvous again as soon as she could.

I spoke to one of the soldiers, *"Sprechen sie English?"*

"Ja, a little," he said.

"OK, forward march, for you the war is over," pointing the way forward. They gave us no problems. Christine was an ace, as good as her word. We handed over the three prisoners to the local resistance and we pressed on. Valentine crowed, and she allowed him his moment of reflected glory.

It was always something of a lottery with safe houses, the next one we moved into was the local village bakehouse. Again, the lingering smell of freshly baked bread took me back ten years or more, the taste was even more enchanting. Newly baked loaves had the effect of making me feel randy, but the pleasures of the flesh would have to wait.

"It's all changed." That phrase had a familiar ring to it, it had been burned into my soul. It reminded me of the early days of operations, when it was on, it was off, it was on again, with a different target every time. "What's new, Christine?" Valentine asked.

"Don't worry boys, it is all for the good. I am told we can now head directly for Biarritz and not Pau. The way ahead is almost clear, you will both be home for Noël, or even earlier." With that she kissed us both. "Crossing the mountains from Biarritz will be easy, you will see—you will be in excellent hands." If anyone deserved a medal for courage and devotion to duty, this mere slip of a girl would be top of my honours list. Today was her seventeenth birthday and tonight we would have a party. I cajoled mine host into baking a cake. The baker could only manage half a candle.

The main highway down went close to Roquefort, Mont de

Marsan and Bayonne. Place names on a map, although I had heard of Roquefort and the special cheese made in the town. Christine had told us that once more this section was being run by a woman who went under the code name of Tante Go. This lady, much much older than Christine, had apparently a legendary reputation above reproach from Brussels through to San Sebastian in Spain. The heat was definitely off, the Boche had no time now to be too interested in evading aircrew. They were far too busy protecting themselves from resistance forces who by now included the majority of French men and women. The enemy was on the run, harassed, blasted and ambushed night and day. For them the writing was on the wall—finis, and more and more of La Belle France was being liberated. We only had to keep our heads down, and we could be home and dry.

The last leg was the proverbial piece of cake. We became audacious enough to take a train ride. We holed up at a small town called Anglet, that had a beautiful ring to it, before we moved again off into the mountains. Tante Go lived up to her legend, making the path for the final climb as smooth as silk. I said to Laurie, "Tomorrow we leave France; we must always remember how much we owe to Christine, our golden girl, we could not have got so far." The fond goodbyes were tearful, Christine and I had become like our cover story, brother and sister, we seemed to have been together for so long. My last words to her before she had the pleasant task of handing us over to the mountain guide at the foot of the Pyrenees, were please, please take care on your way home. The last link in the chain before we could say we had made it spoke little English, he was Catalan. Christine filled him in with all the necessary information. He simply smiled and shrugged his shoulders. This for him was another well paid job, nothing else. We gathered that he spent most of his time before the war engaged in smuggling a variety of goods in both directions. We were, as promised, in excellent hands.

He was a hard taskmaster, but he certainly knew the mountains. Most of the time it was heavy going, gruelling climbs that knocked all the stuffing out of us, but the ordeal was almost over. The spur to press on was strong and at least we did not have to contend with deep snow. The biggest hazard was crossing the river Bidassoa into Spain, but Dame Fortune smiled upon us and other than a soaking, the raging river presented few problems. We had reached a peak when Florentino, that is what we called him, pointed into the distance. "SS," he said. Valentine and myself threw ourselves to the ground. Florentino appeared non plussed at our actions, before a great big smile spread across his crinkled rugged face. He pointed again to a place below, "San Sebastian," he repeated. There below was total freedom, we had made it out of occupied France, and we would soon be in a neutral country. We both shook the guide's hand vigorously, this was one happy mutual admiration society atop a peak in the Pyrenees. The date was the third of September 1944. My war had now been going on for five whole years. Florentino left us on the outskirts, he didn't want to be involved with the Spanish police.

The welcoming party of the British representative was brief and congratulatory. Arrangements were already in hand for a journey, mostly by train, to La Linea, a town on the border with Gibraltar. Incidentally, Florentino was the place where our guide lived on the other side of the mountains, we were never told his nom-de-guerre.

For Laurie and myself the following seven days were sheer luxury, no more living like hunted animals, all the way across Spain down to Gibraltar, from where it was planned to fly us home courtesy of a Short Sunderland Flying boat of Coastal Command. We took off very early in the morning, with a long operational flight of some fifteen hours ahead of us. Laurie slept, and I busied myself during those long droning hours helping out in the galley and serving hot food to the hard worked crew. Spam and chips had never tasted so good. Valentine rarely woke, totally exhausted by the realisation he would soon be home.

We landed at 1600 hours on a calm water in Milford Haven in Wales. Home at last, we had finally made it. I couldn't wait to get on the end of a telephone and phone my father-in-law who I knew would be on duty at Stroud Police Station. I suddenly realised that I had completed my sixty operations and was entitled to an operational egg-frying tonight. I kissed my good luck talisman, wondering what had happened to the rest of the crew. There would be lots of questions, requiring lots of answers. Other people were in the same frame of mind, and both of us were escorted post haste to London back to Air Ministry, to be de-briefed.

It took almost a week to de-brief the pair of us, and it was sheer purgatory not yet having seen my wife and baby. The daily ration of buzz bombs inflicted on London was a nightmare, aircrew were not used to being on the other end, the experience frightened the life out of me. When everybody was satisfied and all the questions had been answered, we were free to go on leave. Valentine worked himself a posting to London; grounded forever. A whole month's leave ahead before I reported back to Lincolnshire, this time as an instructor on a Lancaster finishing school, with an additional remit to visit operational squadrons and talk to aircrews about escape and evasion. I was something of a celebrity, even so late in the day.

A whole month's leave, the powers-that-be were very generous, I was certainly not prepared to argue. An Indian summer, the middle of Autumn were golden periods to enjoy in the Cotswolds, the Stroud valley in particular.

Chapter 23

It was very late and pitch dark as I trudged up the hill, going home for the first time in six months. Nothing seemed to have changed. The trains were running late, courtesy of a buzz bomb which had made a mess of some of the main railway lines out of Paddington to the West Country. I told Laura not to wait up for me. On my way up to the house, I passed the rolling figure of a man, loosely heading in the same direction. Neither of us said a word. I'd been indoors for some five to ten minutes when the back door burst open and my father-in-law literally fell inside. The rolling figure was now explained. Vic made it quite plain through his maudlin tears he had been happily celebrating my safe return along with his cronies down amongst the vats in Stroud brewery. I left him sleeping in his big old armchair, snoring quietly. It must have been one hell of a party, he forgot to take his false teeth out. Creeping quietly away upstairs to bed, I would leave my felicitations until the morning when Vic had sobered up.

My wife sobbed softly with joy as we wrapped ourselves in each others arms, my small son in his cot alongside slept through it all. It was in the early hours of the morning when Laura shook me gently out of a deep sleep. "Can you smell burning, presh?" she said with a note of urgency. Burning, God the room was thick with smoke. Jumping out of bed and opening the bedroom door, I was met with the curtains on the landing immediately bursting into flames. Picking up the baby, we ushered everyone out of the house without panic in under five minutes. Laura and myself were able to put out the fire long before the fire engine had arrived. The fire itself had started in my father-in-law's old armchair. Obviously he had awoken and, before dragging himself upstairs, had dropped a lighted cigarette down the inside of the chair.

There were, unknown to me, two extra guests, both from London. My wife's younger sister who worked for the Air Ministry and a young cousin, both beginning a short holiday away from the doodle bugs. The following morning with everyone discussing the incident, my dear father-in-law blamed the fire on me, his favourite armchair being consigned outside for the dustman. I missed the dog, the old mongrel Gus. "Where's Gus?" I asked. Poor old Gus had been run over by a local brewery dray. What an ignominious end for a faithful old dog who spent most of his time patiently waiting outside public houses. Ah, welcome home!

Time flies when you are enjoying yourself. The long hot days of the Indian summer we spent soaking up the sun, walking, swimming and playing with our son. Most days we pushed the pram as far as the local park and sat and watched the old men enjoying a game of bowls, or simply lazed around the lakeside feeding the ducks. They were simple pleasures, which Laura and myself thoroughly enjoyed. When a babysitter was around, we stretched our legs walking further afield, to Painswick, to Bisley or to Slad, sometimes taking the local rattler and visiting Gloucester. The landlord of my favourite pub in the town, the Golden Fleece, laid on a welcome home party. The four weeks' bliss soon evaporated away, it would soon be time to return to Lincolnshire and duty. This was a prospect I was not looking forward to at all. The night before my return, it was decided to have one last blow out and drink nothing else but scrumpy. Local cider was a powerful brew. What a mistake. Everybody had rubber legs, and there were a fair number of shouts of "Hughie" throughout the night. I was like death warmed up, leaving home at five o'clock in the morning to begin a train journey back to the war zone, back to East Anglia, and to a job I was not looking forward to.

There was no sense of urgency when I reported in this time. My first visit to Lincolnshire saw me on operations even before the ink had time to dry on my arrival chit. This time it was different, it took me almost a week to arrive. I needed to be fully kitted out again, a full medical check, and another visit back to London for a medical board.

My new job did not impress me at all. It was in the ground school instructing pilots on how to operate the radio equipment installed in the Lancaster. Like Valentine, I was also being grounded. It sounded like a thoroughly boring existence ahead. Why oh why did I not take up the offer of a commission when it was presented to me on a plate? Too late now. The training machine at last was beginning to slow up, the war was going Bomber Command's way at last, and aircrew losses were not so high. Not so many replacement crews were required. Targets were easier, mostly supporting the armies spearheading their way into Deutchland. The Luftwaffe fighter regiments had been dealt a real bloody nose, and were now almost neutralised. It was still good to have a night out in Bomber city, to meet some of the boys at the sharp end.

One of my first tasks was to visit Chalky's parents. They were hoping I could give them more news, good news, but we all knew that Chalky and Bill had both been killed. The official release was "Missing presumed killed in action", there was nothing I could say to them to change it. Mam and Dad White had grown visibly old, it was not surprising, Chalky was their only son. The good news to balance the bad was that all the rest of the crew had been captured and were now in different prison camps. The three NCO's were all in a camp called Sagen Stalag Luft III near the Polish border. Speaking to the skipper's father on the telephone, I learned the boss was now in an Oflag IVC, having been moved there after a series of unsuccessful escape attempts. His father quipped, "He should feel more at home now—I understand its a castle called Colditz. When are you coming up to see us George—soon I hope," he said.

"I will try sir, as soon as possible," I replied.

"Good, good, we would love to see you and your family."

"I'll try my best to keep our Hogmanay date sir, if that would still be OK?"

"Capital, capital George. We will look forward to seeing you and yours—I need to know what really happened and soon."

With the set in of the winter, the fighting in Europe was becoming bogged down, both sides facing each other across a morass of mud. The stalemate was not good for the Allies, it allowed the German land forces to consolidate their positions, throwing in every trooper fit enough to hold a rifle, and leaving the old and the very young to guard the homeland.

As I suspected, the job, important though it was, was tedious. There wasn't really enough to do and I was still on a high. My visits to operational stations to talk to crews and to answer most of their questions was some compensation, making a welcome change, but at the same time made me feel out of it. There was a different atmosphere altogether between an instructional school and an operational station, an operational station was addictive. I knew though I would never be allowed to fly again on operations against Europe. I knew too much about the Resistance machine, so it had to be accepted.

The end of the year was in sight, and still the war dragged on. Christmas at home was a real bonus, it was even a white one to put us all in the right spirit. There was a Santa Claus too, Father Christmas brought me two wonderful presents. Laura told me she was pregnant, that was marvellous news, and the icing on the cake was the award of a DFC to add to my DFM. In absentia, the skipper was awarded a DSO. I was over the moon for him, and so was his family.

The visit to Feddes Castle had to be postponed. The Boss's father had suffered a mild stroke and was confined to a hospital bed in Aberdeen. It was a sad and disappointing end to the year, the sixth year of the war. During February, the command bombed the city of Dresden, creating a massive fire storm. The improvement in the weather allowing Allied aircraft to pound enemy positions meant that a breakthrough was made, the stalemate was broken and there was a swift upsurge toward the German border. The river Rhine was about to be crossed. I managed during May to get some flying in. I felt it was owed to me. During the first week we made some sorties into Germany. They were labelled "Cook's tours" and in essence that is what they were. Tours by air of the Ruhr Valley to give hard worked ground crews a quick look see at some of the fruits of their labours. Fruits indeed, most of them came back feeling a little more than airsick. This was indeed saturation bombing. Jerry could not hold out much longer, squeezed from both ends.

You could hear a pin drop in the ante-room when the Prime Minister announced that from midnight the war in Europe was over. The date was the 8th May 1945. It was victory in Europe day, VE day for short. There was dancing in the streets from John O'Groats to Land's End.

The following week we actually landed across the channel to pick up and bring back home aircrew prisoners of war. I kept searching for a familiar face, hoping against hope that aboard my aircraft would step Nobby, Paddy and Sambo. But our reunion would have to wait, they were too far away.

Flying training was stopped and with no more operations, thousands of flyers were kicking their heels. Our Commonwealth comrades started drifting back home, heroes every one of them, deserving every plaudit of their own people. There was still Japan to be defeated and before too long a force known as Tiger Force was being put together on paper. I found out my name was on the list and was certainly not looking forward to it. Squadrons of Lancasters would be operating out of Far Eastern and Pacific Island bases, helping to bring the Nips finally to their knees. Our American allies however, had other ideas. Having suffered enough casualties island-hopping across the Pacific Ocean, they did not intend to risk huge casualties invading Japan. It took only two bombs to bring the war to a swift and horrendous end. One was dropped on Hiroshima, the other Nagasaki. The magnitude of destruction concentrated in these two metal cases was unbelievable. Civilian casualties were enormous. Atomic energy released in a bomb, the secret weapon dropped by Flying Fortresses, had done the trick. The war was finally snuffed out, just one day short of six whole years.

I had a vision of Neville Chamberlain returning from a visit to Hitler and holding in his hand a piece of paper proclaiming peace in our time. The apocalypse that had now been witnessed in two

Japanese cities, blasted into eternity, should now provide the answer to politicians about future world conflicts. We had done our bit, it was now up to them to win the peace.

The five survivors had a reunion. It was both a sad and a joyful occasion. We went back to the Saracens Head, the Snake Pit in Lincoln, booked in for a weekend and drank ourselves silly. There was something missing but no one wanted to put a finger on it. All of us had passed through a window, and there was no looking back. The excitement was over, all of us now had to adapt to something new. It would be hard.

The boss was back to Wing Commander, his acting rank was no longer considered necessary. He had decided to go back to farming the Scottish hills once he could be released. For the rest of us, like thousands of aircrew, we were mostly declared redundant, surplus to requirements. Like some outworn piece of machinery. A system of demobilisation numbers were allocated on the principle of first in, first out. My initial idea of a career in the Air Force was shelved, and we were herded together like lost cattle at various camps to await someone who had an inkling of what to do with us.

To cap it all, we were subjected to a variety of pseudo psychological and vocational tests by amateur educational officers, who at the end of the day decided what we would be best suited for. It was all a galling and unhappy time. We waited around for weeks on end, working on all kinds of mundane jobs. The group I was with picked potatoes for a blunt ignoramus of a Yorkshire farmer. Other aircrew worked down coalmines, in bacon factories—cheap labour. As I sat under a tree eating my two corned beef sandwiches, I made a decision. I could no longer pick any more potatoes for the meagre sum of half a crown a day, and could no longer put up with the insults of an ungrateful farmer. The rest of the group had reached the same conclusion.

I talked my way into a posting to a station near home, where I was able to live at home and enjoy family life. My new job at RAF Records Office, Gloucester, was the vetting of the thousands of applications for campaign medals from members of the RAF serving in all theatres around the world. We were a mixed bunch of aircrew, including Waafs from branches who had been involved in duties dealing with aircraft. None of us, with one or two exceptions, were admin wallahs, pen pushers, but it was a job.

It wasn't long though before the peace time Air Force began to flex its muscles, the book boys. The aircrew members were requested to cover up their ranks during the day, for what reason, God only knows. To a man, we all refused, and the semi-official order was quietly forgotten.

This however was not the same Air Force. It was becoming noticeable that the characters who had established themselves as born leaders of men, charismatic flyers, were being given their cards. Roll on my demob group. I wondered if the demob suit would be made by Burtons, the thirty shilling tailors.